FAVAN & FLEW

One *Flew* Through the Dragon Heart

BOOK 1

C. S. Johnson

FAVAN AND FLEW

C. S. JOHNSON

1st Edition.

Imprint: C. S. Johnson

Ebook ISBN: 978-1-948464-16-1

2nd Paperback ISBN: 978-1-94846-475-8

Hardcover Edition: 978-1-71613-309-1

FAVAN AND FLEW

For Sam. This is for you, for some reason, I am sure, and at least one good one, I am certain.

And for Ryan, who loves me, even the days when my dragons poo on our floors. Thank you for loving me even though it means you suffer.

1

There was never an act of magic more impressive than the ability to appear calm in times of duress, and Brixton Flew took great comfort in knowing he had mastered the technique long before he needed it.

He made his way out of his small office and stormed across the Rembrandt Academy grounds. The grand buildings London's finest engineers and enchanters had built generations ago stood tall, casting their afternoon shadows against the coal-coated clouds and smoky steamtrails that dotted the skies. In the distance, the magic portal, the large crater in the middle of Parliament, continued to pour out its light as it had for the last 275 years.

Since the Great Disruption of 1605, when the portal was opened, magic wielders had become abundant in London. And while much of the city had changed at their arrival, more of it had stayed the same. The architecture largely kept the classic baroque and gothic structures, the settled brick and mortar coupled with the lengthening stained glass windows of its pre-magic days, adding a ghostly veneer to the atmosphere that attempted to hide its decay even as it revealed it.

Many times as an engineering student, and now as a wielding instructor, Brixton found himself staring into the distance, lost in wonderment. He marveled at how his ancestors could build such majestic things, and all without using magic.

The view before him interrupted his surly mood briefly, offsetting his temper long enough for him to notice autumn's piercing encroachment. There were changing

FAVAN AND FLEW

colors in the tips of the campus trees, and he could feel the discomforting bite of the wind at his back.

Brixton paused in his steps, pushing back the wayward locks of his russet hair, before reaching into his pocket for the letter he had received earlier.

He pulled it out and read through it again, still unable to find any trace of hope in its decisive words.

Angered all over again, he carelessly stuffed it back into his greatcoat before gazing back at the school. He was more than frustrated, and his surroundings easily demonstrated the problem.

Rembrandt Academy was a dark fortress of a school; its tall, nondescript stone walls served as a perfect foil to the energizing beauty surrounding it. The rest of the city seemed to grow out of the ground toward heaven, while Rembrandt seemed happy to anchor itself further into hell.

That was where he was, Brixton thought bitterly. He was stuck in a hell of sorts, and there was no escape.

And it's all her *fault, too.*

As soon as the thought formed inside of him, Brixton hurried to quash any accompanying memories and the following tangle of emotional turmoil.

He shook his head and turned his attention back to his surroundings. The shift in focus was almost like waking up in the middle of a dream. He found himself standing on the central grounds of the academy, in the middle of the campus. To one side, Brixton could see the majestic outline of Wandsworth Bridge over the Thames. Down the other way, the magic portal perpetually illuminated the center courtyard of Westminster Palace, the home of the British Parliament. He watched as the magic light wafting out of the large crater changed from pink to orange before fading into blue.

As a student of Rembrandt, he had learned early on each color was reserved for a different type of magic, and the potency of its power varied between individual wielders. The portal, with its rainbow of colors leaking into the sky, had been the initial source of the magic that flooded through London after the Great Disruption.

Now, as a college instructor, Brixton taught the introductory levels for white magic—creation magic—and its related engineering enchantments. His students were supposed to go on to design the most interesting buildings, machines, and objects that world would ever see.

Perhaps that was why Rembrandt's building was so ugly, Brixton thought. His students would purposefully have to go out of their way to design something even worse.

"Professor Flew!"

He grimaced as another surge of disgust churned away in his gut.

Brixton braced himself as a small squad of students came up to him. But even before he looked at them, he knew he had not prepared enough. An unexpected rush of envy fluttered to the front of his mind as he looked at the students before him. The bright, eager faces around Rembrandt seemed to get younger every day, even though he was, at twenty-two, only six years their senior.

I must be getting old.

Brixton could barely remember a time when he felt young, but it was not their youth he coveted—it was their camaraderie. He never had a lot of friends during his college days, but he wondered if he had ever noticed it until he suddenly found himself all alone.

A rueful smile briefly crossed his face. *I might be getting old, but time is still playing tricks with me.*

In all his life, Brixton never faced any foe as crafty, vexing, or pompous as time.

It was never the right time to say the things he wanted to say, to do the things he wanted to do. Compared to all time's cruelties, the college freshmen surrounding him were nothing, and certainly nothing to fear.

"Ladies," he said in greeting, bobbing his head to them in feigned interest. "And gentlemen, too. How may I be of service?"

"Professor, we wanted to start an extracurricular." One of the girls pushed herself to the front of the group, using her silk and lace parasol to help block the others from his attention.

Brixton knew her face, having seen her in his morning classes. She was one of the few students already proficient in engineering magic. With her ginger hair and pretty green eyes, he felt as though he should have remembered her name, especially since she reminded him of his younger sister, Luella.

As he looked at the girl, she giggled nervously, and Brixton had a feeling Luella would be dismayed by the comparison.

"An extracurricular?" Brixton politely inquired, already formulating a way to gracefully turn down their request.

He had spent his first year teaching at Rembrandt learning how to excuse himself from teaching free lectures, circumventing volunteer opportunities, and avoiding any extra or unnecessary meetings, and he silently resolved to keep to that precedent.

In addition to his two classes this semester, he oversaw a number of special projects assigned to him by the Board at Rembrandt and his department leader, Dr. Henry Winston. He hated the thought of babysitting students for an extracurricular, especially without pay.

FAVAN AND FLEW

"We need a sponsor, and you're our favorite professor. So we came to ask you for your assistance." The girl began to spin her parasol in a distracted, flippant manner.

Brixton sighed inwardly. Students were always hard to please, but the ones from affluent families seemed to be the most eager to make his life as challenging as possible. Between her expensive parasol and the carelessness with which she wielded it, the girl was likely used to getting exactly what she wanted.

As if she knew what he was thinking, the girl smiled up at him with a glib look on her face, and Brixton was not surprised to feel that same old repugnant feeling inside him as he realized she fancied him.

He would have to tread this conversation very, very carefully.

But, he thought wryly, he had always been good at being careful when it came to relationships—perhaps too good.

"Yes, we want to start up a discus group," one of the boys clarified, drawing him back out of his thoughts. Brixton recognized him as one of the Academy's newest medical majors. His name was Anthony, and he likely had a good bit of talent. His accent hinted at his humble, middle-class status, and as much as they touted their compassionate initiatives, the Board did not like to approve such applicants. From his own education experience at Rembrandt, Brixton was willing to gamble Anthony had only gotten in by the slightest degree.

"Rembrandt doesn't have a group, but if we start one, we'll be able to play against Oxford and Eton and Cambridge. Mayhap we'll even get invited to see the Queen." Anthony glanced over at the girl, a look of obvious admiration on his face. "It was just a bloody brilliant idea that Clarise had."

Clarise—that was her name.

"I see." Brixton bit down on the inside of his cheek, trying to look thoughtful even though he was beyond irritated now. It was one thing to be met with disappointment regarding his future, and it was another thing to be forced to coddle the frivolity of the present.

I have to get away from this.

As carefully and nonchalantly as possible, Brixton pushed his abhorrent letter further down into his greatcoat pocket before pulling out his watch. He called on his magic. The warm, familiar feeling raced through him, like a muscle contracting inside his soul. White light danced at his fingertips and slid into the watch.

At the slightest touch of magic, the little dial chimed and the cogs on the front turned a few pegs, first clockwise, and then counterclockwise, before small pair of bland eyes blinked up at him.

"Hello, Ticker," Brixton said.

"Good afternoon, sir." The clock face twitched, as the hands of the watch tipped upward, giving the mechanical face an austere expression. "Sir, I do believe it is time to go home. Class has ended for the day."

"I know." Brixton looked back at the waiting faces of the girls and boys surrounding them. "What is my schedule for today? I need to know what time my appointment is later on this evening."

Ticker twitched as his clock hands turned, and a small projection lit up above Brixton's palm, displaying a pair of cogs turning as Ticker pulled up the desired information.

Brixton nearly groaned at the show. Ticker had been the result of his own innovation, the one he presented for his graduation project. It secured him not only distinction from the Crown, but it made Rembrandt more than eager to hire him after he graduated. Since then, his watch had become his constant companion, which was part of the reason Luella had christened it "Ticker," short for "Mr. Ticker-Ticker-Time-Taker."

Lu was more than accurate, too, he thought bitterly. Ticker did like to take his time, and Brixton had a feeling a lot of it was for show.

Ticker finally buzzed to a stop. "Sir, you do not have—"

"Oh, dear, it seems I have forgotten to program my schedule for this evening," Brixton interrupted. "How could I forget such an important date, especially with the most important woman in my life?"

Immediately, Clarise—and the rest of the girls in her group—began to pout.

"You truly don't have time for us, professor?" Clarise asked. She reached forward and laid her lace-gloved hand on his arm. It was an innocent gesture, unless he allowed it to be something more.

He hated that.

As a student, he had been largely ignored by his peers. Once he began to teach, it seemed as though the younger generations were more than happy to make up for the oversight.

Every year, there were more students in his classes who looked on him in wonderment as he taught—mere girls who let their eyes mist over with daydreams as they moistened their lips, fancying him as much as they fancied themselves adults. Consistently, love letters and anonymous student surveys declared him the most handsome professor among Rembrandt's faculty.

Brixton had a feeling that was one of the reasons Henry kept him teaching the introductory levels. The younger students and their romantic attentions were simpler to ignore or dissuade.

Brixton patted Clarise's hand in what he considered a fatherly manner before he stepped back out of her reach. "Not today, Miss Clarise. I regret you will have to find another professor or employee to serve as your sponsor. Or perhaps your mother or father would be willing to come and participate as such? Rembrandt does also accept parental sponsors."

He nearly laughed at her sickened expression and silently commended himself for his brilliance.

Mentioning parents made things much easier, Brixton decided, as he made his formal apologies and his quick excuses. No college student wanted the reminder that they were only practicing at adulthood while they were completing their studies.

As he resumed his trek through the campus, Ticker let out a series of buzzing noises. Brixton could hear his disapproval, even in the clock's monotonous, robotic voice, and frowned. "You might as well give up, Ticker. I don't regret sending them away."

"It is not *that* I object to, sir. I am merely disconcerted that you feel the need to lie."

"There is nothing in the world I want less than to spend another hour of my day stuck here at the school. If I didn't need to work off my debt, I would quit." He gritted his teeth, thinking of the letter in his pocket again. "Even if I don't have any other job prospects."

"You are a powerful wielder, sir. The Prime Minister himself ordered your first-class distinction after you created me." Ticker's face lit up with automated pride. "Surely it is not unreasonable of the academy Board to employ one such as you to train new students in the levels of engineering."

FAVAN AND FLEW

"I'm only teaching them the introductory classes. Any third-class wielder could do what I do."

"It is for the good of the country and the world, sir."

Brixton rolled his eyes. "I cannot imagine why Lu named you 'Time-Taker.' You are more of a Joy-Taker."

"Pardon me, sir, but you were the one who just used me to excuse yourself from the company of your students."

"What does that have to do with anything?"

"If there is a Joy-Taker here, it is not me." Ticker huffed, blowing a cloud of magic out the front of the clock, making the gears swivel at the considerable amount of discharge. Brixton watched the cloud swirl up into the smoky atmosphere, grimacing as it dissolved just as it touched one of the city's monitoring airships.

Using magic was not a crime, but it was heavily monitored by the Board and various Ministers for safety reasons. Not everyone had the talent to wield magic, but those who did were always considered suspect by the general public, no matter how great or how minuscule their wielding capability was.

In the first years after the Great Disruption, several wielders were hanged or lynched for their talents; some turned violent in self-defense, while others fled the country. Those who stayed often went into hiding. In the generations that followed, magic was gradually and begrudgingly accepted, and new laws were written.

But that did not mean everyone approved of those with magic, and Brixton knew all too well that those who did not included a large portion of the city police.

It had been years since he had caused such an upset with the law, but Brixton did not need to pay a fine or dispute another charge of reckless endangerment or magical misuse with intent—especially if he ever wanted to get out of his current job.

"Careful, Ticker," Brixton warned. "You could get me in trouble with the mage-ragers, and then we would both be in danger."

"The police are hardly 'mage-ragers,' sir. You should forgo the use of such a derogatory term. They do their job, just as you do yours."

"They are pretty quick to condemn those of us with magic. And even quicker to punish us."

"Does your father know how you feel about such things, sir?"

Brixton winced at Ticker's point.

"You are a powerful wielder, sir," Ticker continued. "If they punish you, it is to discourage others such as yourself from engaging in dangerous behavior."

"You are the one who just sent out the charge cloud." Brixton sighed. He knew there was very little point in arguing with Ticker. "I will remember your words, just as you should remember mine."

Ticker scoffed. "It is only that I do not like being used as part of an excuse, sir. I do not think that is asking much."

"There is a time and a place for everything," Brixton said. "Everything except watching my students play frisbee while the girls hop around in short skirts and pretend to be embarrassed when they flash me their knickers."

"I suppose it would be troublesome to worry about the young men reporting you for harassment, if their affections for the girls were strained."

"There is that, too." After growing up in Wandschapel, a poor magical district in London, Brixton did not have to wonder if Anthony would be willing to challenge him for Clarise's affections. Young men who grew up poor took great care to watch over what they thought was theirs, while rich men were content to let the government and the banks do that.

Brixton remembered all too well the times when a pretty girl would spurn his affections or dismiss his attention. He hoped Anthony would have better luck in chasing down love.

Any luck would be better than mine in that regard.

Brixton's fist clenched around the letter in his pocket, pushing back against it, as if to ward off the sudden, stubborn memory of the woman who had broken his heart.

His childish recklessness had allowed him to fall in love, but that love ended up costing him everything he ever wanted.

"Sir? Sir, I asked you a question." Ticker grinded a pair of his cogs together again, making the hands on his clock face twitch. "Where are you heading now? You do not actually have an appointment scheduled for tonight."

"I was not lying, believe it or not." Brixton put his hand inside his pocket, curling his fingers around the rumpled letter once more. "I've been severely disappointed today, and so it is only right and fitting that I go and see the most important woman in my life."

"You have an appointment with a therapist?"

"No." Brixton slammed the pocket watch closed and stuffed it back inside his jacket. "I was talking about my mother."

2

It had been some time since he left his rented rooms at Rembrandt to visit his family. Perhaps a few weeks, Brixton calculated with guilt as he stepped over the older cobblestones of the tight streets, doing his best to avoid the horse excrement.

His family did not live too far away from the school, but it was tucked away in one of the poorer corners of midtown where respectable folk would never tread if they could avoid it.

Brixton never thought his family was poor until he began school. His first headmistress had scoffed at his Sunday best, and he still remembered the tightness of his chest at her slight. The other boys in his classroom would only make the occasional remark, but it was enough to convince Brixton to stick to his books for company and his family for support.

His family lived in a small townhome, topped with a handmade greenhouse and crowned with several electro-magic antennas. From every window, there was a box of flowers, while little sets of chimes jangled cheerfully in the autumn winds.

Despite his sour mood, he grinned at the sight. His family might have been poor, but that did not stop them from being odd.

The door creaked open with the same welcoming familiarity it always had as Brixton stepped inside. He took off his greatcoat, and at once, the small townhouse seemed to reach out with its own essence, bathing him in the scent of oranges and animals, flooding him with the sensation of a million memories. He breathed it in and reveled in it.

Deep down, nothing in the world could dislodge his home from his heart—not the Board at Rembrandt, not the government, not even all his secret hopes and dreams—and there was unspeakable comfort in knowing that.

"We're in the kitchen, Brix. Come on in. I've just finished pulling out a rack of biscuits."

Brixton sighed in reluctant gratitude. His mother was never surprised when he arrived, no matter the hour. He used to wonder if she had a spy in her service, but now, having mastered his own magic, he knew his mother was able to sense emotions.

And it was that talent that made Philippa Flew one of the most accomplished veterinarians in London, and that was why the house always smelled of all sorts of creatures. She often brought her work home with her, and as Brixton walked into the kitchen, he saw today was no exception.

"Who does that belong to?" he asked, gesturing toward the large peacock sitting on the table.

The large fan of its tail sprouted at his voice, making him jump back as the hundreds of colorful feathers unfolded before him. The peacock squawked, clearly sore at the disruption.

Luella's laughter rang through the room as Brixton recovered. He glanced through the fan of exotic bird feathers to see his younger sister's blonde curls bouncing as she began to walk around the table.

"It's Mrs. Fordyce's," Luella said. "He has a broken leg. Mum brought him home so I could take care of it."

"Why do you need to help him if it's just a broken leg?" Brixton rolled his eyes. "It seems silly for you to have to use your magic on him."

"Come on. Don't be so stuffy."

FAVAN AND FLEW

"I'm just concerned. You really ought to be more careful when you use your magic." Brixton sat down on the chair at the far end of the table. "If you're not, the mage-ragers will realize you have plenty of talent, too, and they'll come running to sign you up to work at Rembrandt along with me."

"Oh, Brix. It sounds like you had another hard day. I thought as much when you came in." Philippa sighed. Her braided hair was a shade darker than Brixton's and lined with wispy grays; it whipped gracefully behind her as she hurried to press a loving kiss to her oldest child's forehead.

Brixton might have waved her off when he had been younger, but now he welcomed his mother's affections. He gave her a quick kiss on the cheek in return as Luella giggled again.

"I would not mind going to Rembrandt, but don't think they would want me to teach the newbies just yet," Luella said, jutting her pointed chin forward proudly. "I'm only fifteen."

"You know as well as I do that some magic comes in early."

Many of the first wielders had experienced it as a secondary trait, one that appeared toward the beginning of adulthood. As Mendel and Darwin's theories speculated, magic moved down through the bloodlines, and as the talents were recognized earlier, it became generally accepted that most magic began to appear during adolescence.

But there were still the occasional stories of talented children who knew of their magic long before it appeared, and Brixton knew that a great many of those stories were true—after all, he had once been best friends with one of the most powerful wielders in London.

"There's no need to brag," Luella said with a huff. "We all know that you were a prodigy right from birth. The rest of us will bow down to you one day, I'm sure, but in the meantime, the requirements for specialized magical instruction start at sixteen. Even you didn't get to go until then."

"I was actually thinking of—"

Brixton went silent as his chest tightened, his heart clenched, and his fingers shook.

He had only just barely stopped himself.

He had come *so bloody close* to saying her name.

It was appalling to think that after nearly four years he still thought of her—thought of her, dreamed of her, but never spoke of her.

How could he? Remembering her was like lighting himself on fire and forgetting how much it burned.

The rest of the room fell into sudden silence along with him. Philippa reached out and patted Brixton's hand, and the old, angry sadness he felt suddenly became more tangible.

In some ways, his mother's sympathy made it easier to pack his feelings back into the corner of his heart where he kept them, but it was harder to see all his efforts at forgetting the past were self-defeating.

Luella let out a small sigh before she turned her attention back to the peacock. The fan of his feathers twisted shut as he enjoyed Luella's attentions. "Well, if I am proficient in using my talent as I am, it is only because of your 'illustrious example,' Brix."

Philippa moved away as Brixton cleared his throat. He was grateful for the change in topic. "That sounds like a compliment from someone else, not you."

Luella's bright blue eyes gleamed with wry amusement. "It's from your latest professional development report. A copy of it came in the post this week."

"You shouldn't be reading my mail. That's rude. Why would Rembrandt send a copy of my report here, anyway?"

"Perhaps it is because of your debt," Philippa said lightly. "We still send in payments."

"I think it's your fault, Brix. You don't read your mail, do you?" Luella smirked.

Brixton said nothing, thinking of the growing piles of unopened mail accumulating in his office and in his apartment. It was more likely that his mother was right, but he would not give Luella any satisfaction.

Brixton glared at her before reaching for the biscuits his mother had just pulled out of the oven. He was just about to take a bite when Luella snatched it out of his hand. "Hey!"

"Hey yourself," she said. "These are for Roger."

"Roger?"

Luella pointed at the peacock. "Mum's making the biscuits for him, not us."

"I'll pour some tea for you, dear." After years of their quarrels, Philippa smoothly interrupted them. "I have some bread coming out of the breadmaker soon, if you would like some toast. It will be safe for you to eat."

Brixton glanced back at the ancient appliance, one he had built himself when he first discovered his talent for order and creation. He still saw it as he had that day—the parts had magically sorted themselves inside his mind; the capacitor pulled into the electric snare, the cogs twirled around to generate the heat, the fan dispersed the excess power; even making the bread tray from an old pot had been easy, with his early talent guiding him as he melted, sculpted, and reformed it into the perfect shape for rising bread.

Now, more than ten years later, he saw the sloppy, untrained elements of his work. The tray was uneven, the charge never kept, and the cogs needed to be replaced. He cringed at the sight of it, but he knew his mother would never let him replace it, and his father was too eager to prove he was capable of keeping it running himself.

Brixton shook his head. "I don't want any toast, thanks."

"Here's your tea then, darling." Philippa handed him a cup and saucer as Luella fed Roger the treats.

"I guess you're not worried you're going to make him sick," Brixton remarked, watching his sister stuff treat after treat in between the peacock's beak.

"He won't get sick." Luella stuck her tongue out at him. "I know what I'm doing."

"I just thought I'd point out—"

"He's not a machine, Brix, and there's no need to pretend you know it all when you only happen to know a lot."

"The treats have some medicine in them," Philippa explained. "Roger will not only get some good food for his tummy, but this food will keep him asleep long enough for Luella to work her magic. It was quite a nasty break."

Luella jutted her chin out proudly. "Mum said it would be better if I put him to sleep before I tried to heal him."

Brixton nodded in approval. "It will be easier for you to concentrate on his leg if he's still."

"I know. That's why I agreed to it."

"You're pretty smart for a fifteen-year-old, but it's still a bigger job than you're used to."

"It's a smaller job than you think." His sister beamed up at him as she held up her palm, while a small prism of burning light appeared. "See? I can conjure up my power without using a wand or an etching, just like you."

Brixton blinked in surprise; such a skill was rare for someone as young as Luella. "Blast it, how long has it been since I've been home?"

"It's only been a few weeks, Brix," his mother replied, as he shifted uncomfortably in his chair.

His own power had always been evident to him. It was a part of who he was, identity and talent alike. The ability to create and order objects had always come together in his head. He had been able to work on those visions without extra effort, using his hands to put the pieces of a project together, even without the extra help from his magic.

At sixteen, he had gone to Rembrandt and learned how to channel that power. He spent a good portion of that first semester getting ink stains from conjuring paper, picking out splinters from carving symbols into wood etchings, and using a chisel to sculpt and carve stones. Learning how to use his magic without conjuring aids had proven irresistible, and he quickly mastered the technique.

Brixton watched Luella now, eyeing the bright spark of her talent as it slipped back into her skin. Luella's magic reminded him of the portal; it was a rainbow of color, a changing mix that carried her playfulness, just as his magic carried his practicality. The bright white of his magic allowed him to work late into the night, designing new machines and planning out new ideas, while hers seemed to change color to add more joy to the world.

"If Lu's going to get herself in trouble, I better start paying attention more often." He bit his cheek, wondering if there would be a way he could keep her out of

Rembrandt. He did not want the Board to conscript her into working for them in order to help pay off his debts, too.

"We always enjoy it when you come and see us, but there's no need to worry about Luella. I would like to keep her on as my apprentice at the shop. We have been doing much better financially since you started working at Rembrandt. I know you are not happy there, but your work is important, Brix."

He grumbled, muttering a string of nothings under his breath. His mother was right, of course, but that made everything even more difficult—especially when he had disappointing news to share.

He pulled out the letter he received at his office and let it fall to the table. Luella and Philippa glanced at it and fell silent for a long moment.

It was his mother who dared to speak first.

"So that is the main reason why you are upset today." Philippa sighed at the sight of the insignia. "I'm so sorry."

Luella picked it up and read the postmark. "The Office of the Airship Force of Her Royal Majesty, Queen Victoria."

"I didn't get in. They rejected my application."

"This is the third time you've applied." Luella passed the letter to her mother, who pulled out a pair of half-moon glasses from her apron so she could read through the letter's contents.

"You don't need to remind me," Brixton muttered.

"I was more reminding myself," Luella scoffed. "Not everyone keeps up with your life as it goes along, you know. I don't see why you want to serve in the ASF anyway."

"I don't like working for Rembrandt, even if they're giving me a special interest rate on my loans while I work for them." Brixton shook his head. "At this rate, I'll be in debt for the rest of my life, but if I could get the job I wanted, it would at least give me some joy."

"We are helping as much as we can, Brix. Your father and I owe them, too, for getting you out of trouble with the law when you were younger," Philippa said.

Brixton said nothing. His antics in experimenting with his magic when he was younger had led to several misadventures, not all of them unintentional, and many of which led to court dates and subsequent charges. The Board at Rembrandt had stepped in and loaned his family the money to get out of jailtime. They had also lent their prestige in securing him lesser charges, on the premise he would attend the school.

Brixton was grateful for that. He had vowed to become an honorable citizen, a responsible wielder, and a better son. And while he managed to make some progress in those areas—some significantly more than others—it seemed the harder he tried to get rid of his debt, the faster it grew.

The one time he had asked Henry about his class assignments, the kindly doctor only shook his head.

"It's not enough, Henry." Brixton ran his hand through his hair nervously. "I appreciate the stipend for food and rent, I really do, but I'd like another class or two to help pay down my debt to the Board faster."

"I can understand your frustration, Brixton, but the Board wants you to be free to do more research assignments, and those are added onto your salary, too," he said. Henry had taken great pains to assure Brixton he was imagining things. "There is no reason to think they are intentionally keeping you here, Brixton. Your debt, while it has unfortunately accrued interest as time has passed, will be paid off one day. These things take time. And you can

FAVAN AND FLEW

always work on more research assignments if you want to earn more."

"I guess so."

Henry chuckled. "Surely, you're not truly upset at this, are you? Here at the school, you can do so much. You have the freedom to experiment, and you have the chance to make a difference in the lives of your fellow countrymen."

Brixton mumbled something non-committal under his breath. He did not mind the research assignments, but some of them made him more than a little uneasy.

"This is a very competitive position, Brixton," Henry continued. "Do you know how many people would love to be in your position now?"

Brixton refrained from mentioning that he was likely the only one who did not want to be in his position, but only barely. He knew he had no business questioning Henry about anything.

Back in his school days, when Brixton respectfully addressed him as Dr. Winston, if there was a part he needed for an experiment, Henry was the one who procured it for him. For Brixton, who had stolen quite a few things in his youth in order to bring his designs to life, it was even more of a welcome surprise when Henry gave him what he needed without question. There was no trace of any suspicion or contempt like Brixton's father often displayed, and it was rather nice to have someone eagerly listen to him discuss different theories and new ideas.

And when Brixton's world turned upside down during his senior year, it was Henry who helped him refocus and finish his work.

If Henry, his most respected mentor and supporter, believed the Board was only being fair, Brixton had to at least give him the benefit of the doubt.

FAVAN AND FLEW

Even if he did not want to.

"You have a great deal of magic, Brixton, and your interest in building things has only added to your expertise," Henry continued. "The Board and I know this, which is why you have such a high rank even though you teach the introductory levels. It will be easy for you to teach engineering basics while putting your energy toward Rembrandt's research projects. Besides, Rembrandt is among the most reputable employers in the kingdom, especially for a talented wielder like yourself."

Henry did not need to mention that being employed by Rembrandt seemed to discourage other prospective employers. Even as a contractor, no one seemed to want Brixton on their payroll without the school's blessing.

Brixton only nodded and quickly changed the subject. He did not want to dwell on such an unpleasant topic, especially when he knew Henry would never agree with him.

More than a year had passed since then, but Brixton was still reluctant to discuss his debt, even with his family. Luella would blink her large eyes at him in sympathy, and his mother would vow to work harder so she could help him even more—just as they were doing now, he realized with a sense of self-disgust.

He did not want them to suffer for his sake, as unavoidable as it seemed to be.

"Would you like some cream?" Luella asked, pushing a small pitcher toward him. "I got it fresh from the Rawlings family this morning."

"What did you do for them to get it?" Brixton was more than grateful for the distraction. He stirred it into his tea, watching the liquids swirl in his cup, the contrasting pattern whirling together inside his mother's favorite kingfisher china.

Luella giggled. "Their son had a scratched knee the other day and they sent it to me in thanks for healing it."

"You technically don't heal things with your magic, Lu."

"The Rawlings don't know that, and their little Neil doesn't, either."

"It says here that there was a filing error," Philippa held his letter up to a light, tracing her fingers over the decisive words. "Your application was sent in past the deadline."

"I mailed it out weeks in advance," Brixton said. "The only thing I can think of is that it must have gotten lost in the mail. I used the campus post, so I've been wondering if the Board could have done something."

It was uncomfortable admitting his suspicions about the Board, even if the situation allowed for it. Henry would laugh before dismissing it, his parents would only look at him with sympathetic gazes, and even Luella might question his sanity.

"I am sure that no one at the school tampered with your letter," Philippa said.

"Maybe the Airship Force just didn't want you," Luella said. "You do have a criminal record, even if Rembrandt helped you get out of serving time for it."

"Luella Catherine." Philippa sent her an angry glance before turning back to Brixton. "I'm sure that's not the reason, Brix. After all, that's the second time the Airship Force has sent you that response, and you mailed it out from here last time. If there was an issue with the mail, it is more believable that the error falls to the reception rather than the delivery."

Brixton did not like the empathetic gleam in his mother's gaze as she looked at him. He was about to stop her from asking the inevitable question when Luella asked it herself.

"Do you think it is possible that you didn't get in because of Captain Favan?"

All at once, the dull spark of his frustration fanned into a burning fire inside of him. Brixton hurriedly snatched the letter from his mother's hands.

The sudden movement caused Roger to squawk angrily. His long neck twitched and curled, knocking the last of the treats to the floor. As Luella and his mother raced to pacify the exotic bird and clean up the mess, Brixton left the room.

"Brixton!" He heard Luella's soft footsteps start after him, but as he made it to the top of the stairs, he heard his mother quickly stop her from following him.

It was too much to bear, Brixton thought. The mention of Captain Favan in conjunction with his mother's assessment of the letter seared pure pain through his heart, reopening the wounds of his past, leaving him breathless with anger and, to his revulsion, longing.

Brixton did not stop as he forced himself forward, heading toward the welcoming solitude of the lab at the top of the house.

His father was a man of many talents, but not a single one that was classified as magical. For years, Bartholomew Flew had been interested in mechanisms of all sorts. He had built and repaired items of all sorts on the side long before Brixton was born, and his interests had branched out over the years since. His job at Scotland Yard sometimes took him away for days at a time, but Brixton's father had never failed to find his way back to the collected projects in his lab.

While his father was skilled at repairs, he was far from orderly, Brixton thought with a small sense of amusement.

He looked around the room, his eyes roaming from the dome-shaped greenhouse at the top of the house down to the excessive soot piling up from the attic hearth. The lab held tools of all sorts, half-finished experiments, half-built automatons, and a range of scraps, tools, and blueprints scattered all over the place. Brixton remembered when he was a child, he used to watch his father work; it was hard for Brixton to say if his magic grew along with his interest, or if it was the other way around.

Brixton tossed his letter onto a nearby desk before picking up his father's small watch repair kit. He pulled Ticker out of his pocket, but this time, he did not open the watch. Instead he turned it around, unscrewed the back panel, and opened his automaton to where he could see into the heart of the magic loop, the snare that held Ticker's power and personality.

It was like watching lightning curl and uncurl, repeating the motion so many times it seemed to be dancing. He gazed into it, losing himself in the memories tied to its magic—in the memories tied to her.

Opening his past wounds was as comforting as it was harrowing; it was not something he did lightly. He braced himself for the pain, but there was never any pain as intoxicating as the memory of her voice.

"Brixton."

He was lost. A reluctant smile crept onto his face as he fell back into the welcoming arms of his past.

"Brixton."

His sixteen-year-old self was scurrying past the materials room when he heard his name spoken with a soft, foreign lilt. The sound broke through him like a magic spell, disrupting his intellectual musings and forcing him into an uncomfortable position.

He was in a hurry; his professor would be upset if he was late for class. As a star pupil, Brixton knew he had a certain reputation to live up to, and he had learned well not to call any negative attention to himself.

But at the sound of Adelaide Favan calling for him, he felt helpless—helplessly nervous and helplessly intrigued. It was almost as if some part of him had been waiting for her to call, and he had been more than ready to answer.

Out of guilt, if nothing else.

He nearly lost his grip on the stack of books he carried as he stumbled to a stop and glanced back at the doorway to the materials room. He could see a slim shadow at the back, where her dark skirts whipped around as she moved between stations, pulling out supplies and looking for spare coils, cogs, or anything else she decided she needed.

He did not have the faintest notion why she would be calling him. Adelaide never seemed to talk to anyone unless it was out of necessity.

"Are you coming in or not?" Adelaide straightened, looking up at him from behind a thick pair of black-rimmed goggles, the kind that magnified her eyes behind the protective glass.

Brixton felt a quick twinge of regret. She always wore them when she was working on something. He had a sinking feeling he was going to be late for class—but he stepped into the room regardless.

"I'm surprised," she said as he tentatively approached her.

"Why? You were the one who called me."

"Is that what I need to do to get your attention?" Adelaide put her hands on her hips as she stepped back from the table, where a box full of wires and screws and other various building materials winked up at him.

Brixton felt his face turn red. "If you're talking about earlier, I—"

"I don't want to talk about earlier," Adelaide said. "You know who my father is. Do you think your friends are the first people to make fun of me because of my family?"

"They're not my friends. Not exactly." Brixton sighed. "They're just people we go to school with. You don't have to be friends with them. You just have to get along with them until we graduate."

"Is that your plan?"

He shifted his feet as the clocks chimed loudly, the pleasant ringing turning sour in his ears. He was officially late for class. Brixton glanced back at the door.

Adelaide did not pay attention to the clock. She saw to her work, fiddling with one of the gearshifts. Brixton noticed she was also still wearing her workshop gloves. Along with her goggles, they were a semi-permanent part of her wardrobe. They were thick and black, going up past her elbows. The school issued them as part of the engineering department; Brixton hated wearing them, since the synthetic material of the gloves interfered with his ability to use magic. Adelaide was the only one who consistently wore them.

"It's mostly my plan," he said, finally answering her.

"Seems like a silly plan, especially for the next four years."

"Earlier, when those girls were picking on you, I didn't say anything—"

"I said I didn't want to talk about earlier. People have made comments about me all my life. Getting accepted into Rembrandt two years earlier than everyone else is merely another unearned privilege in their eyes."

Her voice was calm, but Brixton saw that her fingers, even buried in her large gloves, shook ever so slightly.

"I don't presume—"

"But you do." Adelaide pushed up her goggles onto her forehead again, brushing back her long black hair.

Brixton hated how he stared at her. Up close, her eyes were cloudy gray, speckled over with a silver lining. He noticed they were slanted, ever so slightly; along with her flattened nose and full lips, there were plenty of hints at her Chinese heritage. He had heard the whispers of her family, especially her father, the famous Captain Favan who led Her Royal Majesty's Airship Force.

That was one of the main reasons he had tried to befriend her before. Brixton had approached her when she was first introduced to their class, eager to talk about her father's legacy and how it was his dream to be in the Airship Force one day, too. Adelaide had ignored him then, brushing off his introduction.

Remembering that, he frowned. *She has some nerve, admonishing me for poor manners.*

He cleared his throat to give himself a moment to recover. "You should know *you're* presuming that *I'm* presuming something. I don't know you well enough to presume anything."

For the first time, Adelaide softened her expression. Brixton briefly wondered if he had hurt her feelings, or if it was possible he had successfully pointed out her double standards.

She tugged the goggles down over her eyes a moment later, returning to the project before her. She said nothing as she picked up a suturing iron and began to burn a twisted bunch of wires together.

For a long moment, Brixton watched her. Despite her gloves, her movements were very precise—so precise that they almost seemed awkward.

Just like the rest of her, he thought with a small smile.

Adelaide was fourteen years old, two years younger than everyone else at Rembrandt. She had transferred into the school during the middle of their second semester, and ever since their failed first meeting, Brixton kept his distance from her, even if he continued to watch her out of the corner of his eye. He knew the others in his class teased her for her youth, her connections, and her ancestry.

He could sympathize with her some in that regard, given he received plenty of his own mockery. He was only at Rembrandt because of his scholarship. Most of the students were from the aristocracy, and the idea of rich merchants or lower-class workers—such as his parents— sending their children to Rembrandt was nothing short of scandalous.

He easily dismissed those who badgered him; he was here for an education, and nothing more.

But as Brixton gazed down at Adelaide, he suddenly wondered if she was able to do the same.

She was such a small thing. She was not only two years his junior, but she was also at least a foot shorter. The Rembrandt Academy uniform nearly swallowed up her body. He could see her vest was pinned in the back, and her long skirt was clearly hemmed. Brixton had a feeling she liked to wear the goggles on her forehead if for no other reason than they lent her another two inches in height.

FAVAN AND FLEW

"Why did you call me?" Brixton asked, daring himself to speak again.

Adelaide bit her lip, and Brixton found himself staring again.

Finally, she sighed. "I need you."

His breath caught and his body went still. He was only able to move after she added, "I need your help."

The words came out with a ripe bitterness in each syllable, and Brixton almost laughed at her discomfort. It was clear she never asked for help if she could avoid it.

He cleared his throat again, swallowing the last of his laughter, and nodded. "Tell me what it is."

"I need help assembling this," Adelaide said, pointing to the neat array of metal scraps and parts before her.

"What is it?"

"A dragon heart."

"Beg pardon?" Brixton dropped his books, missing the table and causing them to clatter to the floor. He was certain he had misheard her as he bent to pick them up, but he was even more surprised when she laughed.

Her eyes were pushed back into slits behind her goggles, giving her a wizened, animated look as her smile widened. Brixton stared at her as he picked up his books and stacked them neatly beside hers.

"I'm only kidding," Adelaide said, before she arched her brow. "Or maybe I'm not. Either way, I need your help with this part."

She opened the top panel and pointed to a small knot of wires lined with alloy and copper. "This is an energy loop I've been working on. It's a special type of power source. The Board wants to develop more efficient batteries, especially since the Edison Project has shown promise.

Now they want to see what the wielders can do to improve it."

"I talked with Professor Ohm about this," Brixton said. "He wanted to find a way to generate perpetual energy. He thought electricity could possibly be infused with magic."

"I know. I overheard your conversation after class a few days ago."

"You did?" Brixton took the suturing iron out of her hand.

"He was dismissive of the idea as an alternative life source, but he was interested in seeing if you could figure out how to make his own theories work."

He bit down on his cheek. He knew which conversation Adelaide was referring to, and it was one where Professor Ohm spent several minutes admonishing him for his eclectic reading tastes.

"What?" Adelaide asked.

"It's rude to eavesdrop."

She jutted her chin forward. "It's also rude to ignore people who need help."

"I don't know if you're saying that to make me feel bad about before, or if it's just to make sure I stay here and help you," Brixton muttered. "Do you care to tell me which?"

"I have an extra pair of gloves if you need them," Adelaide offered.

He rolled his eyes as she sidestepped his question. "I don't use them if I can help it." He called up the power that resided inside of him. He could feel it flowing from his heart down to his fingertips, filling his palm. "I like working with my hands better. It's easier to conjure up my talent. That's my magic, as you might have known already. I can build things. Anything, really."

"Well, no wonder you're so good at this." Adelaide pouted as Brixton undid her work. "You're using magic."

"And you don't? Why are you in school to be an engineering wielder if you're not using magic?"

"I *like* working with machinery," Adelaide said. "I'm here because Rembrandt produces the best engineers in London. The fact that it's a magical school does nothing for me."

"Do you even have magic at all? I thought that was a requirement for coming here."

"It is." Adelaide went silent, and for the first time, Brixton saw her blush. With the small patch of red on her cheeks, he could just make out a light trail of freckles across her nose.

"Ouch." He flinched as the suturing iron slipped across his fingers.

"Pay attention to what you're doing. You don't have to worry about my talent right now. All you need to know is that it's not helping me fix this." She crossed her arms and looked away.

"Right." Brixton turned back to the item in front of him.

The box-like machine was oddly shaped, with two egg-shaped bumps on the top, and two small spherical compartments on the bottom. There were four smaller openings, almost in a whirlwind pattern. He had to commend Adelaide on her joke. It was shaped a little like a heart, although he had to wonder at the dragon part of her claim.

He ran his hands over the machine's main compartment panel and took it off, revealing the intricacies of the inside. There were several niches and nooks inside, and he found himself marveling at how the larger workmanship blended into the smaller components almost seamlessly. After a

FAVAN AND FLEW

moment of closer study, he knew the older parts from the newer, and he could anticipate how the power would move through such a device.

Seeing how the power would have to flow from the left to right, tangling up inside the different sections, he let out a low whistle.

"This is beautiful," he said. It was a much older design, almost like an old battery cell, one that was modified into a multiple-capacitator power generator. "It's so elegant. I've never seen anything like it."

"Thank you."

"Did you build this? Without magic?" Brixton asked. Examining it even more slowly, allowing his magic to burn brightly and illuminate every shadow, he saw where wires were meant to cross and connect, where to suture and separate, all for easy and consistent power flow.

"I've worked on altering it a little, but the main component's design and a couple of the parts are from my family's collection." Adelaide put her hand on top of it, caressing it almost lovingly. "My father wanted me to find a way to use these for airship engines, but his grandmother was a little upset at that idea."

Brixton was impressed. "Do you think it would work?"

"I don't think just one engine would work." Adelaide held up the knot of wires she had been working on before. "Professor Ohm's electrical theory is all well and good, but not every theory translates well into reality. The wands and symbol etchings into wood or stone, or even on paper with ink, can help wielders because of their organic power. When it comes to machinery, all the life inside of it has been purged. I can't see magic powering up something that big for a long time without periodic charging. And that makes things more complicated, when wielders and their powers are involved. With wielders, they're only as good as their magic allows them to be. But if they use it all up, they'll either faint or die, and that's not going to help keep the power steady."

Brixton found himself staring at her again. "You certainly know a lot about magic, considering you don't use it."

"And you seem to know a lot about engineering, despite having a talent that makes it easy to cut corners."

There was something in her eyes as she held his gaze with hers, and he suddenly wondered what she saw when she looked at him. Brixton knew she was not happy he allowed her to be openly mocked earlier. Was she teasing him now? Or was it possible she was trying to be friendly?

"Edison used a constant stream of electricity to do that," Brixton reminded her, breaking his gaze away from hers. "Maybe we can find a way to make that work with a mix of magic and electricity."

"Magic and machinery doesn't inherently mix well," Adelaide said.

"Surely we can find a way to fix that." Brixton gave her a small smile.

He was surprised when Adelaide was the one who looked away this time. "That's what Professor Ohm wanted you to do, isn't it?" she asked, brushing a small lock of hair away from her face.

He shrugged. "I don't think he wanted me to actually do it. He was just making conversation with me. I think he was worried about my grades."

"That's how they tell you to do things here," Adelaide retorted. "You Brits are notoriously polite, sometimes to a fault."

He bit down on his cheek again. Did Adelaide forget she was at least half-British herself? "We're not all like that," he said.

"No, you're right. You're not all like that, or you would have said something to stop those girls from teasing me earlier. Or maybe you thought it was rude to interrupt their rudeness?"

Her assessment was stark and hard, and the earlier guilt he felt metamorphosed into shame. "Maybe I should go. I don't know if I can help you with this."

"I would rather you stay, then we'll find out if you can or not."

"Fine. But I don't want to hear anything else about the girls teasing you."

"If that's your price, I suppose I'll consider it. I doubt you'll hold me to it, though. You're already interested in the project. I can tell."

Brixton scowled at her, but Adelaide only handed him another small bundle of wires.

"What is this?" Brixton asked. He turned it over in his hand, noticing the twisted curls and studying the magnetic tips. "It doesn't belong in here."

"I told you, your professor wanted you to try to find a way to snare the energy of magic and use it as an electric source," Adelaide said. "As the engineer in the class with the highest grades, he wanted you to figure it out. Since you didn't pick up on it, this is what I've made to get us started. I think if a wielder can use the wire to collect a small amount of power, these wires should be able to hold it and the magnets will keep it moving."

"This is pure alloy?" Brixton took a second look at the wires Adelaide handed him. It was hard to believe such a little bundle could be so expensive.

"Amazing what having the last name of Favan will do for you, isn't it?" Adelaide gave him a small smile. "There are a lot of drawbacks, but there are some benefits, too. Vendors know we can pay off our bills."

Brixton caught the sadness in her voice and went back to work. He did not know if he could comfort her or not, and it did not help he was starting to feel angry that she had to suffer at all because of her family's name.

Next time any of those girls say anything to her, I will stop them. His silent vow eased his earlier shame, and he decided working with her on her project was a good penance for his earlier silence.

Together, they worked on her project steadily, with only a question or an order here and there, as the time passed.

It was nearly an hour later when Brixton felt a rush as he placed the wires in the middle of the device before connecting each compartment to it. "All right, then. I think that part is finished. Now what?"

"Now we need to add some wielder magic to it to see if it works."

"Well, there you go, then."

Adelaide said nothing; she only looked at him expectantly.

He groaned. "Why do you need my magic?"

"Yours has the best chance to work. After all, you've got creation magic, don't you?"

"Creation magic?" he repeated carefully.

"There are three main domains of magic," Adelaide told him. "There is the power to create, to change, and to destroy. Every dichotomy of magic stems from those distinctions."

"I've never heard that before. I've got white magic."

"They teach you advanced specialties here, so they can prepare you for specific jobs in the workforce," Adelaide reminded him. "What I am referring to is very basic stuff. I wouldn't be surprised if you learned it a long time ago and just forgot. It is not as important here."

He felt uncomfortable, realizing that she was right. It had been a long time since he had studied the basics of magic, and even then he glossed over it, quickly moving onto the more advanced teachings specific to his own talent.

"Do you remember why the magic portal was opened in the first place?" Adelaide asked. "Didn't you ever wonder why Parliament didn't blow up when Guy Fawkes and John Wright and their men tried to assassinate King James?"

"Well, it happened," Brixton said. "There's no point in questioning what would have happened otherwise. There's no way to know for sure what would have come to be, and there are not a lot of specifics known."

"But don't you think some people know?" Adelaide looked at him intently. "I find it hard to believe that a student of your intellect would give up on asking questions."

Brixton felt an unexpected pleasure at her half-compliment.

Adelaide bit her lip again. "Did one of your teachers tell you that?"

"Tell me what?"

"Tell you there's no use in wondering what would have happened, because it didn't happen? That there was no point in asking about what specifically happened, because there are no answers?"

FAVAN AND FLEW

"Well … " Brixton scratched his head nervously, suddenly very aware she was right about that, too. Dr. Winston had said it before in some of his lectures.

Before he could reply, he heard the clock chime again. He looked up at the time to see he had missed his class entirely. "Oh, no."

"Don't concern yourself," Adelaide said. "They never come looking for you when you've missed class."

"They do for me," Brixton retorted. "My scholarship here depends on a good class record." He did not want to mention his criminal past played a part in that. He was required to attend all of his classes, and if he missed any, he would have to make them up in detention.

"I'll tell them it was my fault if they come and bother you."

"It doesn't work like that, Adelaide," he snapped. "Your father's name doesn't extend its privilege to me."

She stepped back at his words, bumping into the table. Her hand reached out and steadied their project, and he immediately regretted yelling at her. But instead of apologizing, he shook his head and grabbed his books. "I've got to go."

"Wait. Will you help me work on this another time, Brixton?"

He was surprised she said anything to him at all, considering he had just insulted her. But when he looked back at her, the goggles were back up on her forehead. Her eyes were full of pleading, and he found that he could not say no to her. He was more surprised to find that he did not want to say no to her, either.

"Maybe later, when my schedule is less cluttered," he said. "I can't miss class the way … "

She gave him an impish smile. "The way I can?"

"You said it, not me," he muttered, blushing as he turned and left the room.

Once he was out of her sight, he breathed deeply, trying to calm the excitement he suddenly felt. There was no question that an hour working with Adelaide was much more stimulating than going to class, even if it was more trouble.

<u>3</u>

Brixton pushed his chair back from his father's workbench, allowing himself a moment to refocus. The mystic chords of memory never seemed so threatening as when he allowed himself to think of Adelaide.

"How can it be three years since I've seen her? And how can three years seem like a lifetime?" Brixton scoffed, chiding himself for his weakness and weariness.

It did nothing for his mind to ask such questions, even if his heart had the answers.

A few moments later, he finished tweaking Ticker's battery and tightened the screws on his back panel. Ticker did not need to be charged, but Brixton usually enjoyed working on the watch's magic loop, the one it used to help keep the battery charged for longer periods of time. It was a design he had refined from the little bundle of wires Adelaide had provided that day, and as much as he missed her, as much as he tried to hate her, he knew he would never trade those moments of his life away.

Even if he had to ignore them.

He was just eyeing his father's collection for another distraction when the door to the lab opened and Luella walked in.

"Father's still out working." Luella came up behind him, studying the array of tools and parts Brixton had pulled out. "If you were wondering."

Brixton shook his head. He knew his father did not object to either of his children working in his lab, but he was not thrilled with the prospect of sharing the space. "I wasn't."

"I'm sorry I said anything about Captain Favan earlier." Luella clasped her hands together behind her back, bowing her head forward. Her hair slid forward, hiding her face in a rare expression of contrition.

"It's fine." Brixton shrugged. He was about to assure her that her apologies were not necessary when a screech broke across the room.

Chirp! Chirp!

Brixton nearly covered his ears at the sound. "Oh, Lu. Please don't tell me—"

"Don't make a fuss, Brix. I'll get her."

Luella weaved her way around him. Standing on their father's work chair, she reached up to a high shelf and took hold of something. When she jumped back down, Brixton had a clear view of the item in her hand.

He groaned at the sight of the enchanted bird. The cogs of its eyes swiveled unevenly, blinking out of sync at the sight of him.

Brixton shrugged. "Why haven't you gotten rid of that? It's been ages."

"I happen to like Chirpy," Luella insisted. She flipped her hair back over her shoulder as she rubbed her cheek next to the small mecha-bird's head.

Chirpy twitched in artificial pleasure. Behind its glowing purple eyes, a small ebony spark caught Brixton's attention, and he reached out to inspect the bird more closely. He was about to take her from Luella when the small rustlings of the inner machinery began buzzing with full power, and Chirpy whistled a warning in his direction.

Luella giggled at its antics. "I know you like her, too, even if you don't like to think about who gave her to me."

Her tone was soft, but her words struck him soundly.

FAVAN AND FLEW

Brixton toyed with one of his wrenches, twirling it around between his fingers as he remembered the day when Adelaide had come over, bearing the gift for his little sister. The little mecha-magic songbird had easily stolen Luella's heart.

Brixton decided to change the subject. "When is Father expected to be home?"

"Inspector Spade has been asking for more men to work longer hours lately," Luella said. "There have been a few cases this week that require Father's attention."

"What kind of case is it?"

"I'm not sure. But maybe you can talk with him about it later. You might be able to help."

"I can't imagine I'd be much help. I'm a professor, after all, not a detective."

"You're still a wielder, and you know more about magic than most."

"Maybe they can just hire me down at Scotland Yard then; although I don't know why they would bother, if I'm not good enough to join the Airship Force."

"I am sorry you are unhappy at Rembrandt," Luella said, reaching out to pat his arm affectionately. "It has been a long time since Mum and Father have been able to keep all of us comfortable, but you should know we are all really proud of you. We would be a lot worse off without you, Brix. And without Rembrandt, too."

"I know."

He knew, but that did not make it any easier. After graduating from Rembrandt, he had been shocked to discover that his family could wind up out on the streets due to his remaining debt.

That was the only reason he agreed to work for Rembrandt—that, and because Adelaide's father vowed

Brixton would never be allowed to fly as long as he was alive.

Brixton glanced down at his rejection letter and frowned. It seemed Captain Favan's old threat still carried some weight.

Luella shifted, as if she could read his thoughts. "He's been dishonorably discharged, you know."

"What?"

She leaned against the wall of the lab, mindlessly petting Chirpy's fake feathers. "Captain Favan was dishonorably discharged from the Airship Force a week ago."

"What? Why?"

"Rumors say he was caught trying to manipulate the magic coming out of the portal. Her Majesty was not happy with him, and in the end, the House of Lords had him tried and dismissed from the corps. He's awaiting a sentencing trial now, locked up in Tower Hill."

Brixton shook his head. "He was the greatest fleet strategist since the ASF was created."

"No one is arguing his skill, just his ethics." Luella shrugged. "If he did manage to block your application, he'll be gone next year and then you'll be able to take over his job."

"I have no desire to be captain, Lu. Airship engines are some of the finest pieces of technical workmanship ever created. I would love to work on them." Brixton shuffled some of his father's paperwork aside and sat down on the desktop. "It would be much more interesting than the Board's research requests."

"What's wrong with the research? You've always liked studying."

"Some of them are just silly, Lu, and others … well, others can be quite sadistic, especially if they are used unethically." He thought about his latest award, the one he had received for working on the PRISM project, and nearly shivered. "It's not something I want to worry about while trying to teach enchanting engineering basics to kids."

"I would be appalled to hear my teacher calling me a kid."

He smirked. "That's what makes you a kid."

"At least you're allowed to go and see the portal up close for your work whenever you want," Luella said, quickly deflecting Brixton's taunt; she knew he had scored a point against her. "I have to wait for public viewing hours, and Mum is always so busy I never get to go."

"We wouldn't have the funds, either," Brixton murmured, while she made a face at him.

Luella was right. The magic portal was a sight to behold. It was a large circular hole, spanning several yards across Parliament's center courtyard. Every inch was filled with light that poured out into the sky, like an ongoing geyser of magic. The light appeared to flow right out of the old courtyard cobblestones, cutting into the grass and mud of the gardens.

Despite its beauty, no one wanted to get too close. People who walked into the portal disappeared, their bodies dissolving into the brightness of the light. There was talk of putting up a wall between the portal and the public, but eventually, only a railing made of silver was constructed around it. The king at the time thought it was a safe way to make the portal into a spectacle, one which the public could easily pay to see.

"I don't like going to see the portal. St. James's airship field is just across the block."

Luella rolled her eyes. "You always do that, you know."

"Do what?"

"You only see what you want." Luella crossed her arms. "There are good things in the world, even if they are not to your perfected liking."

Brixton did not know how to explain it to her. As much as she was skilled for her age in magic, understanding the human condition was different. He did not know how to explain to her that he just knew certain things. The magic of the Disruption might have granted humans the ability to manipulate the invisible forces of the world, but it had done nothing to satisfy every desire born inside the soul.

"I'm not trying to be mean," she said.

"I didn't think you were."

Luella eyed him carefully. "But you are sore at me for earlier still, aren't you? Or are you upset that I'm trying to point out you're in a good position, even when it's not the one you want to be in?"

Brixton shook his head. "It's not you, I promise."

"Good. Because I just want you to be happy." Luella gave him a friendly punch on the shoulder. "If for no other reason than you should be."

"I should be?"

"You've always been able to have adventures and go out and meet people. You get to have fun and you have a job, even if it's one you hate. Mum likes having me in her shop, all so she can make sure I don't get into trouble."

"Getting into trouble is not worth the so-called adventures I've had. I'm still paying for them, after all this time." Brixton shrugged. "Maybe if you get Rembrandt to offer you a scholarship, you'll have a chance at more freedom and happiness, too."

"I still need to wait another few months to apply." Luella twirled around in a circle, holding Chirpy high. "Until then, I'm stuck trying to make you happy."

"If you want me to be happy now, get rid of Chirpy."

"Come on, it's been a little over four years since I got her. How much longer do you think she'll last, Brix?" Luella glanced down at the mecha-bird again, watching as the power loop tucked behind its twin breastplates whirled on with the same ebony glow.

He eyed the small automaton, his earlier curiosity returning. Luella was right; it should not be too long before Chirpy's power fizzled or her parts broke down, and she would only be a pile of elegantly designed scrap metal.

Adelaide had made Chirpy for Luella after their first meeting, when she had unintentionally upset her. Brixton never bothered to check on it, and he was surprised to hear Luella had not tried to keep it charged on her own, either.

How has Chirpy managed to survive all this time?

He knew Adelaide was smart, but he did not think she had discovered a way to keep her automatons from losing power indefinitely.

Luella hugged the mechanical songbird to her chest. "I think she's gotten more of a personality over the years, you know. She whistles music to me sometimes."

Brixton clenched his fist. He thought about Ticker in his pocket, how he had been asked to work on designing personable mech for his graduation project.

Was it possible Adelaide had found a way to program something like that, a year before he had finished Ticker?

"Do you think Adelaide will ever come back?" Luella asked quietly.

Brixton did not want to answer her question. "Let's forget about it for now, shall we?"

FAVAN AND FLEW

"I know you wish you could forget her." Luella's words, spoken in good faith and kindness, still burned against him with stark rawness.

"She's already forgotten me. There's no point in remembering her." He gave his younger sister a rueful smile, watching as she made her way around the room, looking through the windows, avoiding his gaze.

"I wouldn't say that. I'm sure she remembers you. I mean, others remember you from school, too."

The doorbell rang, distracting them long enough for Luella to look out the window.

Luella giggled. "And here's some proof. It looks like Gloria's come to see us again, and she's apparently found another stray for Mother to tend to while she asks us questions about you."

"Gloria?" He searched his mind for a face to go with the name, but he found himself unable to recall her.

"Gloria Alberton." Luella grinned. "She's been coming around more often since she started working with Father at Scotland Yard. She picks up all sorts of strays while making her rounds. Mum and I agree she does this as an excuse to come over in hopes of seeing you. But she pays us every time and she always tries to find new homes for the animals, so we put up with it."

"I know who she is, and I just remembered how manipulative she can be." Brixton rubbed his temples. "And here I thought the worst part of today was over."

4

Gloria might not have changed much since their days at Rembrandt, but Brixton's reaction to her sure had. Seeing her in his family's kitchen, carrying a small kitten close to her chest, he felt none of the lustrous wonder he had felt when he first saw her.

She was still very beautiful. Her face was narrow, with a high forehead and elegantly arched brows. Her figure still filled out the uniform she wore, though it was a police uniform now. When Brixton had first met Gloria at school, he could have stared at her for hours; now, at the sight of her golden red hair, he was only tempted to ask whether or not she had a younger sister named Clarise.

"Brixton." Gloria greeted him warmly and eagerly as he walked into the room. "It's wonderful to see you. Your father said it was doubtful that you would be home. I'm so glad he was wrong."

"Did he escort you?" Brixton asked, gazing around the room.

"No. Inspector Spade has requested his help on another call." Gloria lowered her eyes, clearly hurt by his disinterest.

Brixton groaned to himself. She knew he was more irritated than excited to see her, and that was no act of mere intuition.

Gloria's magical capabilities were similar to his mother's, in that she could sense emotions. But Brixton knew she had more power than his mother, and with that added power, Gloria changed other peoples' emotions. He was willing to bet that was a major reason the police found her so useful. They hired her shortly after her failed launch into Society, welcoming her on the force, even though she was young, and even worse, she was from a high-ranking family in the aristocracy. But since no one wanted to marry her because of her talent, she had eagerly embraced her role as a junior officer.

She was not the first wielder of high Society to face such a fate, but she was one of the only ones who seemed to embrace it.

"Who did you bring to me today, Gloria?" Philippa asked, putting out another pot of tea. "Your kitten looks very sweet."

"He seems a little malnourished, but I found him while I was on my rounds near Parliament. I named him Fawkes, for the leader of the Treason Plot."

"The timing is uncanny," Philippa said. "The 275th anniversary is coming up next month."

"I've never thought about whether or not the animals were able to use magic," Gloria cooed as she handed Fawkes to Philippa. "But I definitely think Fawkes is magically adorable."

"Animals can't use magic," Brixton said.

"How do you know for certain, Brixton?" Luella asked as she sat down.

"If anyone would know, it would be Brixton," Gloria replied. "You were always one for the books while we were at school. I never bothered much with the origin of our magic. I mean, we have it, so what else is there to do but use it, right?"

Her words and attitude echoed his own youthful ignorance, and Brixton tried to remain patient.

"Using it implies that one has an understanding of it," he said, reassuming his position as an esteemed professor.

"We know that during the Great Disruption, the Gunpowder Plot failed to go off as planned. There was no physical damage done to the Parliament building when the powder exploded, but the portal opened up and the energy from it gave people the ability to wield different kinds of magic."

Gloria gave him a flirtatious smile. "I suppose you are right about the history of it, but knowing that does nothing to help me use my talent. Give me some wood, and I can etch a reveal spell that will tell me everyone's darkest fears in this room."

"That's precisely why we won't be giving you anything," Luella said. "Poor Roger the Peacock here will be absolutely frightened by the howling that's sure to ensue. It's a good thing he's asleep or Fawkes would ruffle his feathers, too."

Roger was snoozing lightly at the table, his broken leg outstretched as Luella bandaged it. Brixton knew that it was all healed up now, thanks to his sister's magic. The bandage was a reminder for Mrs. Fordyce to spoil him when he returned to her.

Not that anyone would doubt that she wouldn't, Brixton thought. Mrs. Fordyce was a well-known eccentric and one of the kindest ones when it came to her pets.

"You get some of the strangest creatures in here, Mrs. Flew," Gloria said. "Last time I was here, you had three French hens running around."

"Actually it was five. Roger here belongs to Mrs. Fordyce, and I would be remiss if I let her poor peacock suffer, especially after he got his leg caught in a window," Philippa said, patting the sleeping bird on the head. "Mrs. Fordyce has been one of my most loyal customers for years now."

"I imagine all of your customers are loyal."

FAVAN AND FLEW

"How is working for Scotland Yard going, Gloria?" Philippa asked, ignoring Gloria's flattery. "I imagine your parents were surprised you accepted the position there."

"They were," Gloria said. "But the inspectors appreciate my talent. As a wielder, I can offer much more clarity and certainty to our reports. And the other officers even seem to enjoy having me around."

"I commend you for it," Philippa said. "There's a reason I prefer working with animals to humans."

"Have you worked on any interesting cases lately, Gloria?" Luella asked. "I've heard there's a handsome young madman living in the sewers, trying to lead gentile ladies to their doom. They say he's a practitioner of animal magnetism. And then there is a wicked witch, hiding in the unfinished tunnels of the Underground, desperate for blood as she cooks up her spells."

Gloria laughed. "The penny dreadfuls seem to get cleverer by the day. No, the case I've been assigned to lately is a series of break-ins. It's actually quite boring."

"Tell us anyway," Luella pressed. "I enjoy assisting Mum in her work when I can, but life is exceedingly dull besides."

"Life is as dull as you make it, darling," Philippa said as she checked Fawkes' teeth.

Luella grimaced. "Hardly."

Brixton thought about Luella's complaints, that her life was so sheltered because of his own poor choices. He hoped his sister had the good sense to stay out of trouble.

"My current case is the one your father's been working on, too," Gloria said. "Someone has been breaking into houses and using magic on the owners."

"Why is my father working on that?" Brixton asked. His father was a strong, tall man, and the chief usually assigned him to disruptions and domestics. "He almost never works with burglaries."

"There are two main reasons," Gloria said, clearly excited she had his attention. "The first is that he has an extensive mechanical knowledge of locks. The second is that he is not a wielder."

Luella wrinkled her nose. "Why does that make a difference?"

"People are quite frightened and suspicious of wielders, even other wielders," Philippa said. "That's why I don't advertise myself as such. But if you had my talent, you would know the sinking sensation people feel when they find out you can work magic."

Gloria nodded. "Oh, I agree, Mrs. Flew. I know it well. Even when the others compliment my lovely shade of pink magic, I know many are cringing on the inside. Plenty of people are still wary of all magic."

"It sounds like this burglar is the exact reason why, too," Brixton said. He felt fortunate in that the people around him were more likely to disparage his company because of his class, not because of his magical talent, but he hated the thought of one thief damaging the reputation of the entire magical community. "I hope you catch him soon."

"We hope we can. He doesn't take anything when he's there. He only wants information."

"Information on what?"

Gloria shrugged. "That is the strange part. They don't remember. It seems to be a side effect of the red magic that's being used."

Brixton frowned. The more potent the color of a wielder's magic, the stronger the wielder. The use of red magic was further disconcerting, since it signified the wielder could establish control over the mind.

"Either that, or they don't want to tell the police," Brixton said. He knew from his own experiences with the London bobbies how unwilling he had been to talk to them.

"Is it why you are there, Gloria?" Luella asked. "Because they don't want to tell the truth?"

"Since I am a woman, and a younger one at that, no one considers me a threat. I accompany the officers, including Officer Flew, and take notes while they ask questions. Those who have been attacked are always much more relaxed when they discuss things with people like your father."

Gloria looked over at Brixton. "Something is strange about the break-ins. Even the new magical locks Rembrandt released a few years ago are all overpowered and the magic in them is gone."

Brixton bit back a smile. He had warned the Board, much to their dismay, that their latest approved lock design would be obsolete in a matter of months. He knew another powerful wielder, especially one with magic similar to his own, would be able to nullify the lock's security measures without much trouble.

"You wouldn't happen to have any ideas how that's happening, would you?" Gloria asked Brixton.

There were a few other possibilities, but none that Brixton wanted to contemplate. A fleeting image of Adelaide breezed past his mind's eye. He hurried to discard any thought of her, but this time for a different reason.

"I imagine there are plenty of others who are capable of creating a skeleton key," he replied, pulling Ticker out of his pocket and checking the time to avoid her gaze. "Why don't you check criminal records? You work at the prison, so it would be easy, and you'd likely find more leads than you would by asking me."

"Brixton, manners," Philippa hissed. "I beg your pardon, Gloria. Brixton is in a bit of a mood today. His application to the Airship Force was rejected again."

Gloria's large brown eyes blinked in sympathy and shock. "You still want to join the Airship Force? I thought that was a passing fancy while you were in school."

"That certainly never stopped you from making fun of me for it." Brixton took a last sip from his cold teacup and then set it down. "Mother, I do believe I should get back to work now."

"Do you have an evening class tonight?" Philippa asked. "I was hoping you would stay for dinner. Your father should be home soon, I imagine."

"My apologies, Mrs. Flew, but Officer Flew received a call on a case just before I left," Gloria said. "He was heading for Parliament, and it is unlikely he will be finished soon."

"Not when Parliament is involved," Brixton agreed. "But it doesn't matter either way. Father doesn't need my company."

His mother's eyes watered at his remark, and Brixton hurried to soothe her wounded heart. "I also have to get back to my office," he added. "The Board is supposed to confer with me over my latest performance review tomorrow, and I have another research project, too."

"Your job sounds much more boring than Gloria's," Luella replied, but she got up and hugged Brixton tightly. "I hope you survive."

"I've survived worse," Brixton said, more truthfully than he wanted to admit. He bowed his head to Gloria and

FAVAN AND FLEW

said his goodbyes to his mother before he walked out of the house.

"Brixton, wait!"

Brixton sighed. It was not surprising to see Gloria come running up behind him. "What is it?"

"I wanted to ask you something," Gloria said. "You used to be good friends with Adelaide Favan, didn't you?"

Brixton stopped in his tracks as Gloria came up next to him.

There is no use in trying to forget her today, is there? He knew there would be no relief any other day, either. There certainly never had been before.

"I know you remember her," Gloria said.

"Then why ask me if I do?"

Gloria took a tentative step back. "I'm just trying to be polite."

He paused only briefly, knowing she was right, and also knowing she was only asking the same courtesy of him.

"I *used to be* her friend," Brixton said, careful to emphasize his point. "We haven't spoken or communicated since she left school and went back to Peking."

"I was only asking—"

"Why?" Brixton struggled to maintain his composure. "My apologies, Gloria, but I've had enough of a bad day. My Airship Force application was rejected, and I have a lot of work to worry about finishing for the Board at Rembrandt. If I have to keep my job there, I need to make sure they don't have a reason to terminate my contract."

"If you don't like your job, why are you there in the first place?"

It was tasteless to admit the truth, but he did it anyway. "Money."

He found it irritating that she was clearly stricken by his response. While he had been coarse in his response, he knew she was more uncomfortable at the realization that some people had to work for a living, and work was not just something one did when there was nothing else to do.

"If you got married to someone with an inheritance, you would be able to quit," Gloria said. Her eyes lowered as a small blush came up onto her cheeks, eerily similar to the expression many of his female students wore when he arrived in the lecture hall.

"That implies there's someone out there who is rich and wants to marry me," Brixton said, hoping Gloria would not be able to sense his sudden discomfort. It was the first day in years he had talked with Gloria, even if his mother and father had no trouble talking about him to her, and he regretted his harsh tone. His guilt eased only somewhat as he recalled how Gloria and her friends used to tease Adelaide when they were in Rembrandt. "And that also implies that there is someone out there I want to marry, too. But please, just ask your questions. I don't want to talk about that."

"I was just going to ask if you heard from her at all," Gloria said. Her gaze stayed on the ground as she took a step closer to him. "Her father was deposed last week. He was moved to the prison on Tower Hill recently."

"I don't even know if she would care," Brixton replied. "She was never close with her father. She was practically overjoyed to go back to Peking when her great-grandmother called for her."

His memory admonished him for the lie. Adelaide resigned herself to go back to the Orient, seeing no alternative under her family's orders. She was far from happy at the decision, even though he knew she had wanted to get away from Rembrandt.

FAVAN AND FLEW

"I don't know why that would matter," Brixton said. "You don't think she's behind the burglaries, do you?"

"No." Gloria shook her head. "No, all the evidence and witnesses we do have point to a young male in his mid-twenties. But I thought of her because I was one of the few people who knew she had a talent for destruction magic."

"Well, I suppose you did learn that the hard way."

"Yes, nearly being killed does tend to make one learn that particular lesson."

Brixton felt a small rush of sympathy; Adelaide had been so angry at Gloria, but even Brixton, after knowing her and working with her as much as he had over the previous three years, never imagined the kind of retribution she was capable of enacting.

He could still picture the moment Adelaide's eyes went dark and she whipped off her glove. For a second, Brixton wondered if she would use it to slap Gloria across the face and challenge her to a duel.

Instead, she placed her hand on Gloria's face. Her black magic dashed out of her body and attacked Gloria, who screamed in pain and pleaded to go free until she fainted away, dead to the world. Brixton had stepped up to pull Adelaide off Gloria and caught her just before she fell.

Adelaide ran off while Brixton carried Gloria to the school hospital wing. Gloria was still recovering a week later when Adelaide was finally punished.

Brixton almost smiled. *Even the renowned Favan name didn't stop her from getting suspended for that one.*

Adelaide had been almost as surprised to be reprimanded as Gloria had been when she was attacked.

It was only later Brixton found out Adelaide had stripped Gloria of all her magic, destroying her energy and nearly taking her life.

FAVAN AND FLEW

It was soon after that when Adelaide started talking about leaving Rembrandt, Brixton suddenly remembered. She was more than upset over the whole situation, although none of her frustration had to do with regret for what she had done to Gloria.

Gloria pursed her lips. "I'm sorry, you know, how I treated you and the others like her at school, Brixton. But I've changed since then. It's not fair to hate me for someone I used to be."

Brixton wanted to ask her if it was the multiple rejections from possible suitors that had finally humbled her, but he did not want to bring up the subject of marriage with her right now—or ever, really.

Before he could say anything else, a loud siren called out from across the city.

Gloria and Brixton both turned toward the source, looking over the city skyline just in time to see one of the city's monitoring airships veer into the Parliament clock tower.

5

The shattered glass rained down on the streets below as the bow of the airship wedged into the clock face and the ballooned sails began to deflate. Brixton felt a rush of fear and uncertainty as he stood there, shocked and transfixed at the sight. From where he was standing, he thought he could just make out a slim shadow jumping from the deck of the ship, disappearing through the hole in the clock face.

Gloria gasped. "The clock tower—it's been attacked!"

"Are you certain it's not an accident?" Brixton asked, even though he already knew the answer.

"It can't be." Gloria shook her head, still paralyzed with shock. "Oh, Brixton. This is terrible. Your father was headed to Parliament earlier."

"He could be in danger," Brixton heard himself say. "We need to get there."

There was no hesitation in his steps as Brixton ran toward the broken clock tower. Gloria called to him from behind, and he could vaguely hear her listing concerns for his safety. But something was happening, something strange. As Brixton spurred on forward, he felt the instinctive tug of his magic as it pushed him forward.

Several people stopped in the streets, gasping in terror and morbid curiosity while Brixton threaded his way through the crowd. Gloria followed closely behind him, reaching into her pocket and pulling out an electro-magic transmitter.

The small object reminded Brixton of a box by the way it opened, revealing a small, tubular mouthpiece attached to a wire. Gloria pulled it out and began speaking into it.

"Calling for Officer Flew. This is Junior Officer Alberton. Officer Flew, acknowledge."

Brixton glanced at the transmitter now, recognizing the design. He had helped some of the senior-level students at Rembrandt with the early blueprints a few months ago. Looking at it now, he could tell it was a finely tuned object, intricately designed despite its size. If it had been any other time, and his father's life were not in danger, Brixton would have been interested in examining the gadget more closely.

Gloria shut the lid down on it a second later. "I'm not getting through to anyone. The line is dead."

"Does it need charged?"

"Yes, it does," she admitted. "It's past the end of my shift and I would need a wand to channel my power to it."

"If you get a moment where you can take care of it, you should."

Gloria gave him a smile as she ran, despite her breath coming in small pants. "Do you want to take a look at it later on? We can get a drink, maybe."

He did not tell her it was the wrong time to ask him out, but more because he did not want to waste his breath on such an obvious remark. Instead, Brixton focused on running faster as he continued to watch over the monitoring airship, its hull half-lodged inside the clock's fragmented face.

As he neared the clock tower, Brixton could see the police running around, setting up a safe perimeter.

"You might want to stay back." Gloria stopped running as she finally caught up with him. Her eyes were full of doubt as she looked up at the broken clock face then down to the riverfront. "This is police work, after all."

"My father could be inside there!" Brixton argued.

She threw up her hands in exasperation. "I can't just let a civilian run around a crime scene, Brixton. It's too dangerous."

"Just go, and I'll follow you. I can decide if it's too dangerous."

"They have procedures for this, you know, and protocol matters. I know you're worried, but you can't be reckless." Gloria frowned at him, leaving Brixton behind as she hurried over to meet with the other police guards.

Brixton clenched his fists. Gloria said his father was on his way over to Parliament. There was no way to know where he was or what exactly was going on.

"Stay back, you vazey bastards. You trying to get killed?"

Brixton frowned as the local police and palace guards were working hard to keep the gathering crowds back.

He quickly ducked back across the street. The last thing Brixton needed was for a mage-rager policeman to insist he "magic" the clock face back to normal. Despite the past centuries, there were some who insisted on remaining ignorant to the limits of a wielder's power.

There was a loud creak, and another round of glass shattering from above. Brixton glanced up at the clock again. He doubted any wielder would be able to use the damaged airship for an escape.

He frowned. *How would the villain get away if his airship is destroyed?*

Brixton studied the scene before him, trying to channel his panic away from his reasoning. From where he stood, there was no way to salvage the airship. Even aided by magic, he saw nothing that would aid it enough to keep it afloat. The ship, with its cracked hull and the leaking enveloped sails, would soon fall.

The crew had to sense it, too, he thought. No one seemed to be on the ship. No one was running back and forth trying to launch the emergency anchor, no one was screaming for rescue …

"It's a distraction."

Inside, his magic dashed out of his heart and rested in his palms as if in confirmation. Brixton began to head around the block. He spied Gloria, working on setting up a perimeter with other policemen. She was too busy, he decided. While the police worried about protocol, the villain would be able to escape without a trace; he had to have another escape planned.

As Brixton turned the corner, he could see the evening sun burn through the hole in the clock's face. A pair of shadows moved from the inside.

There. Two of them.

Brixton braced himself as he slipped through another huge crowd, one that was amassing on the far side of Parliament. In the distance, he could see several were also looking toward Westminster Abbey, making the sign of the cross.

He almost felt like praying himself, but he dared not take the time to stop as he ran around the palace. He passed by St. James Park, where Her Royal Majesty's Airship Force had a small battalion of airships preparing to launch.

He glanced back at the palace and saw a flicker of purple shine from the King's Tower. As he watched, three more quick bursts of red-violet light splintered across the palace keep.

There they go.

There was another escape attempt that was being coordinated on the other side of Westminster. While the airship in the clock tower slowly caused panic on one side, the criminals would duck out the far side.

Another airship, assisted by quieter Rembrandt-designed propellers, moved toward the broken clock. Over the sounds of people panicking in the street, Brixton could hear the captain's commands.

"Hard starboard, men! Save the clock tower!"

Brixton ran a hand through his hair, furious. How could they not see that this was intended to go badly?

A daring idea began to take form inside his mind—one that called to him ruthlessly and relentlessly, despite the barrage of logic and precaution that hurried to fight it.

His heart began to beat faster as he sorted through the risks, before discarding all of them. It was not the right time to question his instinct—not when his father could be in danger, and not when no one was around to stand in his way.

He hurried down the block to the entrance of St. James, the airship field, only to find they were on full lockdown. It was closed to civilians.

Except those with special passes.

Quickly, Brixton searched through his pockets. His fingers curled around his Rembrandt identification badge and pulled it free.

Brixton looked from his badge to the clock tower, where the small monitoring airship began to burn, still lodged in its face.

More people were calling out from below the building, and the Airship Force only seemed to set out to make the matters worse.

His grip tightened around his badge, and then he hurried forward.

Several servicemen ran past him, scurrying through the open atrium, while orders blared out over the public service speaker.

In all the confusion, Brixton found it easy to follow a line of corpsmen into the entrance building and head back toward the airship fields. No one stopped to question him, not even as he struggled to keep pace with the others.

So many things he passed begged for his scrutiny, from historical displays, to artifacts from different raids and battles, and even a statue of the disgraced Captain Favan.

"Move, move, move!" One of the airship commanders waved the shipmen into their loading docks.

He was the first person to pull Brixton out of the line. He grabbed him by the scruff of his collar before blaring into his face. "What are you doing here, Civy?"

Brixton nearly choked at the smell of his breath. He was almost grateful for the distraction, as it allowed him to forget his sweating palms and shaking hands. "My name is Brixton Flew, sir, and I am here at the request of the Education Board at Rembrandt," he said, flashing his ID badge in the man's face.

The commander snapped the badge out of his hand and examined it. "I was not informed of this."

Brixton eyed his credentials. *Commander Carlisle.*

"I was scheduled by the office weeks ago, for the latest airship engine inspection," he lied. "I was told to report to Captain Favan."

Why is it suddenly so easy to lie?

Was he was returning to the days when he used to cause trouble on the streets, or was it just that the instinct had been there all along, hidden inside him, just like his memories of Adelaide?

Brixton did not know the answer, and as Carlisle pulled out his own transmitter and radioed in to the main office, he knew he did not have the time to decide if he wanted to know the answer at all.

The Commander's transmitter fizzled, signaling a dead end. Brixton breathed a muffled sigh of relief.

"I've been told to inspect the engines you ordered from the school for quality assurance purposes," Brixton continued. "I am the leading professor of engineering enchantment at the school, and I have been informed the engines might have been compromised."

"Compromised by what?" The Commander barked. His brow furrowed with deep lines and his eyes went dark with a familiar wariness. "Magic?"

From the soft fear in his voice, Brixton could tell Carlisle was not opposed to the use of magic, but he clearly hated the inconvenience it brought him as a non-wielder.

Carlisle's reaction was too similar to his father's to be mistaken, Brixton thought with a pang of guilt. He was clearly not a wielder.

"Not magic, sir. Inferior materials." Brixton pointed to a ship that was gearing up for takeoff. "If you're going to use these on the field, I insist on going with a crew to make my inspection, sir."

"We do not approve civilian participation in our rescue missions," Carlisle said. "You will have to wait."

"I demand to go right now. I would hate to think that Rembrandt would want to renegotiate its terms with St. James in the coming future. Her Majesty would be appalled by the delay. She was hoping to extend our contract into other areas." Brixton looked down at the transmitter, which was still giving off a fuzzy signal. "Perhaps we could even design a better transmitter for you. One that doesn't rely on magic."

Carlisle hesitated long enough for Brixton to push forward. "It would be my pleasure to personally guarantee you the first prototype, sir. I know you are just trying to do your job here, just as I need to do mine."

Carlisle sighed and waved over another private, who came running. "Professor Flew, sir, this is Private Jensen. He will escort you to the *Horizon*."

Brixton nodded his profuse thanks as Carlisle gave Private Jensen a list of directions and set them off.

"Professor Flew?" Carlisle called to him just as he stepped onto the loading gangplank.

For a moment, his heart plunged, and his mind began to race with the possibility that Carlisle was going to call him up and have him arrested for fraud and premeditated sabotage. Horrible visions of being dragged before the Airship Court of Appeals along with Captain Favan ran through his mind, and he hated imagining the sadistic scowl on the disgraced captain's face most of all.

"What is it, sir?" Brixton asked, forcing himself to turn around and give the airship commander a friendly smile.

"Fly safe." Carlisle gave him a quick salute, and Brixton immediately relaxed.

He was not going to hang for his crimes.

Not today, anyway.

"Step up this way, sir," Private Jensen called, waving him up the loading ramp. "Captain Airey's about to takeoff."

Brixton felt his legs buckle as the ship began to rise and the anchors were pulled up when the engines whirred to life. He had only been on an airship once before, when he was much younger. To his young eyes, everything had been a mysterious wonder, pulling him in and captivating him until nothing else could rival his interest.

FAVAN AND FLEW

It was a much different experience from what he remembered. He grabbed a hold of the back of an empty chair as the ship took to the sky, desperate to keep his footing as well as his lunch. He had a feeling he was more nervous because he had lied his way onto a military ship, but if he was going to be disgraced, he wanted his prison record to be clear of any airsickness.

"Easy, Civy," Jensen said. "Once we get clearance from the captain, you can start your inspection."

Brixton glanced over to see a man in a gray military suit covered in silver trim. Captain Airey was calling out orders, asking for information, and Brixton felt like a kid again as he watched him.

They were headed for the clock tower when the captain finally turned his attention to Brixton.

Captain Jack Airey was a younger man, one that Brixton would have guessed to be only a few years older than himself. He had the accent of an accomplished student, but he had the sharp eyes of a street lad. He was a career soldier, and Brixton had a feeling that, if he managed to get out of his lies without anyone finding out about them, he would jump at the chance to become good friends with him.

"Captain Airey, this is Professor Flew, of Rembrandt Academy," Jensen said. "Commander Carlisle instructed me to watch him while he inspects our engines."

"Rembrandt?" The captain eyed Brixton suspiciously. "We did not have an inspection scheduled from the Board for today. Professor Winston is usually the one we meet with."

At the sound of his immediate superior's name, Brixton felt his gut twist. There was no room for doubt or hesitation, and neither was there room for guilt, he reminded himself.

FAVAN AND FLEW

"I was supposed to meet with Captain Favan," Brixton said, suddenly extremely grateful Ticker was stuffed into his pockets. He hated to think his uptight timekeeper might call him out on his endless stream of lies. "I was sent instead of Dr. Winston since I'm working on gaining tenure at the academy."

"Well, good luck to you then, since no one outside the Board seems to have tenure there. You must be a promising candidate."

Brixton shrugged. "We'll see."

"Pragmatic, are you?" Captain Airey nodded approvingly. "You have your orders, Professor, and I have mine. All I insist is that yours don't interfere with mine."

"Yes, sir." Brixton gave him a quick, sloppy salute.

"Call me Jack." Captain Airey returned the salute properly before he headed off.

Brixton waited until he was out of earshot before he turned to Jensen. "Take me to engine room, Private."

As they headed down into the hull of the ship, Brixton had to tell himself to breathe. He had been able to get on the ship.

Now he just had to figure out what to do next.

<u>6</u>

Brixton tried not to look nervous as he bumbled about the airship engine room. He discarded his jacket and rolled up his sleeves, eager to get to work.

He pulled Ticker out of his pocket and turned him on, pinning him to his shirt to keep him close enough to hear over the roar of the engine machinery. "Ticker, see if you can pick up any transmitting frequencies."

Ticker yawned. "I am not programed to hack into other frequencies, sir."

"But you should know how to do it."

"Sir, it is not legal." Ticker's eyes rolled around as he took in their full environment. "Oh, dear. Why are you on Her Royal Majesty's Airship *Horizon*? What trouble have you gotten us into this time, sir?"

"What do you mean, 'this time?'" Brixton shook his head as he bent down behind the large fans behind the ship's radiator. "I know I've lied much more than you'd like, but I have been careful not to get myself into actual trouble for several years now."

"Then why would you want to break such a record, sir?" Ticker's clock hands turned down in saddened disapproval. "And, if I may say so, why would you break such a record so spectacularly?"

"I believe my father is in danger."

"You believe your father is in danger, and so you put us in danger to help him?"

The complicated nature of the truth made Brixton pause. Finally, he sighed. "Don't look at me like that, Ticker."

Brixton pulled off several covered panels, studying the different buttons behind the giant engines. He called up his talent and relaxed at once. His magic's ability quickly guided him to the ship's trajectory controls.

It would not take long to get where he wanted to go. He silently cheered as he pulled on a few wires and the power flickered. The fan blades whirred and slowed down angrily as their power source was compromised.

"Professor?" Jensen called, as the ship came to a slow halt. The engine stalled and made a coughing sound. Only the sails and the airship's balloons allowed the ship to remain airborne.

Brixton was not worried, but he feigned shock. "The damage was worse than I thought!" he shouted over the whirring and sputtering sounds, hurrying to pull the power from other sections. "Inferior materials are one thing, but this sort of situation can only be sabotage."

"Sabotage?" Jensen blanched. "You mean someone onboard has bamboozled our engines?"

"I'm afraid so," Brixton called, ripping out another pair of wires while Jensen nervously glanced back at the doorway. "This is extensive damage. Please go inform the captain of our situation. I will do my best to fix everything."

"Yes, sir, right away."

Brixton breathed a sigh of relief as Jensen disappeared out of the room. He hated lying to the man, but it was certainly amusing to see he was still able to lie quite convincingly.

"I must congratulate you, sir," Ticker said. "You must have done some extensive deception to get that man to trust you."

"Either that, or he wasn't smart enough to ask if I was the one doing the sabotaging."

"You sound cynical, sir."

"I've learned my lesson the hard way." Brixton brushed a lock of hair out of his face. He looked around, ashamed that he had to lie his way onto the ship. The damage to the engine he caused was not beyond repair, and he hoped he would get the chance to prove himself when everything was over.

At this rate, I will have to capture the villains and stop a diabolical plot to destroy the kingdom in order to stay out of jail.

Brixton fought down a rush of anxiety. If he could save his father—if he could prove his magic was not just a burden, and that it could do some real good for their family—it would be worth it.

"We need to get to the King's Tower," Brixton said. "Show me a compass, Ticker. I'm going to need it to get on a path there."

"I insist on asking if the ship's brakes are working before giving you any requested information, sir."

"These are Rembrandt engines. There's a lot of magic involved in keeping this running. I disrupted some of it, so I can get it to where we need to go, but the brakes will work."

Ticker let out a small moan, but he pulled up the compass for Brixton.

He was just maneuvering the engines to rotate in the direction of the King's Tower when the door to the engine room burst open.

"What in God's name are you doing in here?"

The captain's voice boomed from the entrance, and Brixton stood up in a hurry, giving him what he hoped looked like a frantic salute.

"I'm afraid your engines have been tampered with, Captain," Brixton said. "From my analysis, it is clear sabotage was involved."

"They were reported by my ship's mechanics as perfectly fine before takeoff."

"I would start there for an investigation," Brixton asserted, putting on his best lecture voice. "Especially if they were the last ones to inspect them—"

"Before you came in here." Jack crossed his arms and nodded to the men who flanked him. "Jensen, Salisbury, arrest this man."

"No," Brixton yelped. "No, don't arrest me. You need me to work on this. How else is the ship going to stay up in the air?"

"My mechanics are still onboard," Jack replied. "I'll call them up here and we'll be on our way even before I can throw you in the brig."

"No, don't do that." Brixton sighed. "No, you can't. We need to get over to the King's Tower before it's too late. Time is of the essence, Captain."

"We are under the command of the Admiral, and our orders have been given to report to the clock tower. There's no reason we should—"

"There are other ships that can focus on the clock tower," Brixton insisted, nearly shouting this time. "The perpetrators are making their escape on the other side of Westminster. I saw them."

Jack paused, and Brixton could only pray he would believe him.

The captain gave him a considerate look. "You saw them?"

"Yes. There was a light, some sort of signal. It was coming from the King's Tower. I know that transmitters are down on the ground and there was no way to check."

Jack raised an eyebrow. "You saw the attackers fleeing from the clock tower? That's why you conned your way onto an airship?"

Brixton pushed back his hair and sighed. "Look, you said it yourself. You have your orders, and other ships do, too. Why not do a perimeter check? The monitoring airship stuck in the clock isn't going anywhere. There has to be another way for the attackers to escape. We could see them from up here and keep much better track of them. We might even be able to capture them."

"How do you even know this is a coordinated attack?" Jack asked. "Couldn't it have been—"

There was a loud, deafening rumble from outside. Warning bells and alerts all sounded, echoing in a deadly melody in the heart of the engine room.

"Captain!" A voice called out through the ship, as the officers began to run down the halls outside the room. "The airship in the tower has exploded!"

Brixton nearly collapsed at the sudden pounding in his ears. He wanted to cover them with his hands, but he had to hold on as the ship whipped back and forth, hurtling off course amidst the confusion.

He looked up to see Jack was yelling at him, but Brixton could not make out a word through the sea of noise and numbness. He kept working to stabilize the ship as Jack made his way around the engine, taking Brixton by the collar. He was saying something about taking him somewhere else, and Brixton fought him every step of the way before they made it out of the room.

FAVAN AND FLEW

As the echoing stopped, Brixton was finally able to hear again.

"I don't know what on earth you were thinking," Jack said, "but you're coming with me."

"But the engine! Someone has to—"

"I've sent Jensen and Salisbury to go get the mechanics. You need to come with me and tell me where you saw that signal."

"So you believe me?" Gratitude poured through him, and Brixton could have hugged the man.

"No," Jack replied, cutting Brixton's enthusiasm short. "But I don't want you out of my sight from now on."

If that was the best he was going to get, Brixton decided to go along with it.

He followed Jack up to the top deck. The wind carried the smell of smoke and metal from the other airship's explosion. Brixton saw that it had broken into several pieces before it littered all over the ground before Westminster. The clock face had mostly survived the blast, but all the glass was smashed in, with one of the clock hands having fallen down onto a ledge of the tower. Dangling on the end of it was some of the airship's envelope netting, burning with black smoke. It blended into the darkening sky, but it was repulsed by the bright light of Parliament's courtyard, where the glow from the portal continued on uninterrupted.

"This is horrible," Brixton whispered.

"Looks like Parliament has been evacuated," Jack said. He pointed to the riverfront, where people were lining up.

"Do you have any idea who is behind this?"

"I should be asking you that, Professor," Jack replied. He gave him a small, reluctant smile. "If you've come here, risking your employment and capture by Her Royal

Majesty's Airship Force, you must have some idea who is behind this."

Brixton shook his head. "All I know is that it might be connected to a string of burglaries," he admitted. "My father is a police officer working the case."

"You know he'll likely face questions regarding your escapades here today, right?"

Brixton stifled a groan. The last thing he wanted was to give his father even more reasons to question his integrity. "Please don't bring him into this, Captain."

"You wouldn't be here if you didn't think he was in danger."

Brixton looked around at the ship's deck, wondering if that was the full truth of the matter.

He had always wanted to be a member of the Airship Force, and it looked like he just ruined his chances for good. He had lied to a member of Her Royal Majesty's defense department, abused his position as an instructor at Rembrandt, and leveraged his talent as a wielder to break the steering functions on a government airship.

Blast it, what in the world was I thinking?

Brixton rubbed his temples as terror renewed inside of him. After all those years of quiet desperation, working at a job he hated, dealing with all the Board's demands and the students' needs, was it possible he had gone mad?

"The Board is not going to like this anymore than my father will," he muttered.

Jack called back several orders to the men on deck as Brixton considered the possibility that jumping off the airship onto the pavement below would be a kinder fate.

Ticker buzzed in his pocket, and Brixton nearly slapped him into silence. He did not want to deal with Ticker's self-righteousness now.

It was only when the buzzing grew louder that Brixton pulled him out. "What? What is it, Ticker? Are you going to rub everything in my face?"

"No, sir. I am quite unable to do anything resembling physical harm to your person."

Brixton nearly chucked Ticker overboard. Before he could shut him off, Ticker buzzed again. "I have the frequency report you requested, sir."

"Frequency report?" It took Brixton a long moment to recall he had asked Ticker to find a frequency to hack. "Well, what did you find?"

"The transmitter frequencies utilized by the police and other guards are all up and running again."

"Great." His tongue felt thick inside his mouth as Brixton shook his head. Ticker was telling him it would only be a matter of minutes before his crimes were known and blared out across the nation. The newspapers would be hounding him day and night for the next several weeks, possibly months, and his family would be disappointed and ruined, and soon they would likely be homeless. Brixton closed his eyes, trying to block out the shame that sliced through him.

"All frequencies are in working order, but they are being blocked in the area surrounding the King's Tower."

Brixton opened his eyes. "There's no frequency running through the King's Tower?"

"None. Nothing is able to penetrate into that section of the building."

"All the magic has been shut out." Brixton turned to Jack. "Captain!"

Brixton hurriedly grabbed him by the arm and informed him of the situation, showing him Ticker's data. He was rambling like a madman, but Brixton kept going.

FAVAN AND FLEW

"This is no time to play heroics," Jack warned him. "I'd hate to think you were in league with them."

"I'm not," Brixton insisted. "Why would I tell you anything if that was the case? Someone was there, in the King's Tower, earlier."

They glanced over at the King's Tower. There was no sign of any signal now, but Brixton's talent spurred inside of him again, and he felt a renewed sense of hope.

"They could still be there!" he said.

Jack pulled out a spyglass and looked at the tower.

Brixton studied the tower, seeking any sign that his hunch was right. He poured more power into his magic, letting it churn inside him, unable to stop himself from seeing if there was any inkling of truth.

Seconds later, a bright, violet light pierced through the sky, looking out toward the Tower Gardens. It was just a flicker, but it was all Brixton needed to see.

"There!" He pointed to the top of the tower. He could just make out a figure cloaked in darkness, the shadow wandering across the outside window ledge. In the dying sunlight and the growing luminescence from the portal, he would have missed it entirely if it weren't for the strange weapon the figure held.

Jack saw it too this time. "Hard port," he called. "Prepare cannons."

Using his talent, Brixton saw a shadowed man launching a device of some sort. The shadow anchored it from the window, and a second later, a heavy wire reflected the last of daylight's sunshine across the sky before it descended downward.

It was almost like a tightrope, he thought, watching as the wire disappeared into the gardens as he watched.

Brixton turned back to Jack. "The cannons aren't going to work. It's too small of a target."

"My weapon workers are the best in the nation, Professor."

Another figure appeared beside the other one. This one was much shorter and more agile. Together, both of them attached a small sling to the line. Using it as a seat, the first shadow slid down the zipline into the darkness.

"You could destroy the tower if you miss," Brixton argued. "You can't save it if you're going to destroy it."

Jack gave him a smug, stern look. "We have our orders."

"You have your orders," Brixton corrected him. "Just get closer. If I can get over there and stop them, we can save the tower and capture the perpetrators."

"That's assuming you don't die in the process." Jack cut him off. "Stand back, Professor. You've already caused enough trouble here today."

"But—"

"I'm the one in charge here." Jack turned back to his crew. "Aim for the assailants' getaway and fire when ready!"

The airship was closing in to the tower now, but there was nothing he could do. He watched as the cannons went off, grimacing as the cannonballs shot through the fine architecture of the tower. There was a small cloud of debris as the remaining villain dodged several of the counterattacks.

Brixton cheered along with the rest of the crew, but he was unnerved as the remaining villain straightened.

Jack pulled down a lever, and a large horn appeared. He leaned forward, speaking into it, magnifying his voice as he called out to the fighter. "You must surrender. You are trapped, and there is nowhere to run."

The figure held up his hands. Inside, sharp metal gleamed at the tips of his fingers.

"Captain, stop!" Brixton called out, but it was too late.

The attacker tossed his weapons. As they passed through the air, Brixton could just make out the outline of throwing stars. Brixton felt the ship sigh with weariness as they shot through the inflated sails of the ship.

The *Horizon* fluttered, sinking slightly downward in the skies, just low enough to where the airship was level with the tower.

Brixton watched as the dark figure moved to jump.

"Surely he's not actually going to do it," Brixton muttered.

His mouth dropped open as he watched the figure run back and then leap off the building ledge.

For a long moment, the figure seemed to float. The whole of time seemed to slow as he soared, his body stretching, reaching out toward the deck.

He landed on the side of the ship with a soft crash, grabbing a hold of one of the spare balloon nettings that hung from the side of the ship. Brixton gaped, watching as the figure deftly climbed up and hopped onto the deck.

"Well, he's quite the daredevil," Brixton muttered, still shocked. Up close, he saw the figure was dressed in all black, and he wore a mask over his face. His eyes were covered by a pair of goggles, ones that glowed green in the rising moonlight. It was almost like watching something from a carnival, Brixton thought in amazement.

Any number of guards came rushing out to meet him. Brixton leaned over the side of the ship to see if he could watch the commotion from the upper deck.

Pure exhilaration rushed through him as he saw the corps members fight off the attacker. He was nearly in their grasp as Brixton contorted himself into an uncomfortable position over the deck's railing, trying to keep watching the scene before him. If anything was going to vindicate Brixton and his brazen actions, it was capturing the party responsible for the clock's vandalism.

"Stay here, Professor." Jack reached behind him and set him down in a chair near the hallway toward the engine. "I do believe I have an arrest to make."

Brixton grinned as Jack's first commander came and took the helm, guiding the ship toward the river as it fell. He braced himself as the bottom of the hull scraped the outer wall of Westminster Palace.

Even if it only meant trouble, it was so freeing to face the wind and danger head-on. Brixton was so elated by the rush, he barely noticed the noise from the front deck had ceased.

Then he heard Jack cry out in pain.

Brixton jumped up and hurried down the steps the captain had disappeared down only a moment before.

What is going on?

Brixton saw the answer as he stepped through the entrance to the upper front deck. The shadowed figure had removed one of his black gloves and was holding up a ball of black magic in his palm. The captain was unconscious at his feet, and the rest of the corpsmen had backed up. From where he stood, Brixton could see some of them were below deck, preparing for a trench-like warfare. He watched as the figure headed in his direction.

Brixton ducked out of the way, hiding his face and scooting around a large doorway as the figure ran by.

He's a wielder. The assailant was using his power to attack the captain and push back the others.

So where was he going now? Brixton wondered. He watched as the figure made his way down the hall.

A small pouch plunged to the floor as it fell off the attacker's belt. Brixton watched, still dumbfounded, as the attacker tumbled and rolled, easily scooping it up and tying it firmly onto his belt in the back.

Whatever was inside it, Brixton saw, was precious to him.

Brixton followed the shadow, surprised to see it turn to the engine room where he had been escorted when he first arrived.

A dark light burned in the figure's palm as he removed his other glove, and Brixton realized he was going to destroy the engines. The attacker did not know they were already down, thanks to Brixton's earlier handiwork. They would be stuck in the Thames, afloat, until someone could come and evacuate them.

That seemed to be the plan, anyway. Brixton took a deep breath and leaned against the wall, just outside the engine room door.

He could do this, he told himself. It was one villain and him, and he could take him on. It was the smaller one, after all, not the taller figure he had seen earlier.

If nothing else, I have to do this to make up for all my deception today, he told himself.

Behind him, the engines stalled, and Brixton knew it was time to act. He called up his magic, prayed for the strength to get through this, and stepped inside the room.

Immediately, Brixton shut the lights off. His power still glowed, but he knew the villain would be surprised, and there was nothing like keeping an enemy off guard. He

FAVAN AND FLEW

made his way to the panel where he had attempted to take over the steering earlier, and he was surprised to see a green glow on the villain's face.

He was still wearing his workman goggles, Brixton realized. His opponent likely thought the lights went off because of the engine stalling, not because he had flipped them off—if he noticed the lights were out at all.

"Stop!" Brixton launched himself at the villain, knocking the figure away from the panel as he tackled him. Brixton was gratified to see his opponent was lighter than he had estimated. It would make fighting him more manageable.

Or so he thought.

The figure slid out from under him. Before Brixton could blink, his opponent sank a solid kick into Brixton's gut.

The blunt burst of pain made him grunt, but Brixton did his best to keep a hold of his opponent. Black magic burned against his shirt, but Brixton used his own magic to counteract it.

The villain seemed surprised by this, and Brixton did not hesitate to use it to his advantage; he pushed the villain back, slamming him headfirst into the wall behind them.

The tiny glass lenses in his goggles cracked, and the eerie green light stopped. Brixton held him against the wall, using all of his weight to keep the villain there.

"Got you," Brixton whispered, hoping someone was on their way for backup.

A small, muffled gasp escaped from the man, before he pushed back and slipped through Brixton's hold.

The green glow around his eyes had disappeared as he pushed back his goggles, but the black fire in his palms increased as he took a fighting position.

Brixton swallowed hard as he held himself steady.

The fighter charged him, but Brixton easily caught him. Their hands, covered in magic, clashed dangerously, and lightning blazed out from the shock of their union.

At their contact, Brixton was struck by two simultaneous realizations, both of them dangerous and possibly deadly.

The first sensation he processed was that their magic was equal, enough to cancel each other out. He knew it was true. He could handle whatever the attacker threw his way. He had more physical strength, even if he did not have the same fighting technique. He could win.

But the second realization stopped him. He recognized this power. Not just the power itself, but the person behind the power. He had felt this connection before …

And as he looked down at the figure before him, his mind slowly awakened to the small, delicate fingers fisted against his palm. The figure's black hood had fallen back at the force of their clashing power, and a long wave of straight black hair billowed out.

It was not a man, Brixton realized. It was a woman.

And it was not just any woman.

"Ada."

Her broken goggles were pushed back on her forehead, the same as countless times before. Her eyes were narrowed and focused, and he knew she was only concerned with winning.

But at his old endearment for her, Adelaide Favan's silver eyes opened wide and she finally saw him.

She stared up at him, and he only saw her. Their magic started to curl into each other, the spindles of power whipping around them even more fiercely as they recognized each other.

FAVAN AND FLEW

A million and one moments passed between them in less than a second. Sensation after sensation flooded from him to her and back again, moving from their rocky beginnings to their budding friendship to the passion of their last encounter.

"Brix?"

She whispered his name, full of shock and longing, before her eyes slid down to settle on his lips.

It was then that Brixton knew he was lost. Everything was lost.

All of his frustrated years of yearning broke through him at once, and in that moment, he was too weak to resist or fight off his feelings.

"Ada." He leaned down and kissed her.

It seemed impossible that Brixton could both remember and forget everything about their first kiss as her lips parted under his once more.

The same heightened desperation called to him as her softness melted effortlessly against the tautness of his body. He tasted the same soft, malty sweetness of her mouth, feeling the fullness of her lips as they flowered beneath his. Her body curved into his, her fingers gripping his knuckles. He heard her same, muted sigh of pleasure as their joined hands collapsed between them, and he felt the same heady rush as they collided into each other.

But this time was different, too. He resisted the urge to run his hands down her body, to gather her against him. Before, he had been too intoxicated by the taste of her to wonder if she could handle the full extent of his passion; this time, he was overwhelmed, but he was all too aware of what it was like to lose her.

The equal power of their magic diminished as he began to be consumed. It could have been years or seconds since their last meeting; he had wanted her then, and he only wanted her more now.

The engines behind them sparked; the ship began to sink. Brixton felt his own destruction become increasingly inevitable before she reluctantly tore herself away from him.

His voice was a husky whisper as he stared into the silver seas of Adelaide's gaze. "I've missed you."

Her raspberry lips pouted almost imperceivably, and Brixton felt the same helpless tug from the back of his heart that he had felt the first time he met with her all those years ago. Back then he was nervous, certain that whatever it was about her that made him look twice, was dangerous.

Now he knew for certain it was. Adelaide was dangerous with her power, with her skills, and even with the terrifying, electric beauty she had about her. As her talent slid back inside her palms, he let his own magical guard drop and he nearly fell over.

It's the same as before. Brixton lowered his gaze as he collected himself, trying to hide the damage he felt. Everything was the same—his eagerness, her response, their shared passion—right down to the desperate shakiness running through him as they parted. He forced himself to remain conscious, determined to see to it that she did not leave him this time.

Seeing his weakness, Adelaide's gaze suddenly hardened. "If you value your life, Brix, you will stay away from me. I'm here on a mission."

The precision of her voice was noticeably detached from the rest of the world; all trace of the warm hunger between them was already wiped away.

Disappointed, Brixton tried to settle himself, propping up next to the engine as he stepped back from her. "I've noticed, along with the rest of the Queen's Airship Force."

"I suppose I have neglected to send out the proper invitations." Adelaide clumsily hurried to put her gloves back on and remove the broken goggles from her forehead. "You must convey my apologies to the appropriate parties."

Her flippancy should have made him angry, but Brixton vividly remembered their days in school together—the hours they spent working side by side, passing chirpies back and forth with silly, hidden messages; he remembered her joy when she met his family, felt the anguish when she

FAVAN AND FLEW

had unintentionally upset Luella, relived the hopeful fear she experienced at their first kiss.

His Ada was never afraid to break the rules, and he should not be surprised to see the law did not stop her, either.

"What's happened?" Brixton asked. "Why are you here?"

"I told you, I'm on a mission."

She ran her hand down the long ponytail of her hair; Brixton noticed it was much longer than the last time he had seen her, and he fought down a sudden urge to reach out and touch it.

"What sort of mission would involve damaging the clock tower and blowing up a monitoring airship?"

"I can't tell you about it," Adelaide replied, clearly flustered. "I have to go now. I swear I didn't mean to see you again, Brix. I really didn't … I'm sorry, we—"

He grabbed her arm, suddenly angry. "Don't say it. Don't make me hate you again."

"We still can't be together."

He felt the pain knife through his heart before his soul plunged into darkness. The last time he felt this way, he had woken up in Rembrandt's medical ward, alone, with only his questions and memories for company.

But this time was different, he told himself. Last time, he had been distracted with doubt, wondering if he imagined how she felt, or if she was embarrassed by her decision to kiss him. Now, Brixton knew for sure she wanted him as much as he wanted her, and even after the many years between their last encounter, time had not diminished the longing between them.

He would not wind up in the same situation as last time. Not when he was this certain of her response to him.

"Please, let me go." Adelaide tried to pull herself free, but she seemed just as averse to leaving him as he was to let her. "You're only going to get in trouble if you stay here."

"No." Before she could say anything else, Brixton tugged her close and lifted her off her feet. "You've always been worth the trouble."

He gripped her as his lips met hers again, pressing into her with everything he had.

She has to believe me this time.

"Brixton." Adelaide responded to him at once. Her arms latched around him, and her gloved hands ran through his hair. He was protected from the full force of her magic this time, and he reveled in her embrace.

Some part of him knew he was in the middle of a malfunctioning engine room, halfway through an attempt to rescue his father, in a ship falling out of the sky; the *Horizon* was descending to the ground, and his criminal record was about to resurrect itself. He knew he should have been holding Adelaide down for arrest, rather than holding her against him, silently pleading with her to admit she loved him as much as he loved her.

But he could not bring himself to care. Not while she was in his arms again.

He slid his arms down Adelaide's back, clutching her close to him, feeling the wonderful tightness of her body as she shivered.

The ship rocked under their feet as it finally touched the ground. The sudden crash broke their embrace as they were thrown aside.

Brixton slammed into the floor, landing hard, as Adelaide did her best to catch herself. When he looked over at her, he saw she was winded, breathing deeply, and her

FAVAN AND FLEW

eyes were wide with intensity and uncertainty as she glanced back at him.

"We don't have time for this," she said as she scrambled to stand up. "I have to go. And you have to stay away from me."

Brixton looked over at her weakly, as he felt his back groan with pain and his arm jerk free from a heated tangle of wires and busted machinery that had fallen along with him.

"Ada! I know you're not like this," he hollered after her.

"You have to stop, Brix." The bitterness in her voice was striking as she turned around to face him once more. "You've never known me."

"If you believe that," he told her, "then it's you who has never really known me."

She shook her head and left, leaving him more alone than ever.

Brixton swallowed hard. He clenched his fist and pounded it against the floor. His fingers smashed with stinging soreness, but it was nothing compared to the hurt he felt in his heart.

She was gone.

Again.

The last time she left, she broke his heart. This time, she broke his pride as well.

"I hate you," he whispered, his voice choking on itself.

It was the worst lie he could have told himself. It was the same one he had been telling himself for years, even if he knew he no longer believed it.

The next several moments blurred together, accompanied by pain. He could hear another round of fighting taking place on the top deck, but he knew Adelaide would escape.

At the sounds of sirens calling from the other side of the hull, Brixton knew it was over. He collapsed against the floor, allowing his weariness to overtake him.

He closed his eyes, reliving every moment with Adelaide. He could still feel her magic as it crackled against his; he could feel her heart racing along with his; he could still feel the tremble of her lips as she kissed him back.

Adelaide had not forgotten him anymore than he had forgotten her.

I will find her again.

His silent vow was just as ardent as the one he made all those years ago, when he had promised to protect her from any teasing and mockery.

Brixton opened his eyes, looking back toward the door. The whole situation took on a surreal quality; he had set out to return to school, only to fear for his father's safety, recklessly execute a plan to steal aboard an airship, nearly capture the enemy, and fall in love with Adelaide all over again.

It was impossible.

But it was the truth.

It's the truth.

He blinked, clearing away the muddled remnants of his thoughts as he heard a rescue team calling for survivors. He was about to reply when he saw it.

Just inches in front of him, tucked away under the edges of the engine debris, was a small, black pouch.

Adelaide's pouch.

He thought about the ferocity she had used in securing it. The airship's bumpy crash landing had dislodged it from her belt, and she had been too distracted by his presence to notice.

He grunted as he shifted, crawling on his elbows to get to it. Curiosity took a hold of him as he opened it.

Brixton's mouth dropped open as an amethyst that fit perfectly into his palm shined up from inside the bag.

"What trouble have you gotten yourself into this time, Adelaide?" he whispered.

"Is anyone down there? We are here to assist you."

The call of an emergency rescue force descended the hallway. Footsteps were coming closer, and Brixton had only a second to decide what to do.

He could tell the authorities the truth. He could tell them about Adelaide, about their past. He could show them the jewel and then leave everything behind as he tried to find his father.

"Can anyone hear me?" The rescuers were coming even closer.

Brixton tucked the large gem into his pocket and started to prepare his story. He knew he would need a really good one if he was going to get out of trouble. He closed his eyes as he closed his hand around the precious jewel, praying against all hope he would find a way out of this.

It was nothing short of divine providence, Brixton thought, when he heard a new voice.

"It seems you've gotten yourself into a spot of trouble again, haven't you, lad?"

Brixton opened his eyes to see Bartholomew Flew looking down at him with hazel eyes that matched his own. The wrinkles of his father's forehead were carved with concern, and his mustache curved with displeasure.

Brixton gave him a tepid smile. "Father."

"Aye, lad. Now, what in God's good name are you doing here?"

"It's a long story."

Bartholomew nodded. "I was expecting that." He sighed as he took his transmitter out of his pocket. "Inspector, we require backup. There is more going on here than what it seemed."

"That is certainly an understatement," Brixton said as his father closed the transmitter and pulled him up off up the floor. Brixton struggled to find his footing as he sighed and rubbed his forehead. "You won't believe the half of it."

"I was expecting that, too."

<u>8</u>

The clouds covered the moonlight as she made her way between the shadows of the riverbank. Adelaide did not know how she managed to make her way back to the Tower Gardens without getting caught. Despite her great-grandmother's training, she was too loud, too careless, and too upset to focus. Her heart pounded between her ears as she raced into the darkness.

Once she found refuge in a large wall of hedges, she took the time to glance back at the small airship. It had crashed just shy of the Thames, the hull straddling the riverbank while the bow dipped into the waterfront. She stood still, watching as its engines roared back to life before sputtering to a screeching halt.

The half-deflated balloon was damaged, and the ship's hull was cracked. Even if someone as talented as Brixton tried to do something to fix it, it would not be able to fly for days, she estimated.

"Brixton."

Adelaide slipped down to her knees. Her hand went to her lips, reliving the searing heat that sparked between them in the mere seconds of their first reunion in years.

She could have told herself it was her propensity for trouble that allowed him to kiss her, the same push that allowed her to kiss him back, but she knew that was a lie.

Brixton Flew had intrigued her ever since she joined his class at Rembrandt.

He was one of many people who eagerly came up to her to talk about her father. She had ignored him at first, same as the others, believing it to be the rightful action to take.

He was obviously hoping for an autograph, or even a recommendation, and Adelaide had thought it was quite pathetic to woo her with friendship.

When he backed away, along with the rest of them, she had seen nothing worthy of a second look.

Until that class.

Adelaide closed her eyes, letting her daydreams project into the past, back to the day when she first noticed him.

It was just shy of six years since she had been accepted into Rembrandt Academy at the age of fourteen. Her father had been out on several missions for Queen Victoria and her airship brigade, traveling the world on various goodwill missions and military relief deploys. While he was away, he made arrangements for Adelaide to attend the most exclusive, prestigious school he could find.

Rembrandt was not hard to find. The fact that Adelaide had inherited a significant portion of her family's magic was more coincidental than anything else, since she wanted to work on developing her mechanical skills. With the significant endowment from her father, Rembrandt allowed her to enroll in the engineering enchantment classes.

Of all her courses, Professor Ohm's class was easily the most boring. Adelaide had studied on his theories and put them into practice long before she arrived at Rembrandt. She quickly learned from his lectures where he was right and where he was wrong, and where he thought he was right and where he would never see where he was wrong.

She had dismissed most of his class by the time she noticed Brixton.

Professor Ohm had just droned on for what seemed like hours about his family's law, the one that stated that electric current was proportional to the voltage, when Brixton tentatively raised his hand in the middle of the lecture.

Professor Ohm, caught up in the sound of his own voice, barely noticed him. It was only when Brixton cleared his throat, interrupting him mid-sentence, that Professor Ohm looked over at him.

"What is it, Mr. Flew?"

"Using magic is different from using electricity. Where would that aspect come in?"

Professor Ohm smirked. "Well, of course it is different. There have been several attempts to combine the sciences and magic here, which is evident in your own scholarship, Mr. Flew. The process is not yet an exact formula."

"Yes, sir, I know." Brixton's face reddened only the slightest, before he continued on. "But your principles should be able to apply to the process of the transference of electricity with magic."

"Of course it does," Professor Ohm replied. "But the advancements have not been made in such a field—not yet, anyway."

Adelaide straightened up in her seat. There had been other attempts to combine magic and electricity, but the attempts to do so were limited in their success. Many of them required more electricity or more magic for continued use, and sometimes, depending on the wielder, the machinery would shut off after any magical interference.

"Do you think it is possible, using these theorems, that we will one day be able to create an alternative life source?" Brixton asked.

At this, Professor Ohm chuckled. "My good sir, have you been reading too many horrid novels? Why, that sounds just like something out of *Frankenstein*!"

The rest of the class laughed, but Adelaide just stared at him. Brixton let out a defeated sigh and ducked down over his work again.

Adelaide only continued to stare at him.

Even years later, she had no trouble pinpointing that moment as the moment everything changed.

Before, he was no one worth her notice. And afterward, he was all she seemed to notice.

She recalled how he was such a scraggly kid, in spite of his efforts. He always carried at least six books in his arms in addition to a tattered bag full of more books and supplies. His dark brown hair never failed to stick up in all the wrong places. He tried so hard to look proper, but she could always see his socks drooping underneath his trousers.

He always wore his uniform, she remembered, suddenly appreciating his latest appearance much more. When he held her against him this time, she had been able feel the tautness of his skin through his thin, white shirt.

Adelaide opened her eyes again, not surprised to find they were swelling with unshed tears.

She forced herself to smile into the darkness. Brixton was just what she always suspected. It did not matter how much trouble he went through to hide who he was; he was a rogue at heart, and time had done nothing to change that.

Maybe that was why I liked him so much. He was hiding who he was from everyone else, too.

It did not matter that he wielded white magic; he was creative, an original, and the others in her class had no inkling of the truth about who he was, any more than they were aware they worked in the presence of someone who could destroy everything they ever worked for, Adelaide thought with a small, satisfied smile.

Well, not until Gloria had to go and ruin my dragon heart.

She had been nearing a breakthrough in getting the delicate wirings in the old machine to flicker with life again, and Gloria had to go and ruin it, all in the name of social politics.

Her fingers curled into a fist. She glanced down at the gloves she wore. The thick, synthetic material was a small barrier between her and the rest of the world, but even it did nothing when she was determined to make others pay.

"Yaling."

Adelaide nearly groaned at the sound of her middle name. She stepped out of the refuge of the large bush. The Tower Gardens welcomed her, the gardens bathed in a mix of moonlight and magic. "What is it, Jiahao?"

Her cousin appeared beside her. He was much taller than she was, and in the nighttime, garbed in only black, Jiahao appeared even more imposing than usual.

"I have been looking for you. You are late." It was hard to say from his stoic tone what his mood was, but Adelaide knew him well enough to know he was never happy.

She also knew him well enough to have trouble blaming him.

Jiahao was the one who was tasked with overseeing her. It was among the most reviled of jobs among the members in her great-grandmother's clan. Ever since the Opium Wars, none of the Chinese willingly trusted the British. Her mother's fate and the untimely deaths of her grandparents did nothing to discourage this trend.

Adelaide knew her father had grown up in a tumultuous home, and as a mixed-breed herself, Adelaide knew she would never be fully accepted into her father's remaining family.

No matter whether I have the family magic or not.

"Where is it?" Jiahao asked. "Did you get the Dragon Eye?"

Adelaide reached behind her, ready to pull out her score.

Only to find it was not there.

She glanced all around, dropping onto the ground to look for the jewel. "Bloody hell, where is it?"

Jiahao narrowed his eyes at her. "You stole it and then lost it? *Bèn dàn*, did you lose it on purpose?"

"I didn't lose it on purpose," Adelaide snapped.

"This is why I should have come on my own. Now our family will be even more dishonored, thanks to you."

"I did the job required of me." Adelaide turned away from her cousin, gazing back toward the riverfront where the *Horizon* was still grounded, tipping dangerously toward the waters of the Thames.

"No, you did not, because you do not have the jewel."

"I had it!" Adelaide shuffled through her thoughts, raking her mind trying to think of what had happened.

Too easily, she was caught up in Brixton's embrace again. She blushed, vividly recalling his hands as they ran down her back, cradling her body against his with a gentle fervency that made her ache with longing.

It was the crash, she realized. Brixton had been holding onto her, and she was too wrapped up in him to notice the pouch was gone from her back when she left.

"You lost it on purpose," Jiahao accused. "I can see the shame on your face."

"We'll get it back." Adelaide dropped her head in disgrace. Jiahao would not be satisfied with her contrition, but he would agree it was pointless to argue with her.

The amethyst was lost, and they would have to find a way to retrieve it once more.

"You have ruined several weeks' worth of inquiries, Yaling," Jiahao muttered. "It took us forever to find out where they were keeping the other Dragon Eye. Tàitai will not be happy."

"Let's go back to the haven," Adelaide said, unwilling to discuss Lady Fang Gu Qin, her great-grandmother, and her upcoming disappointment. Adelaide knew that if they had succeeded, her great-grandmother would have likely objected to something. "There's no use discussing this out here. We still might be caught."

"If you value your father's life, you will not let these filthy pigs capture you."

"You don't need to insult them." Adelaide had spent the last several years in Peking listening to her kin disparage her British family, but it was too much to hear Jiahao condemn all the British after coming face to face with Brixton.

Brixton was the one, after all, who had stood up to the ones who teased her about her Chinese blood.

Jiahao narrowed his eyes, giving his face a snakelike quality. "You dare defend them, after all they have done to our nation? Do I need to remind you of what they have done to our family? They are the reason we carry our disgrace from generations ago! You are siding with them against us, just like your father did."

"Never," Adelaide shot back, immediately regretting saying anything at all. "I was only commenting on it because I don't know why you waste your breath. They don't deserve your scorn, let alone your notice."

He looked at her again, his brow furrowed.

FAVAN AND FLEW

"They don't deserve your notice at all," she added, clarifying her comments.

"I will be the one to judge whether or not they are deserving, as it is *my* scorn," Jiahao said. His voice was stark and clear, and Adelaide knew it was the end of their discussion.

She followed Jiahao as they made their way through the tight streets between London's richest and poorest districts. As they approached the British Museum, Jiahao opened up a grate into the sewers and slipped inside.

Adelaide took one last look at the stars before she pinched her nose shut and followed him.

The darkness of the Underground was as unique as its smell; Adelaide did not know why her great-grandmother insisted on making the underground's hidden tunnels her home. Her father's townhouse, set in the affluent Whitewand district, would have easily housed her several cousins, aunts, and uncles as they found a way to infiltrate London.

But then, Tàitai always seemed to think in strange ways. Adelaide never fully understood her father's grandmother, even if she had constantly been by her side for the last several years. After such a time, Adelaide was inclined to think she did not want to understand her, either. When she came close to seeing Tàitai's point of view, it was almost always when it came to sadness, bitterness, and pain.

Jiahao led her through the dark tunnels. Together, they hopped over train tracks and slid through the tight hallways that lined the Underground construction sites. Just as the darkness completely enveloped them, they reached a hidden archway, tucked away by an old aqueduct.

While her great-grandmother had been in Peking, a small band of Qin family members remained in London,

FAVAN AND FLEW

keeping an ear out for rumors and whispers that spoke of intrigue and trouble. They had kept up the haven, using it as a place to gather and hide.

Adelaide watched as Jiahao opened another gate, pushing on the heavy doorway.

All at once, a new light flooded over them, as the door opened up into a hidden world. Tapestries and ink drawings lined a small hallway, one that led back to where a raging fire kept the area warm. Adelaide took a deep breath, glad that the fire was full of scented offerings that pushed back against the dank and dreary smell of the sewers. She watched as the smoke was channeled up a smokestack, released outside without significant notice.

"Tàitai!" Jiahao called, his voice echoing into the chamber. "We're back."

A squat figure, dressed in a mix of the finest muslin and taffeta London had to offer, stepped forward from behind a standing screen, one that blocked a hidden doorway. Adelaide bit her lip as Jiahao stepped forward and began to converse with her ghoulish form.

Adelaide glanced around, eyeing their place of operation. It held many tunnels the Chinese had no trouble burrowing during the days when construction of the Underground railway was ongoing.

There were tunnels and rivers under London that no one spoke of, and they were all marked by her family's diligent mapping. From the beginning of the Roman Empire's expansion, aqueducts had been constructed to ease the flow of water and begin the rudiments of indoor plumbing. Over the last years, especially with the help of wielders, the systems had been improved and nearly all replaced with finer functions.

The old waterways had been largely forgotten by the public that walked over it every day, and the train tunnels

FAVAN AND FLEW

had been modified by workers without hindering oversight. Her family was smart to use them to their advantage, easily traveling from one end of the city to the other without being seen, even if it seemed unnecessary to Adelaide.

If there was one downside she could not ignore, it was that in the haven, she was still her father's only offspring, and living with her great-grandmother's family stifled her. She had to go without her own room or any creature comforts. In the last several days since her return to London, she had been unable to sleep without waking up because of other clan members.

She gritted her teeth. Tàitai would say that her only comfort should be knowing their family's honor would be restored soon, now that they were close to getting the Dragon Eyes back.

"Yaling!"

Adelaide barely stopped herself from flinching at her name coming from her great-grandmother's crinkled lips. It nearly always meant she was in trouble.

She hurried forward and bowed her head low.

"Jiahao tells me that you failed to retrieve the Dragon Eye that was being used as the timepiece jewel." The harsh sound of the crone's voice whipped through the air, stark and hard, landing on her ears with shame.

"Yes, Tàitai." It was tempting to mumble, but Adelaide knew from past experiences not to shy away from anything she did, no matter how disappointing. It would only lead to more punishment.

"You have failed us." Tàitai shook her head, her white bun in the back shaking in a delayed fashion.

Adelaide almost smiled. From her wig to the fine material of her dress, Adelaide knew her great-grandmother had her own guilty pleasures, and it was easy to see them reflected in her vanity.

"My sincerest apologies, Madame."

"Don't use that tone with me," her great-grandmother snapped. Her dark eyes burned black against the shadows of their secret hideout. Adelaide saw several other members of her clan's family in the background, watching her as they worked.

Adelaide wanted to send them a warning look, but she knew they would only use it as an excuse to shame her for her lack of discipline.

"Your father betrayed us," Tàitai said. "Now you have disappointed us. Is this your intent, or is it the fault of your weakened blood?"

Adelaide hung her head. There was no use trying to appease her great-grandmother.

Not after this great a failure.

"You will have to get the jewel back," Tàitai said.

Adelaide glanced up cautiously. "You mean I will have another chance to steal it?"

"Yes." The word spit out of the ancient woman's mouth as she glared at her. "Like it or not, this is the only way forward if we are going to fulfill my plans."

"And my freedom?" Adelaide asked quietly. She thought of Brixton, hoping against all hope she would be able to see him again.

"Of course, child," Tàitai said. "No woman in our family ever wanted to live with Wuja's curse. All our work will be for naught if we do not have the Dragon Eyes, and only with them in your possession will you be able to fully control the magic inside of you."

Adelaide breathed a sigh of relief. "Thank you, Tàitai."

"Do not thank me for sending you back into that den of wolves." Her great-grandmother frowned, deepening the ridged lines of her forehead. "You deserve the pain you suffer for your incompetence."

"Yes, Tàitai."

There was enough silence to convey the eternal depths of her disappointment before she whipped around. "Jiahao," she snapped.

Jiahao stepped forward. "Yes, Tàitai. I am here."

"You will go with Yaling while the rest of us prepare for the final stages of our mission. Yaling will take care of the timepiece jewel. Your brothers will retrieve the other Eye."

Jiahao frowned. "But what about the other work?" He glanced back at the other members of their clan, the ones who were wearing work aprons and thick gloves as they handled metal and fire. "I thought I was supposed to stay here from now on. The people have noticed my power."

Tàitai reached the end of her patience and slapped Jiahao.

Adelaide was unable to stop her flinch this time, as Tàitai's wrinkled hand smacked into Jiahao's cheek.

"Never question me," she hissed. "We have waited centuries for this moment. We have the ability to absolve the Qin family's sins, not to mention punish the Westerners for their ill-gotten gain. Just do as you are told, and then we will once more take our place as the rightful heirs to this world."

Tàitai's gaze snapped to Adelaide's. "If you want to see your father alive again, you will take care of tonight's mistake."

Adelaide held firm. "You know I've pledged myself to your cause."

"I know a snake when I see one," Tàitai replied. "Your mother's family has further weakened your family's blood."

"My blood might be weakened, but my magic is still stronger than yours," Adelaide argued.

"Then you know your life is at stake and angering me will only quicken death."

Adelaide felt her resolve disperse. Her great-grandmother was right. She bowed her head forward again. "Yes … Tàitai. Consider it done."

"Good. You and Jiahao must find the Dragon Eye you lost and secure it for us. Our other project is nearly complete, and once we have the Dragon Eyes, we will reclaim this world as our own."

Adelaide glanced at Jiahao, a red palm-shaped mark still on his cheek from where Tàitai hit him. He shot her a bitter look, and he did not have to say anything for her to know that he blamed her for all their trouble.

"Go. I will not suffer any more mistakes," Tàitai snapped. She waved her hand, dismissing them as she disappeared back into the gloomy depths of the underground haven.

Adelaide bit her lip, tasting the last little bit of sweetness from Brixton's kiss, knowing her family would only see him as a mistake.

9

Brixton felt a soft beam of sunlight settle on his forehead as it stirred him to waking. He tasted the sourness of his tongue before he yawned and grumbled.

He was tempted to fall back asleep; in the last several years, he could not remember sleeping so well, and he dreaded waking up to find the nightmares were waiting for him.

"You'd best get up, lad, or you'll be late to work."

Brixton's eyes blinked open at his father's voice. He shot up in his bed, surprised to find himself back at home in his old room. He seemed to become aware of everything else at once. He could hear his mother's footsteps downstairs as she busied herself with her animals and their breakfast; he could hear Luella's irrepressible humming come pouring out from the lavatory down the hall; and, much to his chagrin, he could sense his father's ever-present disapproval as he sat at the end of his bed.

Brixton glanced down to see he was still in the same shirt and trousers from the day before. His jacket was hanging on the post by his bed, and he hurriedly grabbed it, rifling through his pockets.

"You wouldn't be looking for this, would you?"

Brixton glanced over as his father held up Adelaide's pouch. As he watched, Bartholomew untied the strings and pulled out the amethyst. "It's a nice steal."

His father's soft-spoken words were a condemnation Brixton never wanted to bear again. The old shame and remorse hit him hard, forcing Brixton to relive the death of his good relationship with his father all over again.

"I didn't steal it," Brixton insisted. "I managed to get it back from the person who did."

Remembering his encounter with Adelaide, Brixton tried not to look guilty as he stared at his father.

"I've never been one to know why you decided stealing was a good thing when you were younger," Bartholomew replied, ignoring Brixton's explanation. "I know your mother and I are not the wealthiest people you might know, especially since you were sent off to school, but we have tried our hardest to instill a sense of morals in you."

"And you have," Brixton murmured, trying to reassure him. "I promise, I was going to return it. I … I didn't know what to do with it, and last night was … "

He did not know how to describe the previous evening. So much emotional turmoil accompanied the events as he tried to process them.

Bartholomew sighed. "I want to believe you, even if, as a policeman, I tend to think that falling leaves return to their roots."

Brixton had to wonder some days whether his father really wanted to believe him or not. His father was not excited Brixton had magic, let alone magic that made learning how to build things much easier. Once Brixton began to tinker with his lab and his tools, and much more astutely than his father, Bartholomew had stepped back from his son and even some of his hobbies, and it seemed his affection had followed.

"I swear on my life, I didn't steal it," Brixton said. He pulled himself out of his covers, swinging his feet onto the floor. He put his head in his hands, balancing them on his knees. "Last night was … terrible."

"Gloria talked with me some after you collapsed."

"I collapsed?"

Bartholomew nodded. "You were nearly dead on your feet by the time we picked you out of the airship's rubble. I had no idea you were on the *Horizon* at all."

"I lied to get on it," Brixton admitted. "I saw the monitoring ship turn into the clock tower and I knew it was a distraction."

"Part of your magical talent, eh?"

Brixton bit back a groan. His father did not even try to understand how his magic allowed him to put things together and build things, to imagine new ideas and figure out how to make things work. But he had to admit his father was at least partially right; his magic had called him to action this time, spurring him on instinctively. "A little."

"So you and Gloria saw the attack on the clock tower happen," Bartholomew said, "and then you decided to come and find me. Is that it?"

Brixton groaned under his breath, hating himself all over again for all the trouble he had caused as a youngster. His father might have forgiven him, but he never forgot.

"I've already had a number of people point out the absurdity of everything, including Ticker," Brixton said, glancing over at the little watch hanging out of his jacket pocket. Little snoozing noises leaked out of the small device, and Brixton suddenly wondered at the time.

He had his meeting with Henry today for his new project assignment, and he did not want to be late. He did not want to give Rembrandt another reason to admonish him; it was bad enough his father was ready to punish him, too.

"Police business is no business for you to concern yourself with, Brix, especially given all the run-ins you've had with us in the past."

Brixton tried to bear his father's derision gracefully, but it was hard. He had been hoping his father would appreciate his actions last night. It was disappointing to realize he had worsened their relationship even more.

"You have a duty and a debt to the Board," Bartholomew continued.

"I know."

"I am not only speaking of your financial debt. Scotland Yard is one of the first recipients of your prototypes," his father continued. "I can't tell you how helpful some of them are to us, even to a non-wielder like me."

"Magic is no substitute for intellect."

Bartholomew huffed, blowing out the ends of his thick mustache. "Nor is it one for love. Which brings me to my next question."

Brixton felt his cheeks burn as his father looked up from the amethyst and over to him.

"Adelaide is back in town, isn't she?"

"How did you know?" Brixton asked, surprised. "I was the only one who saw her last night."

"I had a feeling that might be the case after I saw you in the airship."

"Ugh." Brixton rolled his eyes. "I should have guessed you didn't actually know."

"Well, I know the Qin clan has been unusually active lately," Bartholomew said. "I received a few credible tips regarding the matter. I was not surprised to learn she arrived back in London recently. I assume she is here for her father."

"She never seemed to like him." Brixton wrinkled his nose. "I don't know why you or Gloria would think she would come for him."

FAVAN AND FLEW

"Family is family, Brix. We know that from our own experience."

"That's hardly the same," Brixton muttered. "Adelaide was very adamant that her father focused on his work and never made time for her."

"But he still attempted to keep you away from her, promising to block your Airship Force application. I imagine he didn't do that because he was more concerned about what you would do to his fleet." Bartholomew arched his brow. "Although perhaps he was right, given your actions yesterday."

"Given the right incentive, a man or woman is capable of anything." Brixton thought of his kiss with Adelaide, how he felt weak and drained, and how despite everything, he would give anything to kiss her again. "Rescuing you seemed like a worthwhile goal."

"I appreciate your concern for me, lad," Bartholomew said, his tone softening only in the slightest. "But risks and danger are still part of *my* job, not yours."

Brixton said nothing. He knew his father was right, and his recklessness from the day before had all the hallmarks of a man who had gone mad.

"I may not know too much about your world or your magic, but I still know you. And that's why I want to talk about Adelaide. I knew when you brought her to visit us that first time, during your junior year, you were already in love, and I knew it when she broke your heart, too. And I know you've never really let her go."

"I don't want to talk about it."

For the first time in years, Brixton saw his father smile at him. "Of course you don't, because you look like a fool when you do."

Brixton glared at him. "Thanks."

FAVAN AND FLEW

"Believe it or not, I mean it well, lad. True love is not for the proud, but the humble." Bartholomew rubbed his chin thoughtfully. "She has magic, too."

"You knew that, from when she accidentally killed that starling Luella brought home from the park," Brixton said.

"Oh, that's right. I'd forgotten about that."

"What were you thinking of then?"

"The day after she told you she was leaving for the Orient."

Brixton felt his cheeks start to burn. His father was talking about the day when he had kissed Adelaide for the first and, until recently, only time.

"I remember I was called into the medical ward at the school to pick you up. I saw how you looked then, as if part of you had died." Bartholomew gave him a pointed look. "You had the same expression on your face when I saw you on the ship."

Brixton said nothing as his father waited patiently. A moment later, he sighed.

"If she's back in town, and she's after the Dragon Eyes, you're going to get in trouble. You're already lucky—very, very, very lucky, I might add—that Captain Airey and I are friends, and he has agreed to 'forget' your involvement with the airship engines."

"You're friends with the captain?"

Bartholomew waved the issue away with his hand. "Of sorts. We've worked on a few sabotage cases in the past with delinquent corpsman."

"And now your delinquent son," Brixton said with a rueful smirk.

"Yes." Bartholomew did not share in his attempt at levity. Instead, he tossed Brixton the amethyst. "But concerning Adelaide, lad. I must warn you. The Dragon

Eyes are dangerous objects in the wrong hands, and with her family connections, she is headed for trouble."

Brixton gazed at the amethyst in the sunlight. The jewel shone brightly, coloring his room with a red-violet glow.

"What are the Dragon Eyes?" he asked.

"It's an ancient treasure," Bartholomew told him. "There is a legend that goes along with it, as all these things tend to have, but I'm afraid I don't have the time to tell it right now. I've work, and so've you. Perhaps later we can talk. Your mother wants you to come home for dinner tonight."

"That does sound like Mother."

"Can't blame her, can you? She's worried for you, and she's attempting to tend to you as much as you'll let her."

"I guess I should be glad she's a decent cook."

"Aye, lad." Bartholomew snatched the amethyst out of Brixton's hands. "I'm going to take this to Scotland Yard and secure it in a vault there. I'm sure that the Queen will want to have the clock tower restored soon. Until then, we will keep it safe."

"If you want me to check the Rembrandt locks, please let me know," Brixton offered. He knew nothing he could do would stop Adelaide—not on a magical level, and not on a mechanical one, either—but he wanted to make sure no one else could get to them if he could.

"Thank you. I'll let you know what the Inspector says regarding the matter. Unlike Commander Carlisle, I imagine he'll be able to check your credentials thoroughly." Bartholomew's mustache fluttered as he exhaled. "Stay out of trouble, lad."

"I'll try."

Bartholomew put his police hat on his head and straightened it. As he turned to go, he looked back. "Brixton?"

"What is it?"

"If you can't stay out of trouble, at least try to manage it better."

Brixton gave him a small smile. He did not see his father's softness much, but he was still convinced from its rare appearances that it was there. "Yes, sir."

"I understand a little trouble from time to time makes life interesting, especially for a man of your age, but too much will likely kill you."

With that, Bartholomew slipped out of Brixton's room. Brixton waited until the door shut behind his father before he flopped back onto his pillow and let out a long sigh.

"I wonder what else will go wrong today?" Brixton muttered under his breath.

The answer to Brixton's question was waiting for him as he stepped into his office and saw Henry waiting patiently in front of his desk.

Henry was an older gentleman, and he easily looked the part. His hair was pure white, regally brushed back from his face; it was a hairstyle that prominently showcased his balding forehead, even if it commanded respect.

His hair was not the only thing about Henry that was always impeccable. From his ironed slacks to his cuffed shirts and fashionable cravats, he always seemed prepared to face any situation life brought him. Henry often wore a hat and carried a walking stick, one that was carved with a silver eagle on the top. Henry remained ageless throughout all the years Brixton had known him, as if the flow of time simply curved around him.

When he saw Henry in his office, Brixton straightened his shoulders, drawing himself up to his full height. Brixton knew from his time on the streets as much as his time as a student when it was time to put on an act, and this was one such time.

"Good morning, Henry," Brixton murmured. It was the most informal way of greeting his mentor he could muster, and he hoped Henry would see it as a sign nothing unusual had happened at all in the last day.

The old professor smiled kindly, but there was a sadness in his gaze Brixton did not want to see. "Perhaps you should call me 'Dr. Winston,' for this meeting, Brixton."

Brixton felt his heart plummet as he sank into his desk chair. That suggestion did not bode well for things to come.

Instead, he smiled and gestured toward the chair opposite him. "Won't you have a seat, sir?"

"Thank you."

Henry sat down and pulled out his pipe. "Do you mind if I smoke?" Brixton did not stop him as he leaned back in his seat, propped his pipe between his teeth, and blew several long breaths of smoke out into the air between them.

Brixton was glad his mother never came to visit his office. She would be appalled by the smell of American tobacco; Henry came in and visited enough that the smell lingered.

"Well, Brixton, I imagine you are wondering why I am here."

"No, sir," he replied. "You mentioned before I was to receive a new research assignment from the Board."

"Ah, yes. I'd forgotten about that."

Brixton felt his stomach drop even further, but he maintained a bright smile. "I was hoping we could, too, sir."

Henry chuckled. "I've always loved your sense of humor, Brixton. It was a shame more people did not see it while you were in school. I know you did not have many friends."

"I was here for an education," Brixton replied. "I did not need to make friends."

"And I imagine you didn't really want to make friends with the people from the higher circles of Society," Henry added with a sympathetic smile. "They really do look down on us, you know."

"Me more than you, sir. Although I am the taller one between us," Brixton replied.

Henry chortled with laughter once more, before he blew another long stream of air out his pipe. From previous discussions, Brixton knew Henry's family had a history of illegitimacy, and his magical abilities furthered the rift between him and his peers.

"Well, this has been fun, but let's get down to business. Time is of the essence, I fear."

Brixton felt his insides freeze over. "What can I help you with, sir?"

"I understand you had quite an evening last night."

Brixton eyed Henry with a calculative gaze; he was not going to fall into the same trap as he had with his father earlier. "I don't believe there's anything on record regarding my actions last night."

"Nothing on record," Henry repeated. "Clever, Brixton, but still beneath you. There are plenty of smaller records that must be analyzed, and that includes your discussion with a certain Commander Carlisle yesterday at St. James's Airship Field."

"Oh." Brixton shifted in his chair. "I was … merely attempting to collect some information, sir. There must have been a mix-up. Hardly worth your concern, I'm sure."

"Rembrandt is always concerned when people use our name and reputation wrongly," Henry chastised lightly. "Now, I might be able to forgive you for your indiscretion, but I must know. What in blazes did you think you were doing last night?"

The warm, professional tone of his mentor burned away at his harsher words, scorching the atmosphere with sudden, rapid condemnation.

Brixton was expecting that, even if he was hoping for another response. He remembered getting the same treatment back when Henry used to confront him over missing classes with Adelaide.

Brixton looked down at his desk. "I am not sure where to begin."

"That was one of the things Dr. Sheffield mentioned he would like to see some improvement on in the future; apparently, you are indecisive and reluctant to take on extra accountability, even for projects under your management."

Brixton shrugged, and Henry shook his head.

"I would hate to have to bring up more of your latest professional review while I am here today, Brixton. I am already upset that I am here to tell you the Board is ready to fire you."

"Fire me?" Brixton stilled, completely taken aback.

"Yes." Henry tapped his pipe. "You will not be absolved of the debt you've collected with us, either—the roughly five thousand pounds you have left to pay back. We will have to send it to collections, and your family will likely suffer the cost."

"No." Brixton stood up. "My family does not need to pay my debts. I will take care of them myself, even if I have to go to prison."

"Why on God's green earth would we send you to prison?" Henry shook his head. "We both know you would figure out a way to break free."

"Honor is a different matter than skill, sir." Brixton was careful to keep the malice out of his words, but Henry's assertion was too similar from his father's earlier conclusions. He bit down on his cheek, forcing himself to remain silent.

Just because I have magic doesn't mean I lack the moral fiber to wield it.

"I see. Then you should agree, it is better for you to work with us. After all, you have a tremendous talent, even if we cannot excuse your recent transgressions. Last night, you nearly broke every rule on the books, and we know it was only because your father made a deal with the captain of the *Horizon* that you were spared from any mention in the papers at all."

"That is why you would have no trouble blaming them for my debts, isn't it?" Brixton snapped, suddenly angry.

"It is an unfortunate coincidence, Brixton," Henry replied calmly. "But Director Strahm and I have worked out what we believe to be a fair compromise with the rest of the Board. It is one we believe will benefit all parties. If you are in agreement, your debt will be considered paid in full, and we will recommend you go work with the Airship Force on our behalf."

Brixton felt his mouth drop open. "Why would you and the Board do that for me, sir?"

"We're not heartless, Brixton. We know you're frustrated by the students. Damnable, vexing, demanding creatures, aren't they? I remember disliking the lot of them myself when I was in your position." Henry stood up and began to pace. "I saw that your last application to the Airship Force was denied because you were late getting it in. You are overworked, clearly."

Brixton held himself as still as possible. He was not going to apologize for his ambition, he told himself.

"Needless to say, we can't keep you here forever, so that is why we're willing to sign off your debt and make a full letter of recommendation for your transfer to the Airship Force. I think your actions yesterday have shown you would be an asset to Captain Airey's crew."

Once he recovered from his surprise, Brixton was not able to stop himself from smiling. "Thank you, sir."

"Captain Airey will likely make you swab the deck for months after damaging his ship, but I imagine you'll see the trouble is worth it."

Trouble. Brixton narrowed his eyes at the word. This was not a promotion or a celebration, he reminded himself. Henry was here to make a deal. "What does the Board want in return?"

"We need your help in securing the location of a certain former student of ours," Henry told him. He reached into the pocket at his chest and pulled out a folded piece of paper.

Brixton did not have to look down at the profile to know who it was.

He opened the paper, not surprised to find Adelaide's silver eyes looking up at his.

Henry's voice was stark. "We need you to bring her to us here at the school."

"Why do you need my help in finding her?" he asked, carefully keeping his voice stripped of any emotion.

"Surely you remember that she repeatedly had infractions while she was at school," Henry said, ignoring Brixton's question. "With her father imprisoned, there have been several indications that point to Miss Favan as the one behind the attack on the clock tower last night."

Brixton kept his eyes on her picture. "You think that she did all of that to free her father?"

"Most likely she was doing it for revenge. Her father is in prison for treason," Henry said. "The evidence against him is strong. Rumor has it that he is to be drawn and quartered, if convicted."

Brixton gulped. He did not like Captain Favan, but the thought of Adelaide's father suffering the death penalty still turned his stomach.

But what did the Dragon Eyes have to do with anything? Brixton wondered if it was possible Adelaide was after the gem in order to exchange it for her father's life.

Henry picked his top hat off the hook by the door. "I'll expect your first report on her whereabouts by the end of the day, Brixton. I'd hate for the Board to fire you before discharging your debt."

"By the end of the day?" Brixton glanced down at Ticker, who was still emitting a stream of half-snores.

"Yes. You'd best get to work, Brixton." Henry shook his head. "I am sorry for this, you know. I will be sad to lose you to the Airship Force. Or to the Board's decision, if they decide to fire you."

"Last time I talked with Adelaide, she was going to live with her family in Peking," Brixton said. Saying her name aloud in front of his boss felt like talking with sandpaper on his tongue, and lying about it made it even harder. "I have no idea where she would be now."

And that was the truth, even if he had seen her more recently than he would admit. He had no idea where to start looking for her. He had not even known she was in London until their encounter the night before.

"Well, you do have some time. The Board has assigned your junior professor, Mr. Rafael Wilder, to take over until your return. I can give you until tomorrow to check in, but that is all I can do."

"I didn't agree to it yet."

"Surely you would not pass it up, though?" Henry frowned, genuinely surprised. "I assured the Board that a person of your integrity would jump at the chance to help."

"Henry, this is not one of the Board's usual demands on my time," Brixton argued. "I'm used to approving new designs for machinery, assisting with testing, or securing patents for new designs. I have even worked with several of your development teams helping the Board, the Crown, the police, and even the military."

"I know, and you have been a faithful and reliable worker in those matters. But I did not think you would step back from this assignment. Should be easier than you think, after all. Consider it almost like a research project."

Henry reached over and patted Brixton on the shoulder. "And just think. Your family's debts would be repaid, you would have the job you've always wanted, and you would be able to provide a much-needed service to the kingdom."

"Would we be able to help her?" Brixton asked. "At all? If we brought her here to the school?"

"Now, now. Don't let your old feelings for her get in the way of this, Brixton. She is a threat to our nation. She never was one of us entirely, as you know."

Brixton scowled at Henry. "I would think, Dr. Winston, that you of all people would know bloodline does not determine loyalty."

After giving Brixton a disproving look, Henry waved his arm, brushing the matter aside. "My apologies. But we know that her family is connected to quite a few dangerous people in the Orient, and they have made their distrust of us no secret. If she is here, she is working for them. And we, knowing what kind of damage she can do, are the ones who are rightfully charged with tracking her down. Otherwise, she might get into more trouble. And others could be hurt, too."

Brixton felt the weight on his shoulders substantially increase as Henry cordially tipped his hat and exited his office.

Brixton slumped into his chair, putting his head in his hands. *What am I going to do now?*

There was only one thing to do. He had to find her, and he had to find out what was going on. The easiest place to start was Scotland Yard, he thought with a grimace. His father had mentioned that Adelaide might have come back to help her father, and it would be a good place to see if he could talk with Captain Favan.

Maybe Gloria can help me, too. He sighed at the thought of owing her anything, but he had already cost his family too much.

Brixton crumbled the paper with Adelaide's profile in his hand. He had told her before she was worth the trouble, but as he stood there, with his future and his family's fate on the line, he was starting to wonder how far she would go to test his claim.

FAVAN AND FLEW

<u>10</u>

If there was one thing that Adelaide appreciated now that she was disgraced before her family, it was that she could return to her father's house without drawing suspicion to herself—so long as she was careful, of course.

As morning light began to shine through the patches of London fog, she made her way, along with a grumbling Jiahao, to the house where she had spent the majority of her childhood.

The townhome was large and unwelcoming, its quiet pride easily usurped by the haphazard hedges and the unkempt gardens in the front. Several vines hung limp from the black and gray brick fences that separated the house from the street.

After carefully making her way to the back door, Adelaide used her picklocks to slip inside the property grounds. It was easy to find a way through the complicated security system she had designed herself.

Inside, Favan Hall was dark, but still full of the old herbal scents her mother had favored. There was a growing musk that was starting to accumulate, along with a thin layer of dust, but Adelaide preferred it over the smoky caverns of Tàitai's fancy, hidden hovel. The dust was nothing compared to the dirty coal residue of the Underground.

As she made her way through the hallways of the house, Adelaide could not help but notice the change. Before, there had always been someone around, watching over her, whether it was her mother's old nursemaid, Nana, or her father's long-time butler, Hudson.

Things were different now. Nana had succumbed to a fever last spring in Peking, and Hudson had retired in order to spend more time with his grandchildren.

"Why are we wasting our time here?" Jiahao's voice echoed through the dark rooms around them.

Adelaide sighed. Tàitai would not appreciate her reminiscence any more than Jiahao liked sneaking into her home.

"Don't be so impetuous, Jiahao. If we're going to track down the Dragon Eye, we will need all the resources we can get. And there's no denying my father has plenty of those."

"There is also no denying he is in prison. It is likely the house is being watched."

"It's more likely being watched by our clan than the police or any of the Queen's guards."

Jiahao frowned but said nothing. He made his way over to the parlor, glancing out the side of the window at the waking streets below.

Adelaide wished she could tell him she hated working with him as much as he did with her, but she knew she would be lying. Her cousin was one of the only members of her family remotely close to her age, and he had been decent company, even if he was considerably surly. He was several years older than her, at twenty-four, but he always seemed even older because of his mannerisms and perpetual frustration.

"Do you miss Peking at all, Jiahao?" Adelaide asked, suddenly curious.

Jiahao was as much of a stranger in London as she had been in Peking. He had grown up in Peking with his older brothers, Chon, Wen, and Wu. All of them had been to

FAVAN AND FLEW

London several times, traveling the distance as a small number of Tàitai's most trusted messengers.

"Of course I miss Peking." In the reflection of the window, Adelaide could see his eyes shift from one side to the other, taking in the waking streets below. "This is no place for people like us, Yaling. We should be with our own kind."

It was strange to hear him admit he considered her family, but he clearly forgot her life was significantly more tied to London than his.

"If that is so, then there is no true place for me at all," she said.

Jiahao crossed his arms. "Just get going. Tàitai might allow us to work with Chon if we can correct your mistake quickly."

"I know you'd love to join him and your other brothers."

"It is better than being stuck working with you."

Adelaide came up beside him, following his gaze as he watched the streets below. "At least this way, you'll get more of the credit when we get our Dragon Eye back."

"You have been corrupted by this place for a long time, Yaling. In China, no one gets more credit when the job is done correctly. We all share it as we work toward the same end."

"Or the dishonor, I suppose, if we don't?"

Jiahao's dark brown eyes darkened in response to her question. "Do not stand next to me. Someone might notice us from the street below."

"I agree, cousin. I'll get ready, and then we'll head out. You might want to find something that will hide your face a bit better. I think my father might have some old top hats in the closet that would work."

"Do you actually have a plan?"

"Of course I have a plan. You know I've always been smart."

"If you were really smart, we would not be in this position."

It was Adelaide's turn for her temper to stir. "I can always use my magic on you. If you're going to complain about my competence, you might want to consider looking at your own situation first."

Jiahao let out a dismissive snort. "Your power is the main reason Tàitai did not already have you killed."

"It seems intelligence is a family trait, then. She knows she needs me if she's going to get to the Dragon Eyes." She wrinkled her nose. "Even though it is ridiculous to think getting them back is a matter of justice."

"If you truly believe that, you have no sense of honor."

"I have plenty of that," Adelaide objected. "I just believe the West has a better definition of what constitutes honor."

Jiahao shook his head. "The guilty go unpunished in the West."

"And the innocent are unable to forgive in the East." Adelaide turned and headed out of the parlor, making her way toward the stairs. "Just stay here. I'll be down after I get ready, and then I'll tell you what I have in mind."

She waltzed toward her old room with a sense of relief, leaving Jiahao to himself.

And that *is why I do not like people,* she thought with a frown.

Opening her wardrobe, she examined the small selection of gowns before her.

When Tàitai had called her back to Peking, Adelaide was instructed to pack light. Her father had warned her that her extended family hated the British, and she would quickly receive new clothes to wear once she arrived at their family's estate. She had no sooner boarded the airship in St. James's docking field than her clothes had been confiscated and summarily replaced with the latest Chinese fashions.

Now that her father and great-grandmother had found a credible lead on the location of the Dragon Eyes that required her assistance, she was back in London with nothing new to wear. At least, she thought with a grimace, she had not grown any taller since she had last come to London. Her older gowns would still fit her.

Brixton did all the growing between us. She remembered how he lifted her off her feet to bring his lips to hers.

Heat flushed through her at the memory, warding off some of the chilly air inside the nearly-empty house.

Adelaide had to force herself to focus on the task before her. Thanks to Tàitai, she had more time to find the missing Dragon Eye, but that did not mean she had a lot of time to waste. Now that her great-grandmother's machine was almost finished, Adelaide did not want to keep her waiting for any reason. Especially when she should have managed to keep a hold of the clock tower's Dragon Eye in the first place.

Fortunately, Adelaide knew there were only a handful of places that the gem could have disappeared to, and she already had a few ideas of its whereabouts.

She selected a black gown and found a large, feathered hat coupled with a veil for her head. She wished she could have borrowed her great-grandmother's wig to add more inches and years to her disguise, but she had a feeling

FAVAN AND FLEW

Tàitai would not find the request even remotely amusing, even if it was to help her achieve her goals.

"Tàitai would just wonder why I would bother to hide myself at all," she murmured. There was no one to reply, much the same as the rest of her life, but hearing her voice anchored her to the present in a familiar, comforting way.

She pulled out the newspapers she had bought earlier, placing them on the bed while she dressed. The penny dreadfuls were full of inaccuracies, she thought with a smirk, but the sensationalism behind them was almost as informative as the proper journalism of the *London Times*. The *Times* had been careful to report the facts of the incident before speculating what motivated the attack, while the penny dreadfuls had been eager to offer their conspiracies right from the start.

Neither, she noticed, mentioned the disappearance of the Dragon Eye. The amethyst she had stolen along with Jiahao had been implanted in the face of the clock, sealed at the center with blood magic. Despite the magnitude of the spell, her power had easily broken through the old barrier, freeing the ancient treasure.

Adelaide recalled the heaviness of the gem and the wonder she felt as she carried it. It was one of the two jewels her ancestor, Qin Suyan, had collected in return for the enchanted gunpowder Guy Fawkes had ordered for the Jesuits' failed treason plot in 1605.

Thanks to her family, Adelaide knew King James had ordered Suyan killed and the two amethysts known as the Dragon Eyes confiscated. Under the dark of night, he had the jewels separated, but they were soon lost. The Crown set out to find them, and supposedly met with relative success. As the monarchy passed down the Stewart line, the Dragon Eyes were eventually sealed away in secret.

FAVAN AND FLEW

It was almost a shame, Adelaide thought as she finished lacing up her corseted bodice, how much could be determined by what was left out of the news instead of what could be gained from what was printed.

That was not the only significant piece of information she noticed from the reports. There was one fact that correlated between hype and truth, and that was where she was going to start.

She folded the paper, ready to head out toward the old Whitehall Palace, home of the Metropolitan Police Services and Scotland Yard.

Jiahao was waiting for her as she came downstairs.

"You look like a black ghost in that veil," he said. "I don't see how that is going to help us, unless you intend to start scaring the men we question."

She smirked from behind her veil. "Widows are always afforded more privacy here. This is more of a repellent, and a respectful one at that."

"I have heard that you can go and attend a séance where you can have a medium call upon your ancestors. But I do not think that any of ours would be willing to show up in a London parlor room."

"I don't know," Adelaide said. "Qin Suyan was supposed to have any number of London lovers. Some rumors even say she had an illegitimate child with one of the Jesuits."

"I imagine that was another reason King James did not mind having her killed."

"Providing the sacred gunpowder that blew open a magic portal was the lesser sin, I am sure." Adelaide gave Jiahao a teasing smile, and she was gratified when he shrugged; she knew he did not easily show his affection for her, but Adelaide knew it was there.

"Tell me your plan, so I can prepare myself for its failure."

Adelaide pursed her lips, tempted to smack him. But in the interest of their mission, she decided to wait until she had more time to properly punish him. "There's no report on the gem in the news, so it's likely in the hands of either Scotland Yard or with the Airship Force at St. James."

"It could also be at the bottom of the Thames."

"I'll keep that in mind if we run out of other options," Adelaide snapped as they walked outside, slipping out the side door. "But Scotland Yard is first."

Jiahao let out a loud groan. "You are not thinking we can just walk in there, are you? Our family would be very upset if we have to extract you from Tower Hill along with your father."

"I already know you're not going to free him. There's no need to pretend Tàitai wants to."

"She still might order his murder."

"I doubt she would waste the time," Adelaide replied dismissively.

"You would not object to the call for his death, would you?"

"I was under the assumption the Crown was about to take care of that for us. I can't see Tàitai wasting her time." Adelaide glared at him. "Right now, I just need you to follow my lead. We'll stay out of sight as we near Scotland Yard."

"We should use the Underground."

"There's no need to. I've got my disguise, and if you keep that hat on, no one will notice you unless you purposefully draw attention to yourself while we are out."

She glanced down at the simple suit Jiahao wore. He had been displeased by her earlier request to don Western clothes, but he looked rather nice in the linen shirt and tweed suit.

With Jiahao at her side, Adelaide stepped out into the street and hailed down a hackney, acting like an older lady heading out for the day.

The driver seemed half-drunk from the previous night. Adelaide was glad to see he fell for her disguise, and when Jiahao jumped onto the back of the hackney, he did not notice.

As they neared the buildings that housed the London police force, Adelaide turned her thoughts back to Brixton.

Just like the Dragon Eyes, he had not been mentioned in the papers, and Brixton never seemed to get into trouble without struggling to get out of it.

Rembrandt probably stepped in to protect its reputation.

She thought back to the oppressive hallways of her former school. It was in her junior year of college that she began to see the darker side of magic, including the forces that hid behind the school's legacy. But once she saw it, there was no ignoring it.

When her father and great-grandmother wanted her back in Peking, she was admittedly relieved to escape the school.

She only had one regret.

Adelaide looked out the hackney window, gazing at the city streets around her. She caught sight of the dark stone tower of Rembrandt Academy through the remaining clouds of fog. The tall, boxlike design reminded her of the story of Pandora, and it was not entirely unfitting, she decided.

Her mind wandered off, back to the middle of her junior term. Even though over three years had passed, she could picture herself in the materials room, too upset to work.

Adelaide tossed a wrench across the table, scattering a small pile of replacement cogs as the door opened. She nearly jumped, before she saw that it was only Brixton.

"If you break something else this week, you have to tell Dr. Winston about it," he said, eyeing the mess she just made. "He might like me better, but I have a feeling he's adding the extra charges to my account instead of yours."

Adelaide might have smiled if she was not so upset. "If it's a problem, you can just make me pay for the trouble."

"It's fine, Ada," he said, giving her a companionable nudge. "I was only joking."

"Your joking depresses me."

"It can't depress you as much as Professor Albright's class depresses me."

Brixton started talking about their upcoming midterms, and how they needed to start planning for their senior projects. She did not pay attention to his words. She did not want to even look at him; her eyes were watering as she realized that her magic was even more of a curse than she realized.

If I was just normal, she thought, staring down at the table in front of them, *then I could stay here. I could stay here with Brixton.*

"Ada?"

She smiled at his endearment for her. Others in the school insisted that it was proof of his affections, but she

FAVAN AND FLEW

knew Brixton well enough to know he considered her to be like a sister. He had a younger sister already, and over the years they had worked in tandem on various projects, there had been nothing in his demeanor that suggested he carried deeper feelings for her. He would pat her on the shoulder, tweak of her nose, and playfully kiss the back of her hand from time to time, but he was only teasing her. That didn't mean he loved her.

"What's wrong?" Brixton asked. "Did Director Strahm or Dr. Winston talk to your father about what happened with Gloria?"

She could hear the hesitation in his voice as he brought up that sore subject.

"Not exactly," she said. "But I did talk with my father."

"He's not upset with you, is he?"

She pursed her lips, unwilling to admit her father was more upset with the school. As far as she knew, Brixton did not understand what she had done to Gloria, and she did not want to tell him. It was enough to know he was her friend; she did not want to face losing his admiration as well as leaving him.

"I'm sure it'll be all right, whatever it is," Brixton said. "If I can help with something, you know I will."

"You can't help me with this." Adelaide shook her head. "My great-grandmother wants me back in Peking with her. After what happened, my father's agreed to it."

"What?" Brixton's voice was edged with anger. "What about school?"

"It's no matter," Adelaide said, trying shuffle that issue to the side. "I don't need to graduate, since my family's well-connected. I can still make a good match. And of course we have the funds for me to do whatever I'd like."

FAVAN AND FLEW

"But you can't just leave," he said, his hazel eyes wild with hurt and sadness.

"I don't have a choice." She was just about to tell Brixton the truth about her magic—how it was getting increasingly difficult for her to control—when he suddenly grabbed her.

Adelaide initially pushed back, afraid she had unwittingly provoked his temper, but Brixton kept a firm hold on her. He pulled her against him tightly as he took her into his arms.

Feeling the warmth of his embrace, Adelaide went still. It had been so long since someone had held her like that— if, indeed, anyone had ever held her like that.

Her head barely reached his chin; warmth radiated between them as his arms tangled around hers. Even through her gloves, she could feel the strange mix of careful desperation inside of him.

"Brix." His name escaped her in a whisper.

His hands were trembling as he tipped her chin up to face him—the same hands she had seen hold steady as he pulled apart machines, worked with tools, and built all sorts of new creations.

The last thing she saw before she closed her eyes were his lips as they drew closer to hers.

It was the most natural thing in the world to cling to him, to turn her face toward his, to lay her mouth against his, to give comfort as much as it was to seek it.

The second their lips met, the warmth burned into scorching heat.

Adelaide felt energy as it rushed through her veins, her head swimming with the taste of him; her lips quickly parted under his and she wrapped her arms around his neck.

She heard him whisper her name as his hands, still trembling but no longer uncertain, gathered her to him.

"Brixton." This time his name escaped her as a soft cry of delight, as everything between them before then was newly realized; every memory was suddenly bathed with tension and unspoken attraction. Her knees went weak, but Brixton caught her and picked her up, placing her bottom on the table, never missing a beat as he continued to kiss her.

Adelaide felt like asking him if he planned to work on her the way he did with his other projects, but before she could say anything, his mouth slanted over hers, and she found it difficult to think at all.

She did not know if she wanted to, either. If she had stopped to think, Adelaide doubted she would have clung to him so fiercely, pulling him down onto her, reveling in their intimacy as she arched against him, offering him every beat of her heart and every breath in her lungs as he held onto her.

I love you. There was no doubting her feelings for him now, Adelaide thought with an exuberant sense of joy, as time's spell broke and his soul knitted itself into hers.

And then it happened.

Her black magic, the destructive power that persisted relentlessly inside her being, coiled out to duel his. As long as she touched him, her magic seemed to have a mind of its own; she was not able to stop it from trying to destroy him.

"Brixton, we need to stop," Adelaide said, her voice suddenly full of fear. She tried to push back against him, but when she broke away from their kiss, Brixton's mouth found her throat. She was so glad when he clung to her, when he held her against him in that naturally possessive way of his—even though she knew it would lead to his destruction.

At that thought, she jerked back from him. He swayed dangerously, and Adelaide saw her chance. She slid out from under him. Brixton stumbled at the swift movement; he collapsed to his knees, out of breath and depleted of nearly all his energy.

"What is this?" he asked, looking at his hands. "Something's wrong. I can't feel my magic."

Adelaide thought back to the last time she felt this scared and hurriedly stepped back from him, watching in horror as he clumsily reached for her.

It's just like it was with Mama. She straightened her shoulders, forcing herself to face reality's harshness as Brixton fought to stay conscious.

"I'm sorry. I'm so sorry, Brixton. We can't be together," she whispered, inwardly reeling in self-hatred as she backed away from him. Her hand went over her heart as it ached for him.

"But you're mine," Brixton said, gazing up at her, half-delirious with wonder and horror, before he faded from the world. "I need you."

The hackney hit a bump in the road, jolting Adelaide free from her memories. She gasped in surprise, finding her hand gripped at her chest, just as she had when he passed out. A breath of fog on the windows still separated her from the London streets, but there was no longer any chill surrounding her.

Brixton.

Adelaide pressed her fingers into her forehead, as if to stop the pain that came with the memory, even though she knew it was pointless.

After Brixton lost consciousness, Adelaide ran to get help. The school nurse had looked down at her with such disappointment, she remembered.

Adelaide had left him, and the school, while he was still asleep. She thought it would have been easier for him after that; there were no promises to write, no promises to stay in touch.

She also believed it would help her forget him and move on, too.

It was nothing short of ironic that he was the reason they were back in England, she thought, recalling the report she had seen in the *Times*.

The Board was coming out with a new project, one that was supposed to help enhance the city's monitoring airships, something called the PRISM project. When she noticed Brixton in the picture next to the article, she neglected the rest of the article. He was named as one of many professors instrumental in the project's development.

As she stared at his picture, Adelaide could not stop wondering if the changes she saw in him were as stark in person as they were in the picture. She was about to throw the newspaper away, beyond frustrated at her fate, when she noticed it.

In the back of the Rembrandt High Office, a small, oval-shaped amethyst glittered at the center of the Rembrandt coat of arms—one of the Dragon Eyes.

The hackney rumbled over the road again, returning her thoughts to the present. Adelaide saw they had come to a stop near Whitehall.

She quickly paid the driver and hurried off to find a place to watch and wait, trying her best not to think about her first kiss with Brixton any more than their recent one; she had a job to do, and Brixton only complicated it.

She glanced in a passing window, taking in her own appearance as much as she looked for signs Jiahao was nearby. She smiled even though the veil obscured her expression.

Mama would be proud to see me looking like a true lady.

Her mother, Madeline, had been a real lady, one from the higher circles of Society. When she met Adelaide's father at one of the dinners for the State, they had both fallen in love at first sight. After a scandalous, whirlwind marriage, Madeline was disowned by her family, but she married the grand military hero Horatio Ryu Favan and never looked back.

Her father did, though.

Adelaide knew her father came to regret their union later on when Madeline died trying to stop Adelaide from using her magic.

She felt her fingers curl up inside her gloves at the sudden flux of shame, recalling how her magic had killed her mother.

Just like it could kill Brixton, if he ever tries to kiss me again.

Her resolve faltered briefly, but she forced herself to keep moving.

Tàitai promised there was a way to resolve it, Adelaide recalled. If there was a way to stop her magic from destroying the ones she loved, and herself, too, she would do anything to find it.

Even if it meant she had to mercilessly kidnap and threaten a police officer.

And here comes the target now.

Adelaide watched as Gloria Alberton sauntered out of a side door to the building.

A small bit of sour remorse flowed through her as she watched her former classmate walk freely down the street.

Gloria had always been among the prettiest and most popular girls of their class. Adelaide had never minded that, but she hated being the target of much of Gloria's teasing. Gloria had always been able to find a way to criticize or belittle her if she could, and the rest of her friends seemed to enjoy it.

Gloria will likely see this as an enjoyable form of revenge for me.

She frowned as Gloria started heading down the street. Adelaide turned into a small alleyway to see Jiahao was waiting for her.

"Are you ready?" Adelaide motioned toward Gloria. "She's the one who will have some information on the Dragon Eye. She was quoted in both the *Times* and several of the other papers I've read. If we're careful, we should be able to get information from her without using your magic at all."

Jiahao cracked his knuckles, letting his red magic flare briefly against his palms. "I rather like using my talent."

"Gloria has magic, too. You're no good to me if you drain all your energy, especially in one turn."

"I have enough for one thorough job, and if she is as important as you say, I can handle it, even if she does have magic," Jiahao grumbled.

Adelaide hid a smirk. Jiahao had a useful talent; he could impose his will on a person, calming them down while lulling them into a mesmeric trance.

"If you say so. I know she has the power to feel emotions." Adelaide never understood why Gloria taunted her if she could feel other people's emotions. She glanced down at her own gloved hands again. Maybe her power made it easier to deflect Gloria's talent.

"It does not matter to me what kind of magic she has. How do you know she will talk?"

"We were in the same class at school, and she knows about my power. I have a feeling that will be enough to convince her to give us the information we need."

"She is coming this way. What were you thinking of doing?" Jiahao asked.

"I was hoping to convince you to pretend to rob me out on the street as she passed by, and then when she's close enough, we could attack her together and drag her behind the alley. It's busy enough we'll have to be careful, but we should be able to escape any notice if we hurry."

"Will she believe our ruse?"

"If you're convincing, it shouldn't be a problem."

"You know how to fight me. You are the one who needs to be believable."

Adelaide rolled her eyes. "Yes, yes, you're right about that. Just make sure you surprise me. I'll keep ahead of her and scream loudly in my best elderly voice when you attack."

Jiahao glanced back at Gloria once more. "Do you think she'll pursue it? She doesn't look very strong."

Adelaide faltered as she caught sight of a clock in a nearby store window. "I hope she does."

"I told you your plan was going to fail."

FAVAN AND FLEW

Adelaide blushed angrily. "We'll see. If we can't get her this way, we can try something else."

She stepped out of the alleyway, hunching herself over. Under the cover of her veil, she knew she could get away with walking like a crone.

One like Tàitai, if she did not insist on living forever, apparently.

The mental image of her great-grandmother fighting off death—or even death running away from claiming her—amused her, and it was the perfect distraction as she walked down the street several meters in front of Gloria.

Just as Adelaide gave Jiahao the signal to attack, she heard someone else calling out to Gloria from behind them.

"Gloria!"

Adelaide stumbled, nearly falling at the sound of Brixton's voice. She saw him as he hurried over to where Gloria stood just as Jiahao leaped out of the alley shadows.

11

"Gloria, wait!" Brixton hailed her as she walked down the street, gratified he had managed to find her. He had been rightfully worried she would be out on her rounds in the morning.

He considered it to his fortune that he caught up to her as she was leaving police headquarters.

Gloria lit up as she turned to face him. "Brixton! I was wondering how you were feeling this morning. It's good to see you out and about."

"I'm feeling considerably worse than I look," he replied. "I need your help."

"What is it? Are you well? Do you need some help getting back to your house?"

"There's no need to be concerned for my health," he said. "I need your help finding Adelaide."

"Adelaide Favan?" The light in Gloria's eyes died. "Oh. I see."

"Yes." Brixton was just about to explain his situation when a strangling cry came out from down the block.

Brixton and Gloria both glanced toward the sound, only to see an older lady, using a surprising amount of strength, fling a young man to the ground. The street lad cried out angrily as the woman hurried into a nearby shop. Gloria and Brixton watched as the thief scrambled up from the ground and hurried for a nearby alley. He glanced all around, before ducking into the shadows.

"Seems like someone came prepared," Gloria murmured. "It's nice when I don't have to work on my break."

"Should you go and do something?" Brixton asked. He did not want to interrupt Gloria in her duties. He was there to ask her for help, not get her into trouble.

"He's already gone; I doubt I would be able to catch him now." Gloria shrugged. "Besides, you said you needed my help."

"Right." Brixton put his hands in his pockets, shoving back the sudden chill in the air. "My father told me that Adelaide's family was back in London. He suspects they are here because of her father's imprisonment. I was hoping I could ask some questions about him, and her possible location, too."

"I can't just give out personal details about people, especially to civilians, Brixton," Gloria said with a hardened look on her face. "Besides, I know how you felt about her while we were at school, and it's clear nothing has changed."

Brixton stepped back. "This doesn't have anything to do with that."

"Sure it does. I can read your emotions, remember? There's no use in lying to me."

Brixton sighed. "Look, that might be true, but I need to find her because the Board at Rembrandt wants me to. If I don't, it's possible they're going to fire me."

"They can do that?" Gloria frowned. "I'm not sure that would pass any ethics committee—"

"Dr. Winston told me himself. I don't have much of a choice if I'm going to keep my job. Please, can you help me?"

Gloria looked thoughtful. "I get off work at five. Why don't you meet me in Hyde Park when I'm finished? We can walk through the park and talk about it then."

He paused for only a moment before he nodded. "I understand. I will meet you there, just inside the entrance."

Gloria flashed him a dazzling smile. "Wonderful. I will see you there, then. I have to get back to the office soon, so I better go check on that old lady."

She skipped away with a new spring in her step.

Brixton hated that Gloria had coerced him into a public appearance, but he knew she was doing him the favor and he had no right to complain—even if he was tempted to.

Brixton ran his hand through his hair as he reached into his pocket and pulled out Ticker.

Ticker yawned. "What is it, sir?"

"Why are you still sleepy?"

"I've had a rather trying night, I'm afraid. I do believe I may need another charge sooner than I anticipated."

"I just charged your power yesterday, and you didn't even need it." Brixton turned Ticker over in his hand, surprised to find the panel in the back half-melted, scarred and scratched from the outside. It looked as though something had clawed the metal, trying to get into the power source.

Brixton thought back to his encounter with Adelaide. His talent flickered; her magic was responsible for the damage to Ticker. The small energy loop inside of Ticker, the one he had used to capture his magic's power and fuel his friend's power circuits, weakened in warning.

Brixton felt his fingers go numb. Adelaide had warned him before that they could not be together, and he had refused to believe her.

But ... but ...

"But maybe she was right." His voice was soft and low, full of awful disbelief, and he suddenly wanted to find

Adelaide even more. The Board might have had their suspicions, but he had his own questions for her now.

"Did you need me for something, sir?" Ticker's impatience was clear, even in his stoic voice.

"Mark my calendar for an appointment at Hyde Park for five today, please." Brixton ran his thumb over the bumpy panel as he turned Ticker back around to face him.

"Consider it done, sir."

Brixton nodded glumly. He had been hoping he would have found a lead with Gloria, but he would have to wait until five o'clock to find out if she knew of anything else that would help him.

Until then, he only had one more idea of where to go.

"Are you requiring any further assistance, sir?" Ticker asked.

"Yes," Brixton said. "See if you can pull up a compass. I need to get to the Whitewand district."

"May I ask what your intended destination is now, sir?"

"Favan Hall." Brixton shielded his eyes from the sun as he looked back up at the broken face of London's iconic clock tower.

As he began to walk away, he thought he heard someone calling his name.

He turned around, but there was no one there. He frowned before pulling his greatcoat tighter around him.

I must be imagining things.

"Yaling, you'd better be back here."

FAVAN AND FLEW

Jiahao's voice was sharp enough to make her shiver, but Adelaide hurried forward through the dark alleyway. She tore off her veil and hat, carefully keeping her skirts clean as she shuffled back into the cramped, dirty alleyway.

"I'm here," she said, trying to keep her voice down. She hoped Jiahao would follow her example and refrain from yelling and cursing at her for her earlier attack.

Adelaide rounded the last corner to see Jiahao had Gloria in a headlock, his arm wrapped around her neck as he held a hand over her mouth. Her eyes were wide and terrified, and even more so when she saw Adelaide.

Adelaide let out a soft sigh. It was time to get to work. "Can you use your magic?"

"Yes, though it might take a moment," Jiahao grunted bitterly. He took hold of Gloria's neck, letting his power pour onto her bare skin and into her body as she did her best to fight him off.

"What are you doing to me?" she gasped, eyeing Adelaide. "Why are you here?"

"So good to see you again, too, Gloria," Adelaide replied. "I must extend my most heartfelt apologies for not greeting you in a more proper manner."

Gloria, still struggling against Jiahao's magic, glared at her. "Brixton is looking for you."

"I had a feeling he would be." Adelaide did not look at Jiahao as she kept her focus on Gloria. "We are not here to discuss him."

"You need to stay away from him," Gloria spat. "You hurt him while we were at school."

"You did your own share of hurting people, too," Adelaide reminded her. "But I'm not here to reminisce, either."

"If you're going to attack me because I have a date with him today, you're the worst sort of evil."

Adelaide faltered at the thought of Brixton taking another girl out on a date. She was grateful Jiahao lost his patience.

"We can debate the specifics of good and evil later," Jiahao snapped, tightening his grip on Gloria and calling on his magic. Her eyes glazed over with a red haze as his magic took a firm hold over her. "We want to know where the Dragon Eye is."

Gloria blinked. "Dragon Eye? What are you talking about?"

Her voice was slightly slurred, much more relaxed, even if she was still not eager to give up her information.

"The amethyst," Adelaide clarified. "Yesterday, the jewel at the center of the clock face was stolen. We need to know where it is."

Gloria's eyes were wide and innocent as she shook her head slowly. "I have no idea what that is."

"You were there," Adelaide continued. "Tell us what happened after the *Horizon* crashed beside the palace."

"I was organizing the crowds by Parliament while the ASF tried to lower the monitoring airship to the ground. Officer Flew, my boss, appeared and then went to speak with the airship that had gone out of control during the fight. He said he knew the captain. When he came back, he had Brixton with him."

"Why was Brixton on the ship?"

"I do not know how he managed to get on it."

"Who is this Brixton person?" Jiahao asked. "Why does she keep bringing him up?"

"He's another friend of ours." Adelaide kept her focus on Gloria's face, determined not to let Jiahao see her blush.

FAVAN AND FLEW

"I saw him before the ship crashed, working in the engine room."

"I'm losing power." Jiahao shook his head, trying to clear his vision. "She's still trying to fight back. If you're going to ask her any other questions, do it now."

Adelaide nodded and turned her attention back to Gloria. "Tell me about your appointment with Brixton today."

"That is not a question." Jiahao glared at her. "Are you trying to make me suffer?"

"Brixton's father is Officer Flew," Adelaide hurriedly explained. "If we can meet with Brixton, we might be able to get more answers. Now, be quiet and let her answer."

Gloria started to blink. "Brixton and I have a meeting … Hyde Park. Entrance. At five o'clock … Now, get off of me!"

Jiahao dropped her as she broke through the hold of his power. He fell to the side of the alleyway, and Gloria tripped and stumbled as she tried to escape.

"Not so fast." Adelaide grabbed her by the arm.

"Help!" Gloria cried, but not before Adelaide interrupted her by covering her mouth with her hand.

"I apologize for my rudeness," Adelaide said, trying to keep her breath steady. Her own power was starting to leak through her gloves, and Adelaide sighed. Sometimes her magic seemed to have a mind all its own.

Gloria panicked. "You're going to kill me this time, aren't you? You tried to kill me last time and this time you'll do it."

"I would appreciate it if you could calm down." Adelaide scowled, tightening her grip on Gloria. "I didn't mean to hurt you as much as I did last time. You made me

FAVAN AND FLEW

very angry before, and if you remain calm, things will go better this time."

"I'll never help you." Gloria gazed over at Jiahao, turning her ire on him as well. "You are both rotten ratbags and I'm going to arrest you for this."

Adelaide and Jiahao exchanged a quick look. She sighed, letting the ripples of her talent stir inside of her. Adelaide felt her magic gleefully travel from her hand into Gloria's body, seeking out her energy and purging her blood of all its power.

"I knew I couldn't trust you," Gloria whimpered. A moment later, she fainted away, dead to the world.

Adelaide withdrew her hand as Gloria fell to the ground. She hated using her power to win, especially over an easy target. She also hated how it was so easy to take down the people she did not care for. It had been pure agony to watch Brixton suffer under her power; Adelaide could almost disregard Gloria's fate entirely.

Thank you, Wuja, she thought bitterly.

"What do we do now?" Jiahao asked. "We did not get any helpful information out of her. I told you that your plan would fail."

"Gloria didn't know where the Dragon Eye was anyway," Adelaide reminded him. "She didn't know about it. You heard her. Unless your power didn't work as well as you think?"

Jiahao puffed out his chest. "Her mind is weak. My magic worked fine."

"Then we know she was telling us the truth." Adelaide chewed on her lip as she thought through her next steps.

"Well? What is your next failure of a plan?"

"You know, you could offer one yourself, if you think mine are all terrible."

Jiahao leered at her. "I prefer watching you fail."

"I thought the honor or dishonor was supposed to be shared among the parties?" Adelaide shot back.

He huffed and turned away. "Just get on with it. We are stuck in your land, here, not mine."

Adelaide watched him as he stepped over Gloria's body, heading back toward the street.

"Wait, Jiahao."

He glanced back over his shoulder. "What is it?"

First, she decided, they needed to hide Gloria. She would be out for the next several hours. It was entirely possible she would not wake up until the next morning.

And then ...

Adelaide eyed Gloria's fallen form. A daring idea popped into her head. "I need you to hail another hackney."

"Where are we going now?"

"For now? Home. And we're taking her with us."

"If you think kidnapping a member of the police force is a good idea, I know you have run out of ideas."

"I'm not out of ideas yet," Adelaide assured him. "But they do seem to be getting worse."

12

The cobblestones were uneven and unpleasant beneath his feet as Brixton made his way toward the entrance to Hyde Park. He took in his surroundings, unable to find any joy in them; the rest of the world around seemed untouched by the events of the previous day.

Ticker buzzed inside his jacket, still clearly worn out from their encounter with Adelaide's magic. "Time to meet with your lady friend, sir."

"I know, Ticker. Thank you."

"Well, you must be having a terrible day if you are being polite to me, sir."

"You don't have to call me 'sir,' every time you speak to me, you know."

"It is part of my preferences, sir."

"Aren't you supposed to cater to *my* preferences?"

"It seems inefficient for me to change my disposition as much as you do your moods and subsequent preferences, sir," Ticker replied.

Brixton rolled his eyes and made his way over to the gardens. There were several smaller paths for walking, and it was clear enough that he would be able to watch the entrance for Gloria's arrival.

He crossed his arms and leaned back against a tree, gritting his teeth in anger.

Earlier, Brixton had traipsed all over the city, looking for signs of Adelaide. Favan Hall had been deserted when he arrived. From what he found out during his inquires, Captain Favan was branded a traitor to the Crown, and no one wanted a reference from him. Brixton had to bribe several former servants to tell him even that much.

"I hope Gloria's not expecting us to stop for tea when we're through here," Brixton muttered.

"You have plenty of time if you decide to do so, sir," Ticker said.

"For once it's not time that's my enemy, Ticker," Brixton said with a reluctant chuckle. "It's money."

There was a small rustle of grass behind him, coming from the other side of the tree. "It's lovely to hear you laugh again, Brixton."

Brixton felt as though a barrel of cold water had just been thrown down his back. The chilling sensation raced through him, twisting his stomach into even more knots. He whirled around to see Adelaide leaning against the other side of the tree.

A black parasol was in her hand, hiding her face from the larger public as she twirled it over her shoulder. Behind it, her eyes lit up with both caution and happiness as she glanced over at him, and he had a hard time breathing.

"Ada."

Her lips folded up into a small smile. "I've always liked your name for me. You are the only one who's ever called me that."

"What are you doing here?" Brixton finally stuffed an unhappy Ticker in his pocket as he managed to get a hold of himself.

"I heard you were looking for me."

He narrowed his eyes. "You've never been one to make my life easier."

"But I'm worth the trouble, am I not?" There was a small smile on her lips despite the wryness of her tone, and he wondered if she was purposefully trying to anger him.

FAVAN AND FLEW

He thought about how she had gripped him back when he kissed her before, how she had fallen into his arms effortlessly.

Was she was trying to pretend nothing had happened between them?

Brixton saw her falter, ever so slightly, as he watched her.

"Just tell me why you're here." Brixton reached forward, offering her his arm. "Walk with me."

She stepped back, awkwardly bumping into the tree trunk. "I remember how the gossip flows in London, even if I haven't been here in some time."

"I thought gossip never bothered you? Or have you changed your mind since our days at Rembrandt?"

Adelaide was too proud and too stubborn to answer truthfully. Brixton hated that he felt a twinge of pleasure at her disgust, but if she wanted to make their encounter uncomfortable for him, he would return the sentiment.

He was just about to remind her she should be grateful he did not try to haul her into Scotland Yard when she stuck her nose in the air and stepped forward.

"Aren't you so clever?" Adelaide huffed, but she acquiesced and took his arm.

"I am," he said. "That's why we became friends, remember?"

Her fingers tensed on his arm, and Brixton felt a rush of triumph. Back during their school days, he had used whatever excuse he could think of to brush up against her. Being so close to her once more was intoxicating.

"Where are we going?" she asked, avoiding his gaze.

"There is a small pavilion down this way, off to the side," he told her. "There are some trees, which will grant us cover. My parents used to bring me and Luella here when we were younger."

"How is your sister? Still lovely, I imagine?"

"Even lovelier. I went to visit with her yesterday." He wanted to tell Adelaide how going home was such an odd habit to him sometimes, how strange it was to see the life he used to live was slowly chipped away by time.

But when she nodded, a small twinkle of compassion in her gaze, he knew she understood what he meant.

"That's one thing we always did have in common," Adelaide said. "We visit our homes but never stay."

"Have you seen your father?" Brixton asked. He kept his eyes on the winding pathway ahead, unable to ignore some of the chittering lords and ladies who were watching them nearby. He was grateful for Adelaide's forethought in bringing her parasol. The black lace offered a large degree of anonymity to her, even if he did not have the same benefit.

"The good captain has been hauled off to jail, as you've no doubt heard. And by your father, too, come to think of it."

"My father was the one who arrested him?"

"That was what I heard."

Brixton was surprised. His father had not mentioned that to him at all.

Adelaide shrugged. "To answer your original question, no, I haven't seen him. I doubt I will for some time yet, although I imagine if he's convicted and sentenced, I'll be able to go and see him then."

Her voice was steady, but he doubted she was really as calm as she appeared. Adelaide always seemed aloof from reality. After she had left him at school, it was easy for him to think she was heartless and cruel. But he knew the softer side of her as well—the kindness that hurried to wipe up Luella's tears, the courage to be silent as others passed judgment on her, the vulnerability to admit she needed his help.

The daring to kiss him back in the middle of a magical burglary.

It was time to change the subject, Brixton thought, suddenly feverish with longing.

"I'm supposed to be meeting someone else here," he said, and then immediately regretted it. Adelaide would not like to hear he had an appointment with someone else, let alone another woman; she had always hated it when someone else or another class managed to steal him away from her when they were in school.

Brixton was surprised to see her smile.

"I know. Gloria sends her regrets. She's indisposed for now."

"What did you do to her?" Brixton dropped her arm and eyed her accusingly.

Adelaide stood firm. "Nothing nearly as bad as the last time she got in my way, if that's what you were worried about."

"I'm worried about plenty, but I didn't think Gloria's wellbeing would be on the list today."

"I imagine you didn't think I would be, either."

"You apparently don't know me at all then." Brixton turned sharply, heading down to a path partially hidden by an overgrown bush. "I guess I was right about that."

"Well, if it makes you feel better, I don't need you to worry about me," Adelaide said. "And neither does Gloria. Jiahao is watching her. She will be fine."

"Jiahao? Who is that?" Brixton thought back to the day before. Adelaide had not been alone when he first saw her, he remembered. He thought of the taller fighter, the one who had slipped out of the tower using the rope.

For the first time, he wondered if Adelaide was in a relationship. She had only grown more beautiful in the last several years. He felt his stomach clench, thinking of how she could have had any number of romantic entanglements since then.

"He's my cousin, Brix. Calm down." She hesitated, and then squared her shoulders. "You know how I feel about you."

"Do I?"

"Of course you do." She reached for his arm again, lying her head against his shoulder. "I need you."

His mouth went dry. "Ada, I … " Brixton stared down at her, mesmerized. All he wanted to do was lean down and kiss her again, embracing her as he had before.

As if she sensed his thoughts, she tentatively took a step back from him, suddenly fixated on the pocket watch she kept pinned to the top of her corset. "Speaking of Jiahao, I don't have much time. I promised him this wouldn't take long."

Brixton ran a hand through his hair as she moved further down the garden path. "We never seem to have the time we want."

"I am sorry for that." Adelaide sighed. "But I'm serious. I need your help."

"Is this about the Dragon Eyes?"

"How did you know?"

Brixton nearly laughed at the shocked look on her face. "Come on, this is not the first time I've managed to surprise you."

"Not many know about the Dragon Eyes," Adelaide said. "It's a dangerous legend."

"Knowing you as I do, I've figured that part out." Brixton came up beside her again. "But it also helps I was the one who found it after you left me on the *Horizon*."

"You have it?" Adelaide cheered excitedly. "Where is it? I need it back, Brixton."

"I didn't say I had it."

Instantly, her mood darkened, and she took another step away from him, heading toward a small pavilion, where an old machine of some sort stood, largely forgotten, covered in vines.

Brixton recognized it as one of Da Vinci's failed flying machines, one that an inventor had tried to modify for the steam engine. He saw Adelaide's eyes roam over it, examining it for its tactical use and failures. He could see, using his own talent, that the steam engine was too heavy to allow for flight. It would need to be bigger to accommodate the weight. It was an old problem, one that would be resolved with an air balloon or a magic-infused engine.

Adelaide hiked up her skirt, walking closer to the machine. He could see she wore high-button boots, the same as she had when they were in school.

"It's old," he told her, grateful for the change in topic. "It's been here for nearly ten years."

"I can tell." She ran a gloved hand down a propeller blade. "The inventor cared for it deeply. The scratches on it are from the last decade. Everything underneath was burnished, likely several times."

"It was kind of the city to let him place it here."

She shrugged. "I'm not so sure. It might have been better to melt it down and reuse the parts."

"You said it yourself, he cared deeply for it." Brixton came up next to her. "He would have been devastated to destroy it."

FAVAN AND FLEW

"But now he has a lasting reminder that is here, for all of the public to see." Adelaide glanced over the mechanical ruin. "I don't even see his name. It is a nameless failure."

"The worst failures can inspire the best successes."

Adelaide arched her brow. "I've never known you to sound so optimistic."

"I agree." Brixton let his arm brush against her shoulder. "Maybe it's because you're here."

"And now you've gone mad?"

"And now I have hope again." Brixton reached out and took her hand. Even through her gloves, he could feel her pulse dance underneath his palm. He was close enough he could smell the tang of her herbal soap; he could hear her breath catch in her throat; he could see the stars in her eyes. There was no one else around, no one else that he could see as he stood there, waiting on any sign that she wanted the same thing as he did.

Her fingers were shaking as she pulled her parasol back out, using it to shield herself from his view. "If you have such great hope, maybe you can help me."

Anger stirred inside of him. "I'm not going to let you lead me on."

"What?" Adelaide blinked in surprise, and then sighed. "I am not. If there's ever someone leading someone else on, it's you leading me. You're the one who knows where the Dragon Eye went."

"You attacked Gloria and then you came here in her place to flirt with me in hopes of getting what you want," he accused.

"I don't *want* it. I *need* it, Brixton."

"I suppose there's very little point in wrecking an airship into the clock tower and stealing a magic-protected gem without genuine need, but I'm still not going to let you lie to me."

"I've never lied to you." Adelaide glared at him. "Are you going to help me or not?"

"This isn't a school project, Ada. This is theft against the Crown."

Brixton watched as no change registered on Adelaide's face, and he was surprisingly disappointed. She had clearly acknowledged this before, and she remained determined to commit the crime.

Did Adelaide need it to get her father free? Or was it something else?

And then there was the matter of the amethyst itself. Brixton knew the jewel was very valuable, even without knowing the legend behind it. He easily estimated he could pay off his own debts to the Board at Rembrandt at least ten times over.

The Board. Brixton ran his hand through his hair, even more upset by the Board's position on the whole situation, too.

He looked back at her now, watching as she brushed some stray locks out of her eyes. "Believe it or not, I don't have a choice."

Brixton froze at her familiar words. He could still picture that day, years ago, when she told him she was leaving London.

"No." He reached for her again. "No, you're not doing this to me again."

"Doing what?"

"Leaving me behind." He shoved her parasol to the side as she tried to distance herself from him. "Tell me why."

"Why what?"

"Why are you so desperate to ruin your life over this?"

"You don't understand," she tried to say, before he shook his head.

"What wouldn't I understand?" he yelled. "Whatever we are now, we were best friends for years. I know you, and I know whatever has changed in the last few years is not enough to scare me off or confuse me."

She said nothing as he held her close to him. He wondered if she was finally going to tell him the truth, to answer the questions he had flaring up inside of him. She was trapped, and they both knew it.

Adelaide looked up at him, flustered. He saw her glance around, looking for an exit, looking for an excuse—looking for anything that would allow her to keep hiding.

He tried again. "Do you even know what this could cost you? What do you have to gain from all of this?"

Her indecisiveness broke less than a second later. Brixton almost felt the magnitude of her will collapse as she gave up—gave up, or gave in.

"Brixton." His name came out in a breathy whisper as she reached for him.

He was already reaching back. When they kissed, he felt the spark of their passion ignite all over again; she melted into him, and he was drowning in fire as he held her.

"It's you," she whispered against his mouth. "I need you, Brixton."

"Ada." His hands tussled into her hair and cradled her face, relishing every inch of her lips as they opened underneath his.

Stinging pain crinkled its way across his body as he continued to hold on, enraptured by her confession. He barely realized she was struggling to get away from him as he fell into her, his mind overrunning with desire.

He used to dream of these moments, and now she was here again. She was real and she was here, and they were together. Brixton felt his heart nearly explode. It was too much, and never enough, to have her magic call out to conquer his, and to have his respond with the foolish challenge of young love.

"Brixton, let me go." Her voice seemed to call to him from faraway, and he felt himself shake his head.

"No." His tongue felt thick, his mind dull with pleasure and numb with pain as he tried to talk.

"You have to. I'm killing you!" Adelaide pulled free seconds later, and Brixton fell forward onto his knees. His hands barely managed to catch him before he came face to face with the ground.

"I'm sorry," Adelaide whispered. She inhaled sharply as she leaned down beside him, and for the first time, Brixton saw she was crying.

The sight of her tears—two of them, so slim and precise, running down her cheek—jolted him out of his stupor like nothing else.

"What happened?" he asked, sitting back on his knees as he rubbed his forehead. A dull ache began to magnify inside of him, and suddenly his body was screaming at him.

"I told you we couldn't be together." Adelaide slumped back on her heels as he sat up, holding his head at the splintering pain inside of him. "My magic won't let me touch you."

He called up his talent, trying to call himself to order, only to realize his energy was nearly depleted. He looked down at his palms, stunned by their emptiness, and then he glanced over at Adelaide.

"It happened again," he said. "This is what happened when we kissed before."

She nodded glumly.

"This is what happened to Gloria, isn't it? You tried to drain me of my magic."

"Oh, please. I nearly *killed* you," she cried. "The truth is, I can't control my power. It seeks out other magic and life sources, especially from people I care about. That's why the seal around the timepiece jewel didn't stop me, and neither will any magical force around any safe or lock."

Brixton felt his mind tumble all around, and some bits and pieces came together quicker than others. "The burglaries. You and your cousin were behind them."

"Surely you're not just figuring that out?" Adelaide wiped the tears off her face and stood up, trying to compose herself. "We needed to find out where the Crown hid the Dragon Eyes. We knew where the other one was. My great-grandmother has been looking for them forever. They were stolen from my family after King James killed Suyan."

"What are you talking about?" Brixton reached out and took her arm. Instantly, her power rushed to defend her, and he felt the warmth of battle brew between their flesh. For the first time, he faced the dark reality that he could not kiss Adelaide without suffering a significant cost.

He swallowed hard. "Why are you attacking me now?"

"Let go." Adelaide brushed him off, and he felt rebuffed. "I'm sorry. I told you before. My magic will try to destroy you."

"If it's just after my talent, that's not the same as my life."

"Believe me, Brix, it starts with the magic, but it doesn't stop there." She slumped over. "Magic is tied to the blood, mixed within the heart, and resides alongside the soul. That's why even non-wielders fall under my magic's power, and even faster. If my magic kills yours, you'll die, too."

"I don't know about that. But I do know you can control it," Brixton said. "You did in school. It was only that one time that you seemed to lose control, when Gloria made you angry. And I was there and able to stop you."

"I've never had full control of it, and it's harder to control when it's something I care about."

"You used it earlier today on Gloria, didn't you?"

"Jiahao was there to make sure Gloria would be safe. Knocked out, but safe anyway." Adelaide sighed. "It's hard to explain. It's almost like there's an animal inside of me, and when it attacks something, I can't stop it, even if it's the most awful thing in the world."

"I'm sorry." He reached out for her hand again, but then pulled back. "I didn't know."

"It's not your fault." Adelaide blushed. "I never liked talking about my talent for good reason. It's embarrassing."

"You once told me how your monthly courses started in the middle of Professor Hawking's midterm and he wouldn't let you leave until you were finished with your test, because he thought you wouldn't come back to class."

Brixton was gratified to see her smile. "See? This is nothing compared to that."

"This is *everything*." Adelaide put her head in her hands. "Brixton, I can't touch you without hurting you."

Brixton stood up beside her, standing as close to her as he could. He still felt dizzy from their kiss. And now, he decided, it was time to get his answers. "Is this why you left before?"

"Before?"

Brixton nodded. It seemed he was not the only one who was struggling to think through things. "Before, during our junior year. Was your magic the reason you had to leave?"

"Partially." She blushed again. "My father had warned me about my power. It's something unique to the women in his family. We end up destroying ourselves, and if we're not careful, the people we care about most."

Brixton said nothing, only staring at her. All the years of his suffering were suddenly even more cruel as he finally understood what kept them apart.

She had left him in order to save him. Did that mean she loved him, too?

Adelaide struggled to compose herself. "I was hoping that when I came back I would be able to avoid seeing you."

"No." He shook his head. "No, it's better that we're together."

"Is it?" Adelaide gave him a wry smile. "Do you enjoy nearly dying every time we have an honest moment between us?"

Brixton thought of the days following her departure to Peking. He had been lonely without her, angry she had left him without giving him a chance to convince her to remain in London, or to find a way that would allow them to stay together.

He was always so careful not to risk their friendship before. At school, others gossiped about them regardless, but they never had anything between them until she told him she was leaving Rembrandt.

Her disappearance, followed by her silence, had angered and embittered him. He wondered for weeks afterward if she had even wanted to kiss him at all, before he realized he was making himself insane.

Some things were just true, and that was all there was to it. It was the hardest thing he had ever had to accept that she wanted to kiss him, yet she did not want to be with him.

He was about to tell Adelaide that nothing could be worse than her absence when she turned away and began to walk around the flying machine again.

"Then there is the other side of the matter to consider, too. If I hadn't run into you yesterday, I would have the Dragon Eye."

"Why do you need it?"

"It's the key to stopping my power, for one," Adelaide said. "I just told you that. Pay attention."

"I am. But I don't see why they would stop your power."

"There are two of them, two large amethysts called the Dragon Eyes," Adelaide explained. "According to legend, that's exactly what they are."

"Just like the dragon heart?" Brixton asked, raising his brow.

"That's different." Adelaide looked away. "Sort of, anyway. The Dragon Eyes are the key to releasing the dragon spirit that resides inside of the magic portal. The dragon is the only one who is able to take away my magic's curse."

"There's a dragon living in the magic portal?"

"Dragon spirit. Pay attention."

It was true her magic had depleted him when they kissed, but even in his state of half-awareness, it was too much to believe that a magic dragon spirit was residing in the middle of Parliament. His mind reeled while his heart sank.

He rubbed his temples. This was not going at all how he imagined, Brixton thought. One moment he was desperate to kiss her, the next he was confused, and the next one after that he was angry.

"I'm not lying, Brix," Adelaide insisted, watching his face intensely. "If you get me the gem, I'll be able to prove it to you."

Brixton ran his hand down his face. "That's sure convenient."

"I wouldn't lie to you about this."

"You sure didn't bother to tell me the truth about it, either."

Her eyes narrowed at his sour tone. "I'm not supposed to talk about it. It's my family's secret, and one we're not supposed to reveal under anything less than a blood oath."

Brixton ran a hand through his hair again. Was it possible she was trying to manipulate him into breaking the law by playing with his affection?

He looked over at her again. "I suppose that if you have the Dragon Eyes, it'll allow us to be together?"

"My great-grandmother told me that if we can get the Dragon Eyes, we will be able to break my magic's curse. I can't love anyone until it's under control." Adelaide looked away. "Not without hurting them, anyway."

"What if I don't help you? Would you still want to be with me?"

"You've never been one to turn me down, Brixton."

He hated how much she was right, but he did not want her to assume she could manipulate him. "What if I have a price this time?"

"What are you saying?" Adelaide glared at him. "I know you're in debt, but I can't imagine you would use this as a way to get out of it."

"I wasn't talking about money," Brixton said. "I was talking about us."

"If you help me get the Dragon Eyes, we can be together." Her answer was succinct and direct, but her tone was soft. "If that's what you want."

"Do you think that will be enough to convince me to help you?" Brixton hated how bitter he sounded, but it was unbelievable, that she would trade herself for his assistance.

"I guess not," Adelaide snapped, as she reached down and picked up her parasol, brushing off some of the dirt and grass it had collected. "I'm sorry I said anything at all."

He had loved her so desperately before, and even now, he knew he wanted to be with her. The thought that she wanted to be with him, too, was enough to send his heart flying.

But there was no denying he did not trust her. She left him before without answers or explanation, and the old pain had festered over the years. And now Adelaide was back, there was no way he could be sure he was doing the right thing.

After all, there were just some places a man could not go, and walking into Scotland Yard to rob the place was hardly one of them—especially when he already had to worry about his standing with his father and his job.

At that sudden thought, Brixton cringed. *Father and Harry would kill me for this.*

It was happening all over again—he had a choice between his future and Adelaide, and he was going to suffer no matter the choice. Literally suffer, too, he thought, recalling Adelaide's power.

"I do believe it is time for me to go." Adelaide shuffled her away around him. "This didn't go as I'd hoped."

FAVAN AND FLEW

"What did you think would happen, showing up here?" Brixton asked. "I'm curious."

"Well, I didn't think you would go back on your word, that's for sure."

"What are you talking about?"

"You just told me there was literally nothing that would scare you or confuse you to the point you would step away from me, and so I told you the truth!" Adelaide opened her parasol and leaned it against her shoulder, indignant.

"You have to admit, it sounds asinine," Brixton argued.

"Once it would have been insane to say that magic existed at all," Adelaide shot back. "The only reason we know it does is because my ancestor, a woman named Suyan, decided to take advantage of the Jesuits' violence. She sold them sacred gunpowder from China. When it went off, combined with the dragon's treasure that was buried under Parliament, the magic portal was opened."

"Dragon's treasure?"

"The treasure from the Geats," Adelaide explained quickly.

"The Geats? As in the legend of Beowulf?" Brixton felt his own curiosity pique.

"I know this is hard to believe," Adelaide said, ignoring his interruption. "But this is what I've been told. I don't know all the answers, but I've seen enough—I've experienced enough—to know that it has to be true. My family has known the legend for more than a millennium now, ever since the last Qin emperor betrayed his dragon's trust."

Brixton sighed. "Let's not make this more complex than it has to be right now. For now, here, in London, the Great Disruption was caused by special gunpowder that blew open the magic portal."

"That is where the spirit of the dragon now resides." Adelaide nodded. "The magic has been leaking out from the portal since then, allowing humans to channel it and use it for their own purposes."

"Why doesn't the dragon spirit come out?" Brixton turned the story over in his head, trying to find any specific details that hinted at truth.

"The dragon spirit can't exist in this realm for long, not without a host or body," Adelaide said. "Once it has that, along with the Dragon Eyes, it will be fully resurrected."

"This sounds too strange to believe."

"Magic is too strange for some to believe."

"I know magic," Brixton argued. "This just seems … more impossible."

"You haven't thought of where the magic comes from or why, even though I admonished you for it several times, have you?"

Brixton frowned, aware she was correct. "I know the scientific aspects of it, if not the legendary elements."

Adelaide opened her parasol again. "I suppose I shouldn't be too hard on you. After all, I never would have believed you would ever liken me to a prostitute, but here we are."

"What? I did not."

"You implied I was willing to sell myself to you in order to get what I wanted," Adelaide said, her anger boiling over into rage. "That's no different than propositioning me."

"I was not."

She arched a brow. "Are you really going to argue with me over this?"

"Yes!" Brixton stood his ground. "This is madness, and complicated, and … and you were the one who left me, remember?"

She softened, but only slightly. "I've already explained—"

"It doesn't change the fact that you did leave." He shook his head. "Telling me why doesn't negate the reality, even if it informs the reasoning. You might as well take a pistol and shoot me before telling me why I'm in pain."

"That's hardly the same thing."

"It doesn't change the fact I never heard from you until yesterday," he said. "Your father was the one who told me you did not want to see me before you left for Peking."

Adelaide went still. "You came to see me?"

"I guess it doesn't matter now." Brixton felt his embarrassment rise inside of him as he thought about the day he had broken free from the Rembrandt medical ward and hurried down to the airship field at St. James, hoping to catch her flight before its departure. "I couldn't get past Captain Favan."

Adelaide went silent for a long moment. Brixton watched her carefully, waiting to see what she would say.

"I hope you had the good sense to know he was lying." Her voice was flat, but he could see the sadness in her eyes. "I didn't know you went to see him."

"I didn't. I went to see *you*."

Adelaide gave him a small smile. "Maybe we should consider this partnership a form of comeuppance for my father, then?"

He was disappointed in her response, but he did not let her see it. "Let's not worry about him right now. We have other things to worry about."

"So you will help me?"

FAVAN AND FLEW

Brixton felt his heart start to beat rapidly. He was helpless and nervous all over again, the same as he had been when she had called to him that first time.

Even his answer was the same. "I don't know if I can help you."

"I already know you can," Adelaide said. "All you have to do is tell me where the Dragon Eye is, the one you found. That's all you have to do, and then I'll leave you be once more."

"No, don't do that."

"If you want to help me, then do so." Adelaide began walking back toward the main pathway, keeping her parasol on her shoulder. "You should know that either way, I'm very sorry we can't be together—much sorrier than I've ever been about anything, Brix, whether you believe me or not—and I'll have you know it was right of me to leave you last time."

"No, it wasn't," Brixton objected. He followed after her, taking her hand again. He felt the fission of her power at his touch, but he ignored it.

"Of course it was," Adelaide snapped. "What could you have done? Nothing. It wasn't like my father would have let you come along with me. And even if you had, I would've killed you in less than a fortnight."

"But we would have been together."

"Didn't you hear me? Being together would have killed you."

"Being apart from you was just as hard."

All the years they had spent together ran through him. He remembered working with her in the supply room, exchanging notes from different classes, watching her as she argued and talked with him. He could not name the moment when he suddenly knew every freckle on her face, the moment that liking turned into loving—if, indeed, there had ever been something other than loving.

He squeezed her hand. How many years, he wondered, had he wasted, waiting for the perfect moment to tell her how he felt?

"Brixton." Adelaide whispered his name and tried to pull free from him.

He shook his head. "Please, Ada, let me make the decision here. It's my choice this time. You're not the only one who is affected by it."

She hesitated, and he added, "Whether you believe me or not."

"Well, I've already asked, and you've already said no," Adelaide snapped.

"I didn't say no. I said I didn't think I could help you."

She groaned as she pulled her hand free from his. "You're the one making this more complicated than it has to be. This is why I like machines better than people."

"Because you have better control over them," Brixton said.

"No." She shook her head. "Because machines matter infinitely less."

"Well, you're right about that." Brixton ran his hand through his hair again, distraught.

He was helpless, wasn't he? If he had any proper sense at all, he would take her to Rembrandt, turn her in, and then forget about trying to help her. He could then be free of both his debt and his job, and he would be working in the Airship Force as he had always wanted.

But the thought of losing her again was too much, and the thought of forgetting her was laughable. It did not matter to him if her magic presented a barrier between them.

FAVAN AND FLEW

He crossed his arms across his chest. "Look, I can tell you where the gem is, but I'm not going to let you get it on your own."

"Really?"

What was it about her that made everything brighter when she was happy?

Brixton stared at her, knowing he was about to betray his father's trust and commit several felonies, not to mention betraying the Board's trust and destroying his own future. But as he looked at Adelaide, as he thought about how much he had missed her, how much he loved her, and how much he was likely to die anyway, he knew there was simply no other choice for him.

It was so much like before, he thought, remembering how he had felt in facing the broken clock tower. Everything was wrong, but everything was forgotten as he looked at Adelaide.

There was no one else he had ever met who fit so securely into his life while disrupting it so profoundly.

And he was going to do whatever it took to be with her.

"But I need you to promise me you won't lie to me," he said slowly. "I don't know how many of your legends I believe."

"I've never lied to you."

"Then I'll need you to make sure you tell me the truth, no matter what."

"Fine. You have a deal, Brixton." Adelaide smiled up at him, twirling her parasol with a new eagerness.

He saw her cheeks start to turn red. The faint freckles on her nose winked at him in the early evening light as she went still.

"What is it?" he asked.

"I do wish I could kiss you," she admitted softly, as the blush on her cheeks darkened.

Brixton stared at her, letting his gaze fall to her mouth. "Maybe we could try—"

"No." Adelaide quickly turned her attention back to the pinned watch on her dress. "We don't have time to head over to St. Bart's, Brix. I promised Jiahao I would be back before too long."

"Back?"

"Back at Favan Hall."

"I was there earlier. No one was around."

"We're trying not to make it apparent that we're there," Adelaide told him.

"You've done a good job of hiding, then."

She smiled. "Thank you."

"Do you think I would be able to walk you home, at least?"

He prepared for her rejection, and he was not surprised when she shook her head.

"I'm sorry. I haven't told Jiahao about asking you for help yet, and as much as he barely tolerates me, I'd be worried he would attack you before I'd have to step in and save you." She paused again. "And I'm not sure I would be able to, not without possibly hurting you more."

"When can we meet again?"

"Tonight. So we can go collect the Dragon Eye."

"Tonight?"

"I need it, Brixton. I can't help that I need it. My family has already punished me for losing it before. I'll be much better off when I have it back."

Brixton sighed. Once more, every possible objection stepped forward inside his mind, each one demanding that he listen and be reasonable about this.

"Please, you have to trust me on this one."

Brixton could count on one hand how many times in their lives Adelaide had used the word please without sarcasm.

"Fine," he agreed. "I'll pick you up at ten."

He had promised his mother he would come home for dinner. For a moment, he thought about asking Adelaide to come and join them. He almost smiled at the thought of her walking into their small townhouse again, meeting with Luella and his parents after so many years.

Brixton quickly discarded the idea, as much as he might have enjoyed it. His father was curious about Adelaide in connection to a crime, and the last thing he wanted to do was escort her down to Scotland Yard for an interrogation.

Not that taking her there to rob the place is any more desirable.

Adelaide lit up. "Wonderful. Where are we going?"

"You'll see." Brixton clenched his fist, suddenly wondering what his chances were of staying alive while he was in love with Adelaide.

But if nothing else, he thought with a sigh, Adelaide could always kiss him to death so he did not have to worry about hanging in the gallows.

<u>13</u>

Despite his better judgment and against his ardent wishes, Brixton allowed Adelaide to leave him. He watched her disappear down London's busy streets. The coal-heavy air welcomed her, and then all at once she seamlessly melted into the crowds.

Brixton found he was both appalled and amazed at her ability to hide so easily in plain sight.

Once she was gone, Brixton turned down the streets and made his way back toward his family's house. He had recovered from Adelaide's kiss, but he did not know if he had recovered from their conversation.

It was too much to hope for, that she would be back for good, and she would be his. He had not been lying to her about hope.

Even if, apparently, a dragon spirit stood between them.

When Brixton arrived at home, he opened the door to the sound of an indoor tornado whirling through the parlor.

Papers crinkled, books fell, and glass shattered.

"Lu?" Brixton called out tentatively. He took a step back, wondering if he should call for a magistrate. The sounds grew increasingly threatening, as another animal let out a strangled caw.

"Hurry," Luella cried. "Get in the house before he gets free!"

Brixton immediately slammed the door behind him and prepared for another strange animal to come barreling his way. "Him?" he asked.

"Mrs. Drake came and dropped off her raven, Poe, for Mother to tend to his busted wing, and Mr. Radcliffe's crocodile has already tried to eat it, along with the cage."

"Crocodile?"

Luella blew a stray curl out of her eyes. "Yes, crocodile."

Brixton cringed and looked around the now-silent room. There were a couple of places where he could see signs of a recent tussle; there was a small trail of water and a few black feathers on the floor beside an old pair of matching, scratched-up chairs, and there was a puddle of water on the wooden floor from where the glass had fallen earlier.

"He's only a baby," Luella assured him. "Can you help me find them?"

"Find them?"

"Reginald—the croc—escaped my notice when I was trying to clean out his tank. He knocked over Poe's cage and busted open the birdcage door."

Brixton quickly staggered through the front rooms of his home, looking for the loose animals.

"Please don't tell Mum about this," Luella said. "She wanted to stop at the market on the way home."

"I won't tell her, if we can manage to get them back," Brixton promised, just as he caught sight of a rough, green tail flickering underneath the old stove in the kitchen.

Brixton reached for the small beast and nearly laughed, despite his discomfort. "And to think you were worried you would never have any adventures, Lu."

He did not have to see her face to know his remark angered her.

"Just get him for me, would you?" Luella huffed. "This is hardly the kind of adventure I would choose, and you know it."

"I wouldn't choose it, either." He reached down and grabbed it, feeling the small, bumpy texture of the foreign creature. He dropped it, as the creature hurriedly turned to snap at him.

"Ugh!" Brixton scooted backward. "Why would anyone want to buy one of these for a pet?"

"I have a feeling Mr. Radcliffe is working on some unusual science experiments," Luella said from behind him. "I'm not happy about it, but I have no proof. Or at least, nothing I can take to a court."

"Mr. Radcliffe would likely be able to avoid a court date, anyway," Brixton murmured, recalling how many times his father had gotten into trouble for refusing to take bribes from wealthy London residents. The crocodile was more kind, Brixton thought, as he managed to snag Reginald. "Here."

"Don't remind me." Luella pursed her lips as she called up her power; the small, multi-colored light inside of her palms began warping time, slowing it to a standstill. She grabbed the uncooperative reptile from Brixton's hands.

Brixton watched in amazement as Reginald froze, his long nose opened in an infuriated half-snarl.

"If there's anything unusual around here, it's your ability to manipulate time," Brixton said, following her as she hurried toward their back lavatory. She used the old, empty tub, where a twisted coil and a pump worked to fill it with a small amount of water. Once Reginald was safely inside the tub, Luella's power dimmed and went out.

He unfroze at once, still snapping angrily.

FAVAN AND FLEW

"I don't think my magic is that unusual," Luella said. Her eyes twinkled mischievously. "It's all in how you use it, right, brother dear?"

She reached down to pet the small reptile on his head. Her power lit up as Luella studied him.

"It seems he has not been eating well lately," Luella told him. "He's been twitching some, too. I think he's going to need some medicine, if Mum can find some that is safe for him."

"He's a crocodile. I'm not sure human medicine is good for him at all."

"Sometimes we must look for the humanity in things that do not have any, if we are to be better humans ourselves."

Brixton rolled his eyes. "Mum's preference for animals seems to have passed on to you."

"I can at least say it's a learned trait, more by default than anything else." Luella hurried to check the temperature of the water, before Reginald could snip at her fingers. "Mum seems so sad when she has to deal with certain customers for prolonged periods of time."

"I don't know why she married Father then," Brixton said with a huff. "He doesn't have magic."

"He doesn't look down on her."

"On *her*."

Brixton and Luella exchanged a silent, knowing look. While Brixton knew he felt the brunt of his father's disregard, it was no secret his father was disappointed Luella had magic, too.

Luella cleared her throat. "Now that I've got a better handle on Reginald here, I've got to look for Poe. Will you fix his cage for me?"

"I can do that," Brixton agreed.

He soon found himself working in the lab again, suturing the gilded gates of Poe's cage so they would lay straight and smooth.

"I've got him," Luella said as she opened the door.

Brixton glanced over to see Luella had trapped Poe in place, same as she had Reginald. The bird was frozen between the seconds of time, his body eerily still in her hands as it glowed with her power.

"You'll need to wait a bit," Brixton warned. "I'm going to need new hinges for the door. It seems some of them have been clawed and bitten a good deal before today."

"I'm just glad that Mum took Fawkes into her office today." Luella tucked the bird into her arms as she let her power fade. At once, the bird began to struggle to get free, but she kept her hold steady. "I can't imagine Poe would have liked a hungry cat chasing him instead of a grumpy old croc."

"How long can you keep the bird calm now that he's safe?" Brixton asked, glancing over from his workbench. "Maybe you should keep him still while I do this."

"I can do that. But I'd rather not leave him frozen if I can help it. Maybe I'll let him see Chirpy," Luella said. She shut the door behind her and let her talent slink back into her hands. Poe seemed disoriented as he snapped out of his stillness, but when Luella presented Chirpy to him he quickly started squawking all over again.

Brixton frowned. "Can't you keep him quiet?"

"He's upset at his busted wing," Luella said. "His attempted escape didn't help him any. Mrs. Drake wanted to see if there was anything else we could do for him."

"Why haven't you healed him?"

"I need for his arm to stay still, for one." Luella frowned over at the small bird, who had begun pecking

FAVAN AND FLEW

Chirpy, as the mecha-bird blinked one eye at a time. "Mrs. Drake just dropped him off a while ago, so I am hoping to feed him and see if he'll be more still afterward."

"Why can't you heal him while you have him frozen?"

"I wouldn't want to use too much magic all at once. There have been a few more monitoring ships out this way today."

Brixton sighed as he thought of all the trouble Luella could get in if someone noticed her power. He was glad he was home; if any of the mage-ragers came knocking, he could easily take the blame for any magical discharge. "You'd better hope Poe didn't defecate all over the house while he was out of the cage. If he did, the bobbies will be the least of your worries. Mother will be upset."

"I checked!" Luella huffed, blowing a blonde curl out of her eyes indignantly. "I have plenty of power and responsibility, Brixton. There's no need to tease me for the small mistakes I've made."

"I'm sure you know well enough I'd be the world's biggest hypocrite if I did."

Brixton put down the suturing iron, studying his handiwork. The newly-aligned cage door glowed with a renewed sense of pride. The golden gilt shone brightly, making it harder to see if there were any structural imperfections. He called up his talent to check, and only a moment later glanced back to see Luella looking at him with her large, weepy blue eyes.

"What is it?" he asked.

"I did not mean to make you feel bad," she mumbled, apologetic but still slighted. "I wasn't blaming you for what you did as a kid."

"It's all right," he assured her. "I caused a lot of trouble for our family. I have a large debt hanging over my head,

FAVAN AND FLEW

and I can say, quite truthfully, the thrill of adventure is not worth it."

"Not for all of Mr. Powell's mechanical tools, or for Miss Marley's scrap metal?" Luella's apologetic frown turned into a small smirk as she listed off other things he had attempted to steal, use, or remodel when he was younger. "Or the items left behind in the London Trading Company's construction site?"

Brixton smiled back. "Perhaps for the look on Miss Bright's face when I managed to convince her there were ghosts in school with my automatons."

"She was a vapid old spinster," Luella agreed. "I was glad when you got both of us booted out of school."

"It did allow for Mother to begin taking you to work," Brixton said. He looked down at his handiwork again, before he set about to work screwing on a new pair of door hinges. "But Father didn't like having me home so much."

"At least he's become much more comfortable with both of us being in his lab over the years."

"Not when he's around," Brixton muttered.

Chirpy began to tweet loudly, sending Poe fluttering in circles.

"How much longer, Brix?" Luella asked. "I don't think Poe is keen on calming down right now. I'll see about healing his wing when he's asleep."

"I've got it."

Brixton held up the birdcage, showing off the repaired door and the new hinges. "If Mrs. Drake asks about the price, tell her we had to do a welding job on it. Those hinges aren't cheap. I was lucky Father still had some."

Luella gave him a quick salute, before she took the cage by the top hook and hurriedly covered it. Almost immediately, Poe quieted down. The next time Chirpy let out another round of tweets, Poe stayed silent.

"Well, that's better," Luella said. "Now to finish cleaning Reginald's cage. Why don't you come downstairs with me and help get ready for dinner? Mum's clearly running late, and Father is, too."

Brixton nodded mindlessly, following Luella down the stairs. He only glanced back once more as he left, taking another look at Chirpy. The mecha-bird cocked its head at him, and he decided he did not want to know its secrets to longevity just yet.

"Whatever Adelaide did to that bird, it's definitely serious," he said.

"I agree." Luella wiped her hands on her apron as she began working around Brixton. "But I never expected anything less from the great Adelaide Favan. She always had a talent for manipulating magic and machines."

"You have a pretty good talent for that, too," Brixton said. "You control the flow of time around objects."

"It is a more rare power." Luella grinned. "But I can't create anything, let alone fix things like Mrs. Drake's magnificent birdcage."

"That was easy."

"It's only easy to you. Just like stopping time is for me."

Brixton thought about what Adelaide had told him about the dragon, and how it was just on the other side of the magic portal.

He followed his sister out to the parlor, where her earlier work remained.

"Lu? You seem to like animals a lot."

"Of course I do."

FAVAN AND FLEW

"Do you think it is easier to tame them with your power?" Brixton asked.

"I don't know." Luella shrugged as she knelt down before a large, rectangular aquarium, empty except for a few rocks and small plants that artfully decorated the bottom. "I don't really tame them. That's a strange word to use."

"Is it?"

"I usually say I 'heal' them, even though I know that's not entirely true. I just manipulate their natural processes."

"But before, with the crocodile, you were able to see what it did a few days ago."

She shrugged. "I just know some things like that. I'm guessing it's part of the magic."

"Do you think you could do that with something other than animals?" He glanced toward the window.

"I know I can do a little." Luella eyed him carefully, calling up her power. Her arm touched his. She drew back a moment later. "Oh, Brixton. I'm sorry."

"What did you see?"

"I saw nothing."

"Then why are you sorry?" He bristled at her expressive eyes. He knew his sister had great talent, but he was unnerved at her reaction.

"I didn't mean I saw nothing, as in *actually* nothing," Luella said. "I saw a void. That's Adelaide's power."

"How do you know?"

Luella shrugged. "I can't do anything with Chirpy, Brixton. I can't do anything to mess with her power. I've tried to check on Chirpy's power before, but there's no way I can even get close to it. Her talent is strange, that's for sure."

FAVAN AND FLEW

"How so?"

"It does what it wants," Luella said. "And it usually wants to destroy things. But I can't understand how Chirpy has continued to work for such a long time. It's very protective of the energy loop she put inside."

Brixton nodded slowly. He thought about how Adelaide's talent called out to him, and then tried to destroy him.

"You saw her earlier, didn't you?" Luella's voice was quiet but sharp, and even though she was asking the question, Brixton knew she already had her answer.

Brixton felt the heat rise in his cheeks. "Adelaide is back in London."

"I know. Father mentioned something about that today at breakfast."

"Did he?"

"Yes. He mentioned that you were upset, and he suspected she was the cause."

"She was," he said quietly.

"But you got to see her again," Luella continued.

"She told me she was here for the Dragon Eyes," Brixton said. "She wants me to help her retrieve them."

"The Dragon Eyes?"

"It's a pair of amethysts," he said, telling her the whole story of how they were part of a treasure connected with her family, and how Adelaide needed them if she was going to control her magic. Luella nodded sympathetically as he talked, and he was glad he could trust her with his secrets.

He did not indulge her at every question, but Brixton knew if he could trust anyone to help him, it was his sister, especially where Adelaide was concerned.

FAVAN AND FLEW

"Hmm." As Brixton finished his explanation, she tapped her chin thoughtfully. "So her family wanted them."

"Yes. Adelaide told me that there was a dragon in the magic portal just waiting to be released, and that was the reason magic was granted to humans."

"I see." Luella raised her eyebrows.

"I was skeptical, too."

"Well, I meant more that it's all very well and good, I suppose, but she didn't tell you anything else? Anything a bit more … personal?"

Brixton fell back into the moment when Adelaide had fallen into him, the moment when they shared their hungry, devastating kiss.

"I need you, Brixton."

He felt his face flush over even more. "Nothing you should worry about," he said, his tone as dismissive and stoic as he could manage. He saw the small smile flit up to Luella's face, but she did not press for details.

"So, she told you about a dragon who lives inside the portal?"

Brixton nodded. "She said the Dragon Eyes are actually dragon eyes, too."

"That's unusual." Luella tapped her chin thoughtfully.

"That's what I said." Brixton ran a hand through his hair, feeling better that he was not the only one who had trouble accepting Adelaide's stories. "She said it was her family's secret, and that I didn't know about it because I never cared to learn."

"It is strange to think of where the portal came from."

"She had an answer for that, too. The Gunpowder Plot was supposed to blow up Parliament," Brixton said. "Adelaide said one of her ancestors, a woman named

FAVAN AND FLEW

Suyan, sold magic gunpowder to Guy Fawkes and when it blew, it opened the portal instead of blowing up the castle."

"I know from Miss Bright's school that the Gunpowder Plot failed, and the Jesuits and their followers quickly immigrated to America." Luella frowned. "I've never heard the part about the gunpowder, though."

"Adelaide said it was a secret in her family."

"Every family has their secrets," Luella murmured noncommittedly. "Are you going to help her?"

"I don't know if I can. And I already know what a life of crime can do."

"You know, I can't see the future when it comes to people," Luella said. "But for you, I would be willing to bet you'll help her. You've always been good about protecting her."

"I wasn't always," Brixton said softly, thinking of Gloria and her friends teasing Adelaide while he watched, back in their first year.

"Well, humans do have much more choice in such matters."

Brixton nodded glumly. He paused for a moment, before he decided to risk the question. "Do you think Adelaide is right? About the dragon?"

Luella went back to her cleaning for a long moment. Brixton could almost see her thinking it over, as if there were little cogs and rivets working inside of her mind to find an answer.

When she looked back up at him again, she gave him a grin. "If she is, I can only hope that if he gets free, Mum won't take him as a client. After Reginald, I would hate to have to clean a dragon's lair."

<u>14</u>

While he was worried about disappointing his parents—again—Brixton could not stop himself from marveling at the scene they made, sitting at the dinner table together.

It's just like old times.

His father laughed voraciously as he ate, his mustache flanked by a trail of little crumbs. Luella was busy sneaking little bits of meat to Fawkes, and his mother was regaling them with another tale of the many different creatures—and their pets—who made their way into her establishment.

"So of course the instant I tell Mr. Harrow I can take his dog in overnight if he wanted, Fawkes starts to go crazy. I nearly lost him as a client today," Philippa said as she pushed herself away from the table. "Let me get the trifle and then I'll tell you what he said to me."

"I can get it, darling," Bartholomew offered, but Philippa planted a kiss on his forehead and shushed him, quickly telling him she wanted to add another layer of jam.

"After all, we are celebrating," Philippa added, before she disappeared into the kitchen.

"What are we celebrating?" Brixton asked cautiously.

"Father's got a new award," Luella said, pointing to the small glimmer of gold on his father's coat. A new medal was pinned to his uniform sleeve, one that carried the seal of approval from Rembrandt Academy.

At the sight of it, Brixton felt magic begin to stir inside of him. Even as far away as he was, he could make out the intricate design. It did not seem to be just a medal for valor or excellence.

Before he could ask to examine it, his father spoke up.

"Philippa wouldn't get out her famous ladyfinger trifle for one of my awards. Really, she is just glad to see you home for dinner, lad."

Brixton felt a warm pleasure at his father's words. Then Bartholomew added, "Especially given the events that happened yesterday."

Brixton felt his happiness erode at the slight, but he let it go as he heard a small crash come out of the kitchen. His mother could feel it when he did not get along with his father.

"What award did you get today, Father?" Brixton asked, still curious as to why Rembrandt's coat of arms would be on an award for a police officer.

"Have you been promoted?" Luella asked. "That would be exciting."

"I'm good where I'm at," Bartholomew said, waving off their questions with practiced ease. "If they promote me, you'll never see me again. There's always trouble on the streets of London. The whole world passes through here, and that includes the worst the world has to offer."

"But if you keep getting awards, they should promote you," Luella argued.

"This award is not from the force or any of my superiors." Bartholomew dabbed his face with his napkin as he eyed Brixton. "My award came from the Board at Rembrandt."

"I noticed the insignia," Brixton said. "Why would they do that?"

"They said it was for my consistently superior work ethic with the wielding community," his father replied. "But I am more inclined to believe that it was something to do with the prize I brought in this morning."

"The Dragon Eye."

"Yes." Bartholomew nodded.

"Can you tell us what you know about it, Father?" Luella asked, leaning forward in anticipation.

Brixton looked over at his sister. Her eyes were already filled with anticipation and awe, and he wondered if he should worry about her. He had never noticed how eager she was for excitement in her own life.

"The tale of the Dragon Eyes is interesting, that's for sure." Bartholomew sat back in his chair, looking at Luella with a knowing expression on his face.

"I'd love to hear it, and I think we have time, dear, now that I'm done cutting up the trifle," Philippa said as she came out of the kitchen juggling their dessert.

"You know I wouldn't dare start an entertaining story without you, love."

Brixton watched the easy affection of his parents with an odd mix of envy and appreciation. His father truly loved his mother; he could see it in the way he stood up and took the plates out of her hands, the way he tugged on her gray-streaked locks in a playful manner. His mother laughed and let her arm drape over his shoulders as she handed him a new fork.

Brixton thought back to his school days, the hours he spent with Adelaide in the materials room. It became their favorite getaway, the place where he could bring his books to read and she would draw her schematics. The two of them worked companionably on different projects, some just for fun, and others for the school.

Would he be able to have that sort of relationship with Adelaide again? Before Brixton could wander too far off into his musings, Bartholomew cleared his throat.

FAVAN AND FLEW

"Now, where were we? Oh, yes, the Dragon Eyes." Bartholomew took a bite out of his trifle and smiled. "Excellent as always, Philippa."

"Thank you, darling." His mother smiled, a small mustache of whipped cream on her upper lip.

Brixton ignored the dessert in front of him as his father continued.

"Well, then, the Dragon Eyes. The legend goes back a long time, when the Emperor Qin ruled Imperial China," Bartholomew stated. "His family was in charge of the construction of the Great Wall, and he took great pride in building up what he believed to be his legacy.

"But as you know, pride, if unchecked, can lead to destruction. Even before his death, there were rumors that his family had lost the Mandate of Heaven, the ability to rule China."

"Let me guess," Brixton said. "It was because of the Dragon Eyes?"

"Yes. The Dragon Eyes are said to be very powerful objects, in addition to their value," his father said. "They have a history of disappearing and reappearing. The last time they were found was in 1834, in a scientist's castle in Strasbourg, before they disappeared again."

"What makes them so special?" Brixton asked. "I mean, I know they are large amethysts, but of all the treasure, why were they considered the most valuable?"

"They are said to contain dragon fire inside of them. Fire so bright it turns to lightning. Some say it's part of a dragon's soul." Bartholomew eased forward in his chair. "The legend goes that only a member of the Qin family can command its full power."

Adelaide. Brixton tightened his fingers, letting his nails bite into his palms. His father continued on with his tale, mentioning some of the particular events in history that touched on the truth of the legend, even if it was never fully revealed.

As Luella and Philippa began to gather the empty dishes, Brixton remained seated at the table, still listening to his father's story. He felt Ticker's alarm start to buzz inside his pocket, and he knew he only had a little time before he was to go and meet Adelaide.

"That is why I believe the Board gave me this award, Brixton," Bartholomew said, his voice soft. "When I gave the Dragon Eye you had over to my superiors, they were very grateful. Director Strahm, along with the other Board members, were very adamant I had committed a public service worthy of knighthood, if the Queen would acquiesce to allowing it to be public knowledge."

"Why would it not be public knowledge?" Brixton asked. "There doesn't seem to be much value in keeping a legend secret."

"You know as well as I do that there is a dark side to all this magic business. It's already caused one large attack on our nation's palaces. Speculation could lead to more trouble."

"Where is the Dragon Eye now?" Brixton asked.

"In Scotland Yard headquarters, in the vaults." Bartholomew sighed. "Dr. Winston sent a letter from Rembrandt offering to send someone to secure the vault there until the clocktower is restored. They are sending a commission to check on the other gemstone tomorrow."

"The other one ... " Brixton frowned. He had not bothered to think of the other one. But there were two of them, after all.

Bartholomew rubbed his mustache thoughtfully. "Dr. Winston is your superior, is he not?"

FAVAN AND FLEW

"He is." Brixton decided not to mention that he had talked with Henry that morning. He did not know why he felt more than a little angry Henry had not told him about the Dragon Eyes. He had talked about Adelaide, and about Brixton's breach of conduct, but not the Dragon Eyes.

"Now you've had your story, I would like to ask you a few questions regarding your recent outings, if you don't mind."

"Bartholomew, enough. Leave the poor boy alone. He is your son, and you know he did what he had to do because he was worried about you." Philippa folded her hands together. Between her palms, Brixton could just make out the soft, rose-colored glow of his mother's magic.

He followed her angry gaze to see she was glaring at his father.

Brixton felt his stomach start to twist into nervous knots as his parents carefully argued—talking about Brixton's motives and reasoning while they were really discussing Bartholomew's distance and disregard concerning their oldest child—Brixton slumped further into his seat, feeling defeated.

His father was perpetually disappointed in him, enough to where it was making his mother upset. Philippa was gracious as always, but Brixton saw the flicker of tears in her eyes as she excused herself. Luella hurried to follow her out of the room, motioning to Brixton that she would take care of their mother.

"I noticed that Gloria did not report back to her post today after lunch," Bartholomew said, as he turned his full attention to Brixton. There was a harder edge to his voice, now that Philippa and Luella were out of the room. "I am concerned for her. Would you know anything about what happened to her?"

"I did talk to her today," Brixton admitted slowly, valiantly fighting off the queasy feeling in his stomach.

Bartholomew sighed. "Did she mention—"

Buzz! Buzz! Buzz!

Brixton was never more grateful for Ticker as his alarm went off. It was the perfect ending for the conversation.

"Your appointment is coming up, sir. I do believe you must leave now if you are to make it on time." Ticker yawned quietly, attempting to be polite and aloof.

"You have an appointment?" Bartholomew frowned. "This late at night?"

"What can I say, Father?" Brixton tried to laugh it off, much as he had tried to do with Henry earlier. "I'm a popular wielder these days."

"I see." Bartholomew stood up and straightened his jacket, letting his new award flicker in the dining hall lighting. "Be sure you watch yourself while you're out and about. I know the streets of London this time of night, and it's not safe."

"I will be careful."

"See that you are. We have a missing officer, and your mother and I would hate to see you end up missing, too."

As he stepped out of the house, Brixton sighed. He could see his mother being upset if he went missing, but he had a harder time believing his father would.

The night air felt brisk against his skin, and he hugged himself into his greatcoat. He glanced back at the small door to his family's house.

"Considering the risk of what I'm about to do, it might be better for everyone if I *did* disappear," he muttered.

"No one wants that, Brix, no matter how much trouble you cause."

"Lu." Brixton nearly jumped to see his little sister appear beside him, hopping out from the shadows under the front window. "What are you doing here?"

"You can probably guess."

He crossed his arms. "I'm not taking you."

"Come on, please?" Her eyes pleaded with him as she tugged at his arm. "I won't cause any trouble."

"If you thought that was the truth, you wouldn't want to come."

"That's not true. You're going to see Adelaide."

He did not like to admit she was right. "That's none of your business."

"She's my friend, too."

"You're not her friend the way I was," Brixton insisted. "This is something that's between me and her, and I'm not going to let you get caught up in our mess."

"See? No one in this family lets me have any fun." Luella stuck her tongue out at him. "None of the books in our library match the excitement of a real adventure."

"You only say that because you've never faced real trouble on your own." He paused for a moment. "How is Mother? Is she still upset?"

Luella sighed. "I know she is very distressed by the relationship between you and Father, but there's nothing much to be done about that, is there? You've done nothing wrong—"

"That's not true." Brixton thought about his plans for the evening with a grimace.

"Nothing that you haven't apologized for and sought to rectify," Luella clarified. "Look, it's hardly your fault that Father's jealous of you."

"What? That's mad." Brixton shook his head. "He's got no reason to be jealous of me."

"He wanted to work in engineering when he was your age," Luella said. "Mum told me that because he is not a wielder, he was never considered a 'competitive asset,' whatever that is."

"It means desirable employee."

"Well, there you go." Luella crossed her arms. "He was forced to find something else to do for money, which is how he ended up on Scotland Yard with the other mage-ragers. And then you were born with everything he'd ever wanted, and then you got into all that trouble. You can at least understand why he finds it difficult to be happy for you."

"No one should be happy for me."

"That's not the point." Luella shook her head. "But if you take me along with you tonight, I'll be able to fill you in on what you need to know."

"No." Brixton gave her a pat on the head, ruffling her curls just enough to irritate her.

She wrinkled her nose. "None of you ever let me do anything I want to."

"I did plenty that I wanted, and I'm still paying for it."

"There's a price to pay when you deny yourself the things you want," Luella argued.

"I can't imagine you want to make others suffer for your sake, all for a bit of fun."

"Not for fun. For something that means something." Luella crossed her arms, matching his stance, even though she was a good foot shorter than he was. "This is something important, isn't it? You're going to help Adelaide, and I want to help her, too."

He hesitated. "I don't think—"

FAVAN AND FLEW

"Besides, if anyone is going to see the truth about a dragon, it's going to be me," Luella said. "I'm the one whose magic can work with time."

"Only in spurts." Brixton shook his head. "Don't make me call for Father, Lu. You can come on my next adventure. This one is too dangerous."

She glared at him, her eyes losing all their silent pleading as they hardened into angry slits. "Fine. But I *will* hold you to that."

Brixton relaxed ever so slightly, and he suddenly wondered if he would be able to convince Adelaide to go on a fake mission later on, just to fool Luella. "Thank you, Luella."

She reached out and hugged him. "I do wish you would come and visit more often. You are one of my only real friends, you know. And certainly only one of the human ones, considering all the books I've read and all the animals I've tended."

"You'll make more one day," Brixton said. He looked to the horizon, where the damaged clock tower winked at him. He had never set out to make many friends, but he knew he had people in this world he could count on. That was enough for him.

"I'll come back later this week," he promised. "I'll see if Adelaide will come, too."

Luella cheered, if only slightly. "All right. Don't disappoint me, Brix."

"I'll try not to." He tugged on his coat, suddenly unable to find any comfort in its warmth.

It's going to be a long night.

<u>15</u>

"Why are you staring out into the street?"

Jiahao's question was full of impatience, but Adelaide was used to his scorn. She glared at him before returning her attention to the front of Favan Hall.

"I told you. I found a lead on the Dragon Eye, and I'm expecting someone," she said. She did not want to admit to Jiahao just how much she was anticipating Brixton's visit; not only was she anxious to see him again, but she had never been allowed to bring anyone home for a visit.

"You're giving our position away." Jiahao nodded down toward the street, where people walked by in a hurry. From where they were, the people on the street could easily see them, if they bothered to look up. "You know we've had issues with people coming by the house."

"None of the lights are on in the rooms by the windows," Adelaide argued. "No one is going to come here and bother us this time of night."

"No one except your lead, apparently. Why would you be so dense like that, telling him where we were?"

"You can leave at any time if you feel threatened." Adelaide stepped back from the window. She was still dressed in the gown she had worn to the park earlier, but she had added a loose pair of trousers underneath her skirts and changed out her boots for slippers, ones that allowed her to fight and grapple with different terrain easily. Brixton had not given her any specifics of where they were going, but she wanted to be prepared.

She stepped back and crossed her arms, still looking out the window, even though the curtains obscured the view.

FAVAN AND FLEW

"You are nervous." Jiahao's voice was no longer angry; now, it was full of mockery. "He must be someone dangerous."

"He's a friend," Adelaide insisted.

"You don't have friends."

"You're wrong." She shot him a haughty look. "I have a friend, and he's coming to help."

Adelaide decided not to mention Brixton was clearly unsure about helping her; Jiahao was already unhappy at the thought of extra company.

"How is Gloria doing?" Adelaide asked.

"That girl we kidnapped? She is still asleep. How much of her power did you drain from her?"

"I didn't think it was much, but I did want her to remain knocked out until we could finish the job and get the Dragon Eye to the haven."

"Well, it looks like you managed to do just that." Jiahao cracked his knuckles. "Assuming that we succeed tonight."

"We will."

"You had better hope that is the case. Tàitai does not like failure. She especially does not like repeated failure."

"You don't have to remind me." Adelaide sighed. She turned away from Jiahao and began to pace up and down the long hallway beyond the front room.

Jiahao leaned back against the doorframe. "You like this friend of yours."

"Why else do you think I said he was a friend?" The shadows allowed her to blush freely, hiding the truth of her feelings from substantial scrutiny.

"If you like him, he could become a liability, especially with your power."

"Well, I will have you with us to keep him from being one, won't I?" Her tone was sharp, and even in the dark, Adelaide could see the smirk on her cousin's face.

He had found a weakness, much to her displeasure.

Before she could ask him to go and check on Gloria once more, there was a soft knock at the front door.

Adelaide and Jiahao both turned at the sound.

"If you are going to answer the door, that better be him," Jiahao said. "There were other men who came around earlier."

"It's him," Adelaide said. Somewhere in the back of her mind, she felt the pull of his magic on hers. Her breath caught in her throat, and she felt her heart both beat faster and stop at the same time.

"If it is, tell him to go around to the trade worker entrance on the side," Jiahao said. "I will go and open the door for him. We do not need people walking in the house from the front door where everyone else can see him."

"True. Good idea."

Adelaide waited until Jiahao was out of sight before she hurried toward the door. Another knock rang out, and Adelaide took a second to use the special looking device she had designed as a kid.

Using a system of mirrors and light, she managed to create a periscope of sorts for the front door. It collapsed in on itself at the side of the door, but she could pull it out and take a peek. The tubular design followed the door frame, finally slipping through the window on top of the door, allowing her to look down from above at who it was that was calling. As she had grown older, she had used special lighting techniques and different prisms to refine the mechanism.

The bright white of Brixton's shirt collar stuck out from the lapels of his greatcoat, but she could see the moonlight reflected off the face of his pocket watch as he checked the time.

She smiled at the sight of the soft tussle of Brixton's hair, watching him raise his fist to knock again.

A small sadness suddenly clouded her thoughts. She knew what it felt like to hold onto him intimately, to feel the texture of his mouth on hers; she relived it enough to know the warmth of its familiarity and the nuances of its distinction. But she had yet to touch his hair, to feel it against the skin of her palms as she held onto him.

As he knocked again, Adelaide forced herself to concentrate on the task at hand.

"Brixton," she hissed through the door.

He leaned in closer. "Adelaide?"

"Go around to the side of the house. There's an entrance there. We thought it was better if you didn't come into the house from the front of the street."

"Fine."

After giving him directions, Adelaide picked up her skirts and hurried toward the trade entrance.

It's lovely to feel this excited about breaking the law, for once.

It was hard to admit how much she hated the missions her family sent her on, but with her father in prison, they were all she had. And there was nothing else she could do with her magic. Ever since her attack on Gloria during her junior year, the Board members at Rembrandt had been wary of it.

Using her magic on Gloria had been a mistake, but it had been one she felt was only right. Adelaide remembered

FAVAN AND FLEW

how she heard her bag smash into the wall as Gloria slammed into her.

The bag had been carrying her latest work on the dragon heart. Along with Brixton, she had been experimenting with refining her energy loop design.

She had struggled with the problem for weeks before an idea had hatched in her mind. When she had made Luella the larger version of her chirpy design, she had used two energy loops to allow for half of her black magic to charge while the other took a turn; with the dragon heart, she knew more power had to be added in order to make it work, but it was a similar enough principle she knew it would work.

While Brixton was preparing for his exams and working on his assignments, Adelaide had skipped nearly all her classes working on it. She was so excited about showing him, she did not even care when Gloria slammed into her.

Until she heard the crinkling shatter.

Her bag was crushed, sandwiched between her body and the wall, and everything inside suddenly cracked and splintered.

Hearing it break—her dragon heart, the one she had been so careful and conscientious and eager to fix—made something inside of her snap, too.

Something roared inside of her, something that demanded punishment, harsh and fast, and there was nothing to stop her.

The Board made it worse, too, Adelaide remembered. Dr. Winston had taken her project, promising to keep it safe. He told her later he had to destroy it, since there was so much dark magic inside of it.

"Probably from your constant attention to it," he said when she demanded an explanation. He stood there, attempting to be humble in front of a portrait of John Wright, a member of the Treason Plot. Dr. Winston had been kindly in his approach to her, while John Wright's painted gaze seemed to blaze with unremitting judgment.

"The Board had to step in and dispose of it. It might have even caused you to lose control over your power the way that it did. You're fortunate that Mr. Flew was there and he was able to stop you."

"But that project was mine!" Adelaide objected.

"Yes, but it was broken and dangerous," Dr. Winston said. "And you nearly killed a student because of it. You're lucky we have not contacted your father regarding this incident or you would risk expulsion."

"If you haven't heard from my father, it's more likely you haven't been able to reach him," Adelaide snarled, turning on her heel. "I don't need you to coddle me."

Dr. Winston's frown deepened, this time with faint irritation. "We will be talking with him, Miss Favan. Your disinterested behavior cannot continue like this."

"This is the first serious breach of conduct I've had since my arrival," Adelaide objected.

"This is more than serious. And do not think we have been unaware of your attitude or your habits over the past three years. We know you have a pattern of distracting several of our brightest students—"

"I have not!"

"I believe you are mistaken. I regularly get reports to check on Mr. Flew because he is late to class."

"He's just one student," Adelaide said. "If there are others who are distracted by me, that's their problem, not mine."

"Mr. Flew is our top student," Dr. Winston interrupted. "You are derailing him from living up to his full potential.

With his achievements, he could get a good job, possibly even a position on the Board here at Rembrandt."

Adelaide scoffed.

"I know you think it is inconsequential, but for Mr. Flew it would mean a decent living, and some prestige. He could advance his life in ways you take for granted. Do you think it's fair of you to demand his attention?"

"He's my friend," Adelaide said.

"As his friend, you should want the best for him. What do you have to offer him? There is nothing you could do for him that Rembrandt could not do better."

"Brixton wants to fly in the Airship Force," Adelaide blurted, unable to stop herself. "He doesn't want to work for the Board."

At this, Dr. Winston went silent with surprise. Adelaide puffed out her chest, glad to see she had finally bested her stuffy old professor. "So you see, once my father reviews his portfolio, Brixton is bound to get exactly what he wants. You don't need to concern yourself with the time he spends with me. He will be just fine after he leaves here."

She refrained from adding that she came up with some of her best ideas when she worked with Brixton, and she knew it was the same for him, too. Brixton's main compliment to her was how inspiring she was, and she took it with pride, even if she longed for something more.

I will see that my father allows Brixton to fly with him, she thought. It was the best way she could pay him back for befriending her.

Dr. Winston cleared his throat. "Miss Favan—"

She did not hear anything else he said, as she stormed out of his office and hurried off to send a message of her own to her father.

After that, Adelaide wanted nothing more than to leave the school. If it had not been for Brixton, she would have left that night. She knew she could have shut herself in Favan Hall without repercussions.

If it wasn't for Brixton, I might never have wanted to stay past the first month at Rembrandt at all.

"Ouch! What do you think you're doing?"

Brixton's voice cut through the darkness of her home, reminding her of the importance of their mission.

"Brixton?" Adelaide called, suddenly worried. "Is something wrong?"

She found her answer as Jiahao spoke.

"Don't fight me," he snapped. "This is for your own good."

Adelaide came around the corner to see Brixton was on the floor, pinned on his stomach, as Jiahao held him to the floor.

"No one believes that when they hear it from someone who's attacking them," Brixton growled.

"Jiahao," Adelaide snapped angrily. "What are you doing?"

"I'm trying to make sure he's on our side," Jiahao said. His magic was glowing against the evening light. He turned his attention back to Brixton. "Tell us where the Dragon Eye is."

Adelaide hurried to pull Jiahao away, but he shoved her aside, sending her flying past him. She staggered into the wall behind him, feeling the wind jolt out of her. She watched as Brixton bit his lip, and Jiahao poured more of his power into controlling him.

"Brixton," Adelaide whispered. She caught her breath and hurried over to Jiahao.

FAVAN AND FLEW

As she came closer, Brixton finally spoke. "Get … off … me."

The words were spoken bitterly, but there was no sign he would be easily broken by Jiahao's talent. Adelaide could see the sweat on Brixton's face as he released him and stood up.

Instantly, Adelaide rounded on Jiahao. "I told you he was a friend. You shouldn't have done anything."

"You trust him. I do not," Jiahao argued. "If I want to use my talent to find information, I will."

"Just like you did with the others who owned the homes you've broken into, I'm sure," Brixton muttered, patting down his mussed hair and straightening out his coat.

Jiahao stared at Brixton, squarely meeting his gaze even though Brixton was several inches taller than he was. "You are a Brit, and the only good Brit is a dead one. I would sooner trust a snake on sight."

"A snake might be more welcoming than you."

"You need to stop," Adelaide said, stepping between them. "Brixton, this is my cousin, Jiahao. And Jiahao, this is Brixton. I will not have any contention between you as we work together."

"*If* we can work together," Jiahao grumbled.

Adelaide frowned at him. "Brixton has never made fun of me for my heritage, and I would rather you not disgrace yours, cousin. Act with some decorum, would you?"

She turned to Brixton. "I'm sorry," she said, lowering her eyes briefly. "Are you hurt?"

"Not enough to warrant revenge," Brixton told her, still scowling at Jiahao.

"Come on." She tugged on Brixton's sleeve, pulling him away from Jiahao. "Since we will not have to worry

FAVAN AND FLEW

about that if we are working together, why don't you just tell me where we are going, Brix?"

Brixton glared at her and then Jiahao. "The Dragon Eye is at Scotland Yard, in the vaults," he said. "It's guarded by magic and locks."

"That shouldn't be a problem," Adelaide said with a small smile.

"It's still a vault. There will be plenty of police there, and it'll be hard to crack."

"I'll grab an extra set of my tools then." Adelaide started to head back to her room to grab her supplies before she glanced back at the two of them. "Behave while I'm gone."

She did not want to leave them for too long, but Adelaide did take the time to check in on Gloria once more. She did not like the idea of leaving her alone, but there was nothing to be done other than see to her comfort and hope for the best.

With any luck, Adelaide thought, her talent drained Gloria enough that she would not wake up until the next day.

Once Adelaide had everything ready, she skipped down to where Jiahao and Brixton were both waiting for her in silence.

"See?" Adelaide smiled brightly. "You didn't hurt each other while I was away. That wasn't too hard, was it?"

Brixton and Jiahao scowled at each other, and Adelaide only barely pushed back the temptation to grab the two of them by the ear as she stormed out of the house between them. "Let's go," she called after them, suddenly more eager to get going than ever.

16

Brixton glanced behind him, eying Jiahao carefully as he walked beside Adelaide. He was glad when she agreed to let him offer her his arm. Just below the dark fabric of her gloves, he could feel her talent start to gather up inside of her—but it was not just her magic that made him uneasy tonight. Her cousin was putting up an impressive front as well.

Jiahao had dark, distrusting amber eyes and short black hair. Brixton guessed he was around his age, although he could have easily been older. His magic, while it was less powerful than Adelaide's, was easily the most uncertain factor about him.

Brixton knew from what Adelaide had said earlier that she had a cousin with her, but she did not mention his ability to control people.

As Adelaide walked beside him, directing him toward Scotland Yard, he thought about what Jiahao had said to him when she went to retrieve her toolkit.

"I know you're hiding something from her."

Brixton hated that Jiahao was right. He did not want to tell Adelaide the Board was after her, nor did he want to tell her that he had been assigned to find her. He knew she would only be upset, but there was nothing they could do. He was the one who was going against orders in helping her tonight.

As much as he knew it was wrong, Brixton found he could not say no to her.

That in itself was dangerous, he thought with a sigh.

"What's wrong? You're not regretting this already, are you?" Adelaide bit her lip nervously. "My talent is not hurting you, is it?"

"I'm fine," Brixton assured her, tightening his grip on her arm as she tried to shuffle away from him. "I was just thinking … about the other Dragon Eye."

It was not the full truth, but he never promised her he would tell her the truth. He relaxed only by the slightest degree at the thought.

"Don't worry about that," Adelaide said. "My great-grandmother, Tàitai, is sending other members of my family to retrieve that one."

"You know where it is?"

"It's at Rembrandt, in their High Counsel Office."

"It is?" Brixton was surprised.

"Yes. It's on the coat of arms, right above the fireplace."

He had been in the High Counsel Office several times before, usually to receive commendation for his work. "I was just there a few weeks ago."

"I know." Adelaide's voice dropped low. "That was how we found out about it, actually. The *Times* had a picture of the Board and Rembrandt's top professors, after they finished reviewing their upcoming inventions."

He said nothing, remembering the PRISM project. The Board had wanted to invent a way to analyze the various colors of magic and harness their respective types of power, but there was nothing in the design that allowed for the safety of the subject. It had been his job to approve the design, but he had been adamant there needed to be a secure failsafe and a cap on its energy capacity.

He frowned, recalling Director Strahm's objection at his modifications. After several arguments between members of the Board, Henry admitted to Brixton that their boss did not like the extra time required for his suggestions.

Adelaide brushed up against him as they walked, bringing him back to the moment. "You were in the picture, you know."

"Yes." Brixton nodded. "I'm surprised you saw it."

"We still get the *Times* delivered to us, even while we're in Peking," Adelaide said. "There's always a substantial delay, of course. But when that picture came, and I saw it … "

He thought he saw her blush.

"Tàitai is glad we are getting close to getting them back. She's very eager to restore our family's honor."

Jiahao cleared his throat loudly. "That is none of his business."

"Jiahao," Adelaide hissed. "He's helping us retrieve this Dragon Eye, isn't he? If he wants to know, we should tell him."

"He doesn't belong to our family."

"He belongs to me." Adelaide's face flushed deep red in the moonlight as she dropped Brixton's arm and quickened her steps. "That should be good enough for you and the rest of our family."

Jiahao coughed, as if he was not used to laughing. "You do not know our family at all, do you?"

Brixton matched his pace with Adelaide once more, warmed by her comments. He knew she could easily skirt around issues she did not want to talk about, despite being one of the most forthright people he had ever met.

"It's all right," Brixton told her. "You don't have to tell me anything if you don't want to."

"I can later, perhaps," Adelaide said. "Right now we need a plan for getting into Scotland Yard and making our way down to their vaults unnoticed."

"I don't know about the unnoticed part, but I can get us in. Well, you and me, anyway." Brixton looked back at Jiahao, who had resumed his sour demeanor. "It would be more difficult to get the guards at the station to believe he is one of my associates."

"Associates?" Adelaide asked.

"Yes. My father is the one who took the jewel to Scotland Yard," Brixton explained quietly. "He said Rembrandt would come check the magical seal on the vaults while it's kept here. I can say I'm here to inspect them."

"I don't think they would just let you walk in and examine their vaults."

"I have my Rembrandt identification," Brixton said. "That's how I managed to get onto an airship the day you attacked the clock tower."

"I don't think we should bring Rembrandt into this," Adelaide said. "They're dangerous."

"How so?"

"First, they are the keepers of magic, and the ones who have been poorly educating people—both wielders and non-wielders alike—about magic." Adelaide shook her head. "And I know they don't like me, either."

Brixton took her hand, trying to reassure her as much as he was trying to prevent himself from saying anything about the Board's assignment. He knew Adelaide was right about their concern, even if he did not believe it was as personal as she thought it was.

"I can always use my father's name," Brixton offered. "That should be enough to protect us from too much scrutiny."

"I'd rather sneak in," Adelaide said. "I know the cost of using a family name for privileges."

"You asked me for my help," Brixton argued. "This is what I can do."

"Maybe I should go in by myself," Adelaide said. "Now that I know where the gem is, I can get it."

"Like last time?" Jiahao snorted.

Brixton shook his head. "I told you, I am going to help you out where I can."

"But this is something you don't need to do. You didn't even want to do this, did you? Let me make it easier on you."

"There is no making this easy. There's always a price to pay, Adelaide." Brixton ran his hand through his hair. "Sometimes you can't do the right thing without suffering for it."

"I don't believe that," Adelaide scoffed. "But if that's true, then we can at least lessen the price. Jiahao and I can get inside by our usual methods, and we'll meet you by the vault."

"Do you even know where it is?"

Jiahao groaned. "You two are both terrible planners."

"If you get in, they will escort you to it," Adelaide told Brixton. "There's no reason to believe we won't be able to follow you. Once you're there, you can check the vault, and then you leave. Once you're gone, Jiahao and I can break it."

"So this time I am the distraction?" Brixton asked, raising an eyebrow. "Well, it's a little more subtle than blowing up a monitoring airship."

"You'd be amazed at what you can get done if the right people are distracted."

He gave her an odd look, and she gave him a playful smile in return. There was a spark of their old camaraderie in her eyes, and he almost laughed at the sight, despite the trouble they were bound to get in.

"You are also forgetting me," Jiahao spoke up from behind them. "If we need answers, we can get them."

Brixton thought about Jiahao's power, the creepy feeling he felt when he attacked him earlier. The compulsion to speak and reveal his thoughts was powerful, and he had nearly given in at the onslaught.

It was a much different feeling from Adelaide's, he thought. Jiahao's magic was blunt and specific, while Adelaide's was coy and searching; even in its attempts to drain him of his own talent, he felt her magic was at least more welcoming.

Of course, he thought dryly, he felt that way about Adelaide in general.

While they headed toward Scotland Yard, they made their plans, arguing at some points, and glossing over others. As they approached the entrance to the alley behind the building, Brixton felt his nerves unravel.

When he was younger, everything had been about chasing trouble and taking risks, anything to test the limits of his power and skill. While his debt and guilt had taught him to avoid taking those risks again, he knew he had never forgotten how.

Pushing his way into Captain Airey's crew was proof of that.

And so is she, he thought, glancing over at Adelaide.

As Jiahao set off to find a way inside, Brixton watched Adelaide pull off her skirt, revealing her trousers underneath. Even in the dim lighting of the gas lamps and moonlight, he could see they were the same ones she had worn on the *Horizon*. She pulled a large hood out of her pocket, stuffing her excess clothing in a pile of garbage in the streets.

"I hope you don't need those back," Brixton said.

Adelaide shrugged. "I'll worry about it later."

When she was done, he had to hand to it her; there was no color to her except for a sliver of skin around her eyes. She tucked her toolset into the band at her waist.

Adelaide glanced up, raising her brow at him, and Brixton quickly looked away, embarrassed to be caught staring at her.

"You know, I thought you were a man when we were fighting on the ship. I guess I didn't pay attention very much," he said.

Adelaide adjusted her masked hood again. "People usually see what they expect to see."

"I never would have expected you."

Adelaide leaned back against the brick building. "I never would have expected to see you on an airship, either."

"Not after your father's threats on the matter."

They both fell into silence for a long moment, before Adelaide let out a soft sigh. "I didn't know you had talked with him before we left. When he first mentioned your application to me, I begged him not to do anything."

Brixton said nothing. It was something to hear that his suspicions on the matter were confirmed. Captain Favan had found a way to discredit or disqualify him from joining the Airship Force.

"Perhaps you'll get a better chance at joining the Airship Force now that he's no longer in his position."

FAVAN AND FLEW

Brixton nodded. "Perhaps."

"He never admitted to fixing your application, if it makes you feel any better."

"It doesn't."

"He told me once that if you did get into the Airship Force, at least he could see to it that you were transferred to Australia or the Americas."

"Is that your way of telling me I should thank him if I get the chance?" He attempted to smile, but it was still a sore issue. He lost Adelaide and his dream job, and then he found out the interest on his debt threatened his family's welfare. The first month after graduating from Rembrandt had been the most sobering, depressing weeks of his life.

"I am sorry about him, Brix." Adelaide reached over to put her hand on his shoulder, and then drew back. "In his own way, I think he was only trying to protect you."

"Me?" Brixton scoffed. "From what he said to me, I would have thought it more likely he was protecting you."

"I'll admit that I never cared much for my father," Adelaide said. "But I didn't know him very well, either. When I was with Tàitai and my other family members in Peking, I learned more about our history. That's why, as much as it seems more like he's protecting me from you, I believe he was trying to protect you from me."

"Your stories are getting more unbelievable," Brixton said with a disgruntled snort.

"I've never lied to you." Adelaide ignored his slight. "When we have more time, I'll tell you what I know about him."

Brixton met her gaze. "We never have time, do we?"

"Once my family has the Dragon Eyes, and my magic stops trying to kill you, I'll give you all the time in the world."

"I'll settle for a proper goodbye, should you decide to leave London again."

He did not mean to sound so dismissive, but he regretted his tone a second later when Adelaide huffed and turned away from him.

Before he could apologize, Jiahao reappeared. "I've found a good way for Yaling and me to get inside," he said.

"Yaling?" Brixton glanced over at Adelaide.

"It's my middle name," she explained. "It's the one my clan prefers to use."

"I am not changing my ways just to appease you," Jiahao warned.

Adelaide rolled her eyes. "We're just happy you're speaking English, cousin. Now, tell us what you found."

"They pay a lot of attention to the far entrance, the one opposite us," Jiahao explained. "Several runners come and leave this time of night. But there are a few windows at the side we will be able to get through."

"I have my lockpicks in my pouch," Adelaide said, patting the small toolkit bundled up at her side.

"Just don't lose it," Brixton said.

"I won't." Adelaide frowned. "You'd better go and give them something to worry about. Once you get to the vault, work as slowly as possible. Then Jiahao and I will take over once you leave."

"What if I can't get in?" Brixton asked. "We didn't think of that."

"If you don't get in, just leave," Adelaide said. "There's nothing you'll be able to do to help us at that point. Jiahao and I can take care of the rest."

"We do not even need him, Yaling," Jiahao said. "You should drain him of his energy and let him stay out of this entirely."

"No." Brixton cringed at the unintentional loudness of his voice, but he remained firm as he stared down Adelaide. He could tell by the look on her face she was considering Jiahao's advice, but there was no way he would let her do this by herself. "No, I said I was going to help and be a part of this. If you do anything to me, you will only regret it."

"I always do," Adelaide whispered, her rueful tone making Brixton take a step back.

"Fine." Jiahao crossed his arms. "If you are going to be a part of this, you should head in now. It is already late."

Brixton nodded and walked out of the shadows. He glanced back to see if he could see Adelaide once more, but there was nothing but blackened shadows as he headed for the entrance to Scotland Yard.

He gripped his fingers tightly inside his pocket, and then released them.

Brixton entered inside the building that housed the Scotland Yard headquarters with a sense of dread. From what he remembered of its history, it was a refurbished castle that used to belong to the monarchy. Since then, he knew more about it from his previous arrests.

That was how he knew there was a holding cell just beyond the entrance, along with the rows of offices where records were kept, data was collected, and subdued criminals had their papers processed.

He knew from his previous crimes there were several divisions within the force, including ones designated specifically for magic-related crimes.

"Professor Flew?"

At the sound of his name, Brixton turned to see a junior officer hailing him from the far right. The man was in his uniform, minus the hat, but he seemed eager to see him.

Brixton gulped silently.

"How do you do?" Brixton murmured, hurrying forward to talk with the man. He shook the man's hand, guessing him to be close to his own age.

"It's a pleasure to have you here, sir," the officer said. There was a slight cockney accent to his voice, but it was clearly smothered after months of working all over the city. "I expect you'll be wanting to make your inspection of the building right away?"

"Did my father tell you to expect me?" Brixton asked.

"Oh, that's right, you're Officer Flew's son," the man said, a new respect lighting up in his young, eager face. "I imagine he's right proud of you, sir."

"Thank you," Brixton said quietly, not wanting to disillusion him with the truth.

"Come this way. I'm Junior Officer Marcus Littleton," the man said. "If you'll pardon my manners. Come this way."

Marcus led Brixton through the halls of Scotland Yard. There were several officers checking in and calling for help. Every so often, pairs of them would turn down the corner and walk through them. Brixton eyed them carefully; none of them seemed to take notice.

"Officer?" Brixton tapped his shoulder. "Who was it that told you I would be coming in?"

"We've received notice from the Board at Rembrandt that they would be sending you over this way."

Was it possible Rembrandt was actually going to send him here? Brixton ran his hand through his hair, contemplating the idea. He had not returned to his office since talking with Henry before, and it was true they could send him to check Scotland Yard if they felt such an inspection was warranted.

But it was still unprecedented.

"When did you get notice of my intent to come?" Brixton asked.

"Not entirely sure. I've just come onto my shift and Inspector Spade mentioned to be on the lookout for you in the next day or so."

Brixton nodded slowly. It had to be a coincidence, he thought, but there was an uneasy feeling in his gut that began to swirl along with his talent. It was nothing like the guilt he might have expected, given that he did not report in to Henry just yet.

They continued to walk through the halls, before Officer Littleton opened a door and led him inside.

The magic in the air was so pungent, Brixton almost sneezed; his nose prickled with otherworldly awareness, and his hands began to glow of their own accord, as if he was fighting to keep his own identity separate from the rest of his surroundings.

"This is the vault," Officer Littleton explained. "A wielder can't get very far in here without feeling the effects of the deterrent spells. We have a few Board members from Rembrandt that come and replace them every few months."

"I feel it," Brixton assured him.

"Even non-wielders feel it some, if you can imagine, Professor."

"I can. Now, I will have to take a look around the room …"

The room opened up, the sturdy walls arching into a dome ceiling. Little metal doors and shining keyholes dotted the walls, indicating vaults of varying sizes—any one of which could have held the Dragon Eye.

But even without being told, Brixton could feel it. The Dragon Eye carried a magical signature in its aura, so similar to Adelaide's he almost stopped in his tracks. This one called out to him destructively, eager to destroy him.

A bell chimed throughout the vault room, and Marcus straightened. "It's time for my rounds, sir," he said. "I'll leave you to your work. I'll send a replacement down to observe."

"Thank you."

Brixton began to work methodically, shifting through the different spells, seeking where they overlapped and dislodging them from himself. There were etchings along the wall and tiles across the stone floor. He felt the sweat on his brow begin to form as his talent weakened from the long exposure to the repellent spells. The moments passed slowly, and he soon began to wonder if Jiahao and Adelaide would show up at all.

He thought of the little bell, the one that signaled to Marcus. What if it was meant to alert the officer that something else was happening? Was it possible Adelaide and her cousin had been caught?

The door behind him creaked open.

Brixton turned around, relieved to have company. "There you are—"

He fell silent as he saw who it was.

It was not Adelaide.

The man behind him wore a top hat, one with the familiar pin of a Rembrandt Board member, and carried a walking stick with a silver eagle at the top.

"Good evening, Brixton. I have been expecting you."

Brixton felt his mouth go dry with dread. "Henry."

FAVAN AND FLEW

"Perhaps this is another time where you should refer to me as Dr. Winston, my good lad." Henry walked forward, twirling his walking stick with a sense of depraved anticipation.

"Why are you here?" Brixton asked. He knew he was in trouble, but he did not have a clear idea of what kind of trouble yet. He knew that the Board had requested him to come and check over the vault, thanks to Marcus's earlier comments, but he did not think Henry would come and check on him for that.

"I'm here for the same reason you are, of course." Henry stopped in the middle of the room. "I have come to collect the Dragon Eye."

<u>17</u>

Adelaide felt the first wave of regret hit her the moment she walked down the stairs to the main floor.

"Wait." She held up a hand to Jiahao. He was standing behind her, tugging one of the many uniformed guards along with him.

"What is it?" Jiahao asked.

She hesitated. "I'm not sure," she finally admitted.

Jiahao groaned. "After climbing up the side of the building, breaking the window pane off its hinges, walking down all the different levels of this prison, and attacking this guard, now you have doubts?"

"I can't explain it. But I feel a lot of unsettled magic around here."

"If you want to leave this place, we need to find the gem. Tàitai will be kinder to you than the police will." Jiahao turned back to the guard he was holding onto. "You! Where is the vault?"

"Vault?" The officer's eyes blinked slowly, before going blank. "There is a vault room in the center of this building."

"Tell us how to get there."

"It is down this hall, and then you turn to the left. It is behind the large metal door."

The guard's tone was still unfocused, but Adelaide caught the tired expression in Jiahao's eyes, and she knew it would not be long before they would have to discard him.

"Take your mask and gloves off, Yaling," Jiahao whispered. "This one could easily sound the alarm once he is free."

Adelaide nodded, grateful to have something to focus her attention on. As they walked deeper into the heart of the building, the hallways reminded her of the haven. It was a seemingly endless maze of darkness and danger, and one that teemed with enemy movement.

The police officer served a dual purpose in providing information and a cover, but Adelaide was more than relieved that the officers seemed to be content to run around from office to office and not examine their own members too often. They collected a few strange looks, but the officers only saluted each other, and Jiahao managed to hiss enough instructions to the guard he held prisoner that no one questioned them.

She caught sight of the door to the vault and began to feel her heart pounding.

"Yaling," Jiahao hissed. "I need you to take care of this man now. I cannot hold onto him—"

Jiahao's power broke, and the man wriggled free. "What are you doing? Where am I?"

The officer slowly came to the realization of his situation. Before he could say anything else, Adelaide grabbed his wrist.

Her talent rushed out of her and into him, ready to feed off of his own magical energy.

"He's not a wielder," Adelaide said. She felt sad as she watched him fall to the floor, unconscious. Her magic thrived from taking the magic out of someone else, but it seemed just as happy to deplete people of their energy. It took much less time, and the effects were often even more damaging. She watched as the officer twitched, wriggling

FAVAN AND FLEW

on the floor, and wondered if he would be able to recover soon.

"I guess it's called black magic for good reason," she said with a sigh. "It seems more like a demon than anything else some days."

"You could always use your training in martial arts to knock him out," Jiahao reminded her. "Not everything in your life has to be about magic."

"Magic is more convenient right now."

"I imagine a criminal would say the same of his weapon." Jiahao shrugged. "But it is not good to forget what resources you can employ, even if one is more effective."

"You're right."

"There is no need for you to be surprised. I am quite smart, too."

She smirked. "I'll keep that in mind. Right now I'm more concerned about drawing attention to ourselves, which is why I prefer to use magic in here. We shouldn't need to worry about the magic on the vault too much."

"That is where your *friend* will come in handy."

Adelaide said nothing at his jeering tone. She might not have wanted him to face the fury of her family's scorn, but if Brixton could break through her magic's destructive nature, dealing with her family would be a walk in the park by comparison.

Jiahao reached for the doorknob. "You better hurry. After using my magic on the guard, I do not know how long I will be able to stay inside this room."

"I feel the repellent spells, too," Adelaide assured him. "Even if they don't affect me. Just stay here and keep watch. You're the better one for that job, with or without magic."

FAVAN AND FLEW

She might have imagined it, but Adelaide thought she saw Jiahao give her a smile before she entered the room.

Then that feeling from before, the sense that danger was coming, sunk deeply into her heart.

"Brixton," she hissed, hurrying inside.

The door slammed shut behind her. Just as she heard the turn of the lock, Jiahao called out to her and began to bang on the door.

Adelaide whirled around as the light in the vault transformed from a dim gold to a turbulent red.

"It is lovely to make your acquaintance once more, Miss Favan."

Adelaide's gaze narrowed at the old, familiar voice. "Is that you, Dr. Winston?"

He stepped out from behind her, dragging a reluctant Brixton behind him. "Of course it is, my dear. You must forgive me for my poor manners. But I should think it would be easy, given how often you neglect them yourself."

Adelaide looked at the grim expression on Brixton's face. It took her a moment to see Dr. Winston had a pistol jammed into his neck.

She felt the blood drain from her face. "Why are you here?"

"Surely one of my brightest students—regardless of whether you showed up for class or not—should be able to tell me why I would be here, in the middle of Scotland Yard, holding your dearest friend hostage."

"You want the Dragon Eyes," she said slowly. In the background, Adelaide heard Jiahao pounding on the door to the room. She tried to think of what she could do, but panic was swiftly rising inside of her.

"Good girl. Retrieve that one from the vault for me," he said, tossing her a ring with a key. "I should hate to think I would have to waste your friend here. Brixton was always such a promising student, and now he is one of my most upright and reliable professors."

Adelaide's fingers shook as she hurried to open the vault with her family's jewel inside.

The magic around the room disappeared as she opened the small metal door to reveal a small, black pouch—the same one she had dropped on the *Horizon*.

She glanced back at Brixton, who shook his head. Dr. Winston elbowed him, making him grimace in discomfort.

"Why do you want the Dragon Eyes?" Adelaide asked. "They're obviously valuable, but there's nothing you can do with them. You're not a member of my family."

Dr. Winston laughed. "I happen to know quite a bit about the Dragon Eyes, and certainly enough to know you're mistaken. First, allow me to explain. I am a descendent of John Wright."

"Guy Fawkes' partner," Adelaide whispered.

"Yes," Dr. Winston said. "His nephew was one of Qin Suyan's lovers, a man who knew of the dragon's treasure and the gunpowder. He was a romantic and a poet, but ignorant of history or the military—a true revolutionary through and through. As you can imagine, he was quite upset with King James when he had Suyan quietly assassinated. He did everything he could to gain his own revenge on the king, but he did not succeed. After another attempt to kill the king, he was captured. He threw himself into the portal as he was being escorted to Tower Hill."

"So you want to release the dragon for revenge." Adelaide felt her heart clench as she slowly stepped forward.

Would she be able to find a way to free Brixton and escape from Dr. Winston? Adelaide wondered.

"You want to kill the Queen and take over, all because of what King James did to your family," she continued, trying to stall while she thought up a plan.

Adelaide bit her lip, trying not to worry. She could use her martial arts on Dr. Winston, but he was still threatening Brixton, and at their close proximity, she did not want to risk Brixton's safety.

"Heavens, no." Dr. Winston chuckled. "Where did you ever get an idea like that? It is enough to release the dragon and use him for my own power. Why bother with centuries-old revenge? It only gets in the way of present-day progress."

"I don't understand."

"Don't tell me you're more Chinese than you'd like," Dr. Winston scoffed. "The battle over the past is a futile one, even as it may signal the highest virtues. It's naturally sadistic, allowing the tormentors to feel perpetually justified in punishing the innocent heirs of the trouble."

"If you want to use the dragon to rule over the country, you're more Chinese than you would admit to as well," Adelaide objected. "That's the philosophy of the Mandate of Heaven."

"Hardly, Miss Favan." Dr. Winston curled his arm around Brixton's neck. "The Mandate of Heaven is merely the idea that might makes right and the right to rule comes from conquest. That's the most ancient of any natural tradition, no matter your heritage. And now, even with the small amount of Qin blood in my veins, I will be the dragon's master, and I can use its power to finally break free from Society's chains.

"Now, Miss Favan, take the Dragon Eye out of the pouch and give it to me. I grow tired of our discussion. One would think you would, too, given how little you used to attend my classes."

"Adelaide, don't do it." Brixton's voice was rough and dry as he risked speaking, and she felt her heart collapse.

"If you don't, I'll kill him." Dr. Winston cocked the trigger.

"No!" Adelaide gasped, already fumbling with the pouch and its tie. "No, don't hurt him."

"Even if you give him the Dragon Eye, he'll still kill me," Brixton protested.

"Now why would I want to do that? I've always looked out for you as best as I could, Brixton. I always believed you deserved far more than your upbringing. I recognized your brilliance and nurtured you, even when idiots like my colleague Ohm didn't see it, and prejudiced people like your own father hated you for it." Dr. Winston shook his head. "It is only now, as you stand between me and ultimate power, that I would even consider sacrificing you."

Adelaide gave Brixton an apologetic look. "I can't let anything happen to you."

She had no choice, she thought, as she reached out with the Dragon Eye in her hand.

"I had a feeling you would see things my way." Dr. Winston took the gem from her, before shoving Brixton into her.

Brixton curled his arm around Adelaide as he slammed into her, gripping onto her tightly enough to steady both of them.

"Brix." Adelaide breathed out his name with relief. She gripped his shoulders, forgetting she had no gloves on and there was no way to protect him from the full force of her magic.

FAVAN AND FLEW

"You shouldn't have done that," Brixton whispered. He tried to move away from her, but she only held onto him even more tightly.

"I told you before," Adelaide whispered against his chest. "I need you."

Behind them, Dr. Winston laughed as he tucked his gun back into his pocket, examining his new prize. "Excellent performance, Brixton."

Adelaide stilled. "What is he talking about?"

"Brixton didn't tell you, did he?" Dr. Winston said. "Well, obviously he didn't, or you wouldn't have bothered to save him. He knew we were looking for you. In fact, he was the one who led us here."

"I didn't tell him anything, I promise," Brixton said as she went still. "He set me up."

"The Board wanted you to find me?" Her words were flat and empty as she looked up at him.

"Of course we did. We even offered to completely discharge his debt and give him a position on the Airship Force for his efforts," Dr. Winston added.

"There was nothing I could have done about this," Brixton confessed, and some part of his logic resonated with her. "But I wasn't going to turn you in. I wanted to come along because I was trying to protect you."

Adelaide knew Brixton was already here against his father's wishes, and the wishes of the law. Why did it matter if the Board was looking for her, too?

Dr. Winston laughed. "I had a feeling you were still soft when it came to her, Brixton. I feel better about spying on you and your family now. It is a shame they will have to pay for your foolishness all over again."

Adelaide felt Brixton shake beside her. She felt his fear as he squeezed her arms even more tightly.

FAVAN AND FLEW

"Leave them alone," he warned. "They're not part of this."

"Leverage always plays a role in these things, but I would hate to have to punish them further for your trouble," Dr. Winston said. "If I were you, I would refrain from causing any more. You're already in trouble here in the vault room, and I would hate think you would want to make it worse."

Adelaide freed herself from Brixton and turned to face their enemy as her power rushed to her palms, the black magic glowing from her hands.

"Are you still up for a battle, Miss Favan?" Dr. Winston asked. "I'm surprised."

"Really? I'm not surprised at all." She lunged forward, her hands grappling with his as her talent overflowed.

The rush felt good, she thought, as she grabbed Dr. Winston's hands in her own.

It was never easy to control her power, but at times like these, when she dropped all attempts to hold it back, it was like flying.

Everything went rushing into battle, soaring alongside her lead. She ducked and twisted around, landing a solid jab in his torso.

"Oof." Dr. Winston buckled, dropping to his knees.

"You will be sorry you chose to mess with us," Adelaide said, her voice low and deadly. "You are no longer my teacher, and you've never been able to control me before."

She pushed all of her energy into depleting him of his magic and energy. Her vision blurred over, coloring the room in bleeding red.

All except for Dr. Winston. He knelt before her as fallen prey, and she would see to it that he would be punished for his crimes against her.

"Adelaide, you need to stop." Brixton appeared beside her, trying to break her away from Dr. Winston.

She could see the threatening light of his own magic as he took her arm. The white of his power braced itself against the black of hers. A pleasurable sort of pain singed through her arm at his touch.

"Get away from me," Adelaide snapped. At her voice, a blazing curl of energy lashed out, its force crackling as it sliced through the air. The ebony flame curled around Dr. Winston and hit Brixton.

Brixton hollered as he went flying into the vaults behind them. Her power struck him across the torso, and the metal crunched under his impact.

The magic in her blood was boiling, the rush of adrenaline and anger driving it to its darkest.

But his moan managed to break her concentration. A small amount of concern bubbled up inside of her, rebelling at the sudden bloodlust.

Adelaide gasped, realizing it was the same as before; when Gloria had broken her dragon's heart, her power went out of control. Any influence her conscience might have offered was being censored.

Dr. Winston began to laugh.

Adelaide frowned. "What's so amusing?"

He stood up, easily brushing off her magic. "Surely you don't think I neglected to prepare for this after you nearly killed that other student? Now, now, Miss Favan. I expected better of you."

Adelaide felt her mouth drop open. "What happened? How did you do that?"

"Remember, questions come at the end of the lesson," Dr. Winston said as he reached for her.

She scrambled back and fell, weakened by the use of her magic.

Now that she had expended her power, and all at once everything snapped back to normal. The blood red vision of the room dissolved into its earlier golden shade, and her head ached with sudden, deep pain. Her hand flew to her forehead as she began to moan in pain.

"Ada." Brixton's voice was muffled from behind her.

"Brixton." Adelaide faltered at the sound of his voice. She had been so angry, so upset … and now she just felt confused.

She stumbled as she tried to stand up, still trying to avoid Dr. Winston as he reached for her.

Adelaide glanced down at her hands, watching as her magic faded from her palms. Her whole body shook.

My magic …

Using it so intentionally and so fervently had drained her, leaving her beyond exhausted.

"Got you!" Dr. Winston finally caught her by the back of her shirt. As she weakly struggled against him, he pulled out the Dragon Eye, showing her the gem in his hand. "As long as I have one of these, I am protected from your magic. Thank you for rendering yourself helpless for me. It will make this next part much easier."

She struggled to knock the jewel out of his hand. He grunted as she landed a weak punch to his midsection, but despite her attacks, he managed to hold onto the Dragon Eye. She slipped free of his grip and fell to her knees, beyond exhausted.

He grasped her from behind, choking her, and before Adelaide could do anything else, she felt her mind go fuzzy. His arm dug deeply into her throat as she wriggled and writhed for each breath.

"Ada!"

Adelaide heard Brixton calling for her as everything went dark and she finally collapsed.

<u>18</u>

"Ada, no!" Brixton clawed his way to his feet as Adelaide fell limp. He raced toward her, ignoring the agony of his injuries.

"Stop right there." Dr. Winston, breathing hard, took his pistol out again. After the battle with Adelaide, he was clearly tired, but the look in his eye was deadly serious. "As I said, I'd rather not hurt you, Brixton, and I'm guessing you'd rather live, too—even though my testimony is the only thing that will keep you from going to jail for a very long time, while your family suffers the price."

"Why, Henry?" Brixton stood still, forcing himself to speak louder. "Why are you doing this?"

"Didn't you hear me before? I want power, enough to break free from my illegitimate status. All my life I have served others, Brixton. Everyone wants something, haven't you realized? And all of them are so annoying about it, especially those who look to those with magic to give it to them. The Crown wants new security devices, the guards want more communication tech. No appreciation, no gratitude. No, don't you see? We are their fancy slaves with magic; we are the new gods of this world, already neutered to humble piety. For all our power, we are still unable to bypass Society's fortress of bloodlines and their cavalry of rules."

"Henry."

Henry ignored him. "Now is the time for people like us to challenge those rules, Brixton. Come with me, and free the dragon. We can tame it, using its power to rule this nation and the world. We can make everything better for the wielders like ourselves, for those of us who were born outside of privilege."

"Never," Brixton yelled. "Let Adelaide go."

Henry shook his head. "I still need her for this next part, Brixton. It would have been nice if you'd joined me. You might have even convinced me to spare her life when she's finished awakening the dragon spirit. Now you can rot in prison."

Brixton watched in horror as Dr. Winston hoisted Adelaide over his shoulder, showing an impressive amount of strength for the older gentleman, and headed out of the room.

"Stop!" Brixton scrambled after him, terrified for Adelaide.

A small squad of officers came rushing into the vault, but Brixton barely heard them calling for his arrest as he kept his focus on Adelaide's fallen form.

An officer grabbed him, pushing him down to his knees, trying to handcuff him. Brixton shoved him aside, escaping long enough to hear Henry explain that Adelaide needed medical attention.

"Adelaide!" Brixton called.

"Lock him up," Henry said, smirking as Brixton struggled against the officers.

Through the guards and the parade of uniforms before him, he caught sight of Adelaide's unconscious form one last time before Henry slipped out the door.

"Ada." His talent flickered back to life, and Brixton did not hesitate. He thrust himself forward, hitting one of the guards, and turned quickly, using the power behind him to push through another three guards. They all called for him to stop, but he could not.

Not when she needs me. He clawed at the guards, pushing them back, advancing his way through the wall of them.

His body screamed in agony, the muscles still sore from his earlier collision with the vaults. But while the pain muddied his movements, his mind remained clear.

He thought back to the days at school, with Adelaide by his side, and how he did nothing as she was teased, of how she was alone. The familiar shame flared up inside of him.

It's all my fault.

He made it to the door. Down the hall to his left, he could see multiple officers trying to hold Jiahao down. With several attackers on every side, he could not use his power to overtake them.

"They're wielders," another guard called.

Brixton saw Henry's shadow disappear around the far corner just as a wave of red-colored spells pounded on him from behind. "No!"

Jiahao went down, Brixton went down, and then the whole world came crashing down. He felt as though everything important suddenly crumpled into dust as his mind was overcome, his will was broken, and his body was injured.

Brixton finally stopped fighting, too tired to be anything but still. Henry was gone with Adelaide, and he was stuck.

"Call Officer Flew," one of the men said. "Tell him we have his son in custody again."

"Transport them to Tower Hill, to the wielder's prison block," another voice called. "We can't risk them here."

"Aye, sir."

A pair of guards reached out and grabbed them, hauling him to his feet. Brixton stared blankly out into the distance,

FAVAN AND FLEW

unable to do anything but march in time with the guards beside him.

"This is all your fault." Jiahao's voice was soft, but it rang against the cold, stone walls, echoing into a full crescendo.

"I know," Brixton said. "You don't have to rub it in."

He sniffled into his sleeve, watching as Jiahao paced in a continuous circle in the prison cell next to his. It felt like it had been hours since their capture and arrest, but there was no telling how long it had actually been. Brixton had been forced to give up Ticker when he was processed, and he struggled to decide whether or not it was a good thing.

Ticker would love to chastise me for this.

Brixton rubbed his arms, trying to warm himself from the chilly atmosphere of Tower Hill. They were in one of the rooms reserved for the poorest of offenders, located in the basement of the grand castle. He could feel the ancient history as much as he could feel the magic that kept them trapped, and he did not know which made him contemplate the idea of death more.

Kings and queens, priests, traitors, foreigners and natives alike had been kept here, waiting to hear the news of their fate.

For now, Brixton decided it was enough to know he was free to walk around inside his cell. There had been plenty of other cells he passed, as he was escorted into the prison, where chains and stocks were kept ready.

Brixton eyed the carvings in the stone walls around him that channeled the needed magic to keep his power in check while he was in jail.

This is where I could have ended up before, when I was younger, if it was not for Rembrandt.

It was nothing short of ironic he was now trapped here because of them, he thought with a grimace.

"You set everything up." Jiahao stopped his pacing long enough to scowl at Brixton. "Was it because of what we did to your friend, the other lady officer?"

"What? No." Brixton shook his head. "I didn't want this to happen."

Jiahao frowned even further at him, clearly unconvinced.

"I promise you, I didn't know Dr. Winston was at Scotland Yard when we arrived."

"I do not believe you. You and your ancestors have been lying to my kind for centuries. I do not know why I am surprised we are in this situation. You have been using my cousin since the beginning and you betrayed her for your own advancement. You are the reason she was kidnapped."

"That's not true!" Brixton shouted, angry that his loyalty was questioned because of a miscalculation. He stood up and faced the bars that stood between him and Jiahao, ready to prove his honor if needed. "I would never do anything to hurt Adelaide!"

"Dare you threaten me?" Jiahao ducked down into a fighting stance.

"You're the one accusing me of betraying my best friend," Brixton argued. He held up his fists, waiting for Jiahao to throw the first punch between the bars.

Before Jiahao could do anything, there was a low, dry laugh coming from the cell across from them.

"Don't you mean the woman who broke your heart?"

There was something familiar about that voice, Brixton thought. He pushed himself against the front bars of his cell, looking around. Their prison floor had cells lined around the room. Guards periodically walked around the room in pairs, in circular pathways.

Brixton squinted across the way, following the sound of laughter to its source. A man in a dusty uniform sat on the floor of his prison cell in front of the bars. His back was straight, his legs were crossed, and his arms were balanced on his knees as he faced Brixton.

"Careful, now. I don't imagine my daughter would appreciate either of you fighting each other, especially since she's the one in danger now, isn't she?"

"Captain Favan." Brixton nearly choked in disbelief.

Somewhere in the back of his mind, he remembered what Luella had said, about how he had been deposed and he was going to be transferred to Tower Hill to await his trial.

"Well, well, if it isn't Brixton Flew? So we meet again, after all these years." The captain sneered at him, clearly eager to have someone to torment.

His heavy black eyebrows were scattered with white flecks, but his eyes were still the soulless coal-black Brixton remembered seeing the day before Adelaide's ship left for Peking. The small, thin lines of his mustache and the small beard just covering his chin were accompanied by more wrinkles and worry than last time, too, Brixton noticed.

"And here I was, wishing I would never see you again." Adelaide's father chortled darkly. "I have to admit, this is one wish I'm glad to see didn't come true. This is a most amusing turn of events."

Brixton did not want to antagonize him, but the captain certainly did not seem to have any trouble provoking

Brixton. Even from across the room, Brixton could see the arrogance of Captain Favan's gaze as he looked him over.

"Welcome to the wielder's prison," the captain said.

"You're a wielder, too?" Brixton had to admit, he was more than a little surprised. Adelaide never liked to talk about her own talent. It appeared to be more of a family trait than he thought.

"Never bothered to care much that the best captain in Her Majesty's Airship Force was a wielder, did you? I don't know whether to commend you for your lack of judgment or condemn you for your intentional ignorance."

Brixton frowned but said nothing. There was still quite a bit of swagger in the deposed captain. He was still wearing his rank insignia on his uniform, the one that marked him as a special officer in the nation's military.

"Captain Favan." Jiahao folded his hands together and bowed respectfully, allowing Brixton a moment of reprieve from both battlefronts. "It is an honor to see you again."

"You can forgo the formalities and call me Ryu, same as you should call my daughter by her preferred name, Jiahao. I can't imagine my grandmother would think it is an honor for you to see me again."

"He has a point," Brixton murmured. "He is disgraced."

"Willingly and intentionally so," Ryu assured him.

"I find that hard to believe. I heard from reliable sources that you were put here after you tried to mess with the portal."

"Ah, but you don't know who reported me, or why I agreed to be tried for such a crime. Really, Brixton, after all these years, you should be smart enough to know I am here because of my own choosing." Ryu pulled a cigar from his jacket pocket. A flicker of light jumped into his hand, and Brixton saw traces of his orange magic.

Fire.

Adelaide's father was suddenly even more imposing than he had been the last time Brixton saw him.

Brixton was reluctantly intrigued as he watched Ryu try to stare him down. Brixton had forgotten Adelaide was not the only one with mixed blood in her family. The captain had the narrow face and pointed chin of a British gentleman, but his own Chinese heritage was clear. He even seemed to be more dragon than man as he blew out a long stream of smoke.

"But we're not going to talk about that right now, are we? Not when you've apparently endangered my daughter." Ryu scoffed. "I told you to stay away from her."

"If Adelaide is in danger, it is because of your family, not because of me," Brixton told him. "She was attacked and kidnapped because of her magic."

"A real man doesn't shift the blame."

"I think it's a waste of time to ascribe blame right now." Brixton paused. "Especially when we could use the time to figure out how to escape."

"How *you* will escape." Ryu took another puff from his cigar. "I've told you, I'm here intentionally. I'm not leaving."

"What about Adelaide? She's in danger."

"Adelaide has always been in danger because of her magic," Ryu snapped. "She's more likely to kill others than to suffer any danger herself."

"Dr. Winston kidnapped her," Brixton said through gritted teeth. "He's a powerful wielder and a member of the Board at Rembrandt."

Ryu laughed again. The crude sound rang across the prison cells, sifting through the bars between them strongly enough to make Brixton wince.

"I've always thought educators were the most evil of villains," Ryu said. "They all say they're in it for the future. Their intentions are so noble no one thinks to question them. But they hardly mind getting the recognition for their great sacrifice, not to mention access to the latest developments and technologies in their fields. But they're lying, all of them, whether they know it or not. If you want proof of how they really feel, all you have to do is challenge their most cherished teachings. No one can pass personal opinions for dogma and deign other perspectives as taboo quite like scholars can. And Rembrandt is the worst. It's hard to say whether or not it is a surprise that one of Rembrandt's own has taken my daughter."

"This Dr. Winston has a Dragon Eye, too, sir," Jiahao said. "He took it when he captured Yaling."

The shock registered in Ryu's dark eyes for approximately half of a second, but Brixton swore he saw it. His suspicions were confirmed a moment later when Ryu leaned back against the bars, turning away from Brixton and Jiahao.

"You should call her Adelaide, Jiahao," Ryu muttered. "We are in London, after all, and this is our home, not yours."

Brixton briefly smirked as Jiahao's face scrunched up in displeasure, before returning his focus to the captain. "Please, sir, we need to do something. Can't you help us?"

"Why do you think I would be able to help you?" Ryu's voice was muffled as he talked back into his cell.

"You said you were in here intentionally," Brixton argued. "If that's true, surely you have a plan for leaving when you're ready to do so."

"I'm not leaving until my grandmother leaves London." Ryu shrugged. "This place is designed to smother your talent, as you might have already realized; it keeps all

FAVAN AND FLEW

wielders from using magic. As long as I am here, I am safe from the Qin clan, as well as whatever trouble they're brewing up underneath the city."

"Adelaide could still get to you."

"She would never come here." Ryu waved his hand, dismissing the idea. "I wouldn't want her to, either, but that is a moot point. My grandmother is up to no good, and if I thought Adelaide couldn't protect herself, I would have her arrested and placed in here along with me. Of course, that could have been a serious misjudgment on my part. For all Adelaide's magic is her own, my grandmother has a way of smuggling herself into my daughter's mind."

"Why are you here at all? What are you so afraid of?" Brixton asked.

"You've clearly never met Lady Fang," Ryu said. "No one asks if she is someone to be frightened of."

Brixton glanced over at Jiahao, who nodded.

"Tàitai, who is known as Lady Fang to you, is our clan leader. She is on schedule with her plans to restore our family honor," Jiahao explained. "Captain Favan … Ryu … has good sense to be protecting himself in here. Even if Yaling has been kidnapped, she will find a way to use this to her advantage."

Brixton rubbed his temples. "You two are not helping. Right now the only thing that matters is Adelaide. Where did the guards go? I need to see about talking to my father. He can help me get out of here."

Hopefully.

"Guards make their rounds after every twenty minutes," Ryu said. He took another long inhale of his cigar. "Which means I have about five more left before they tell me I shouldn't be smoking in here, and six more before I bribe them for more cheroots."

Brixton watched as the gray trail of smoke swirled around Ryu's cell before shaking his head. He gripped the bars, looking for any sign of weakness. The bars creaked slightly as his arms screamed in pain. He let go, disappointed; there was not enough wiggle room for him to be able to leverage his way out.

"If I were you, I would just give up," Ryu said. "Adelaide can't be with you anyway."

"What do you mean?" Brixton asked.

"I mean you're not going to get anything out of doing this for her. There is no future for the two of you. The only way Adelaide can have a normal relationship with anyone is if she doesn't care about them, and they don't care about her. It's already clear you're not going to be able to keep her heart safe. If you're still around, after all I did to get rid of you, my daughter is clearly already too far lost."

Brixton felt stricken at Ryu's words. He did not know if it was possible for him to be able to stop caring about Adelaide. He would have to forget her entirely, and he had spent the last several years proving to himself he just could not do that.

"And you're likely in trouble, too. Especially with your considerable amount of talent," Ryu continued, scoffing. "The blathering bastards at your establishment think they've been blessed with power, but the truth is power corrupts, and the more you have, the more of a burden it is to the soul."

"I just want her to be safe. That's enough for me," Brixton insisted, too upset at Ryu's disregard for Adelaide to appreciate his compliment. Brixton ducked his head, examining the hinges on the cell door. "Even if we can't be together."

"Now I see why the Board was so eager for you to teach at the school. You're lying to yourself just as much as other educators do."

Brixton paused, unable to wonder if Adelaide's father had a point. He did not want to let Adelaide go.

It was not something he could worry about now, he decided. He examined the hinges of his cell more closely, wondering if there was another way he could break them. The magic in the air made it hard to concentrate.

He looked back at Jiahao through the bars that separated their cells. "Can you help me with this? I think if we can put enough pressure on the lock, we might be able to bend it and get out of here."

"No." Jiahao shook his head. He nodded toward his arm, where a small trail of blood crusted over on his sleeve. "Those bastards back at Scotland Yard drew blood when they handcuffed me, and my arms are already too wide for these bars."

"Come now, you can at least—"

"Jiahao is right. The guards are coming back," Ryu told Brixton, gesturing toward the only door into the circular holding cell block.

Outside of it, after a moment of concentration, Brixton could hear a synchronized set of footsteps coming their way.

"You might as well wait for them to finish their round before trying to worsen your charges," Ryu said with another smirk.

"You think this is funny, don't you?" Brixton accused. "You think that Adelaide being in danger is something to laugh at."

"Like I said earlier, *Professor* Flew," Ryu said, emphasizing his disgust, "she has always been in trouble.

Make no mistake, the Qin magic is a curse, and not one to be trifled with or underestimated. That was how Adelaide killed her mother, and that was how my parents died, too."

Brixton went still. "Adelaide … killed her mother?"

"My wife died trying to tend to her while she was sick. Adelaide was just five years old." Ryu glanced over his shoulder, just enough that Brixton could see the resentment in his gaze. "I wasn't able to free my wife from Adelaide in time."

Brixton looked away, taking a quick peek at Jiahao. There was an uncomfortable look on his face, and Brixton realized that, as Adelaide's cousin, he had likely heard the stories. Her family was his family, too, after all.

"My mother and father had the same magic, but not even close to the extent Adelaide does. My mother ended up losing control of her power and killing herself when I was ten, and my father soon followed suit. That's why I was raised by my grandmother." Ryu rubbed his cigar into the stones of his cell floor. "If she can't find a way to manage her magic, Adelaide will suffer the same fate."

Brixton gripped his fingers around the bars, suddenly even more desperate to find a way to see her again.

"Does she know everything you just told me?" Brixton asked.

"Of course she does." Ryu snorted. "Why do you think my sadistic grandmother has as much control over her as she does? Tàitai is the only woman alive in my family who has learned how to control the curse of her magic. She's sacrificed her heart in return for that."

"What do you mean?"

"Black magic is the worst kind of magic," Ryu said. "You have to have a lot of hate to want to destroy things. My grandmother cannot love anything, and so she is

FAVAN AND FLEW

consumed by plots for revenge and power. She embraced her magic to the fullest in order to gain control of it.

"If you want Adelaide to control her magic without breaking the curse, then she will never be able to love you. Or anyone else."

"You have to be lying," Brixton said. He knew Adelaide had no trouble breaking the law or bending the rules, but she could never embrace hatred.

"I might hate you," Ryu snarled, "but I've never lied to you. Lies are shortcuts the devil needs to succeed. A real man can win with the truth."

Brixton did not know how to answer that. He looked at Jiahao, who suddenly whipped around, gazing at the door to the prison block just as it opened.

A pair of guards came in, followed by two others.

Brixton felt a wave of oncoming guilt start to smother him. He forced himself to remain still, to appear unaffected by their arrival.

But one look at Luella's large eyes and his father's stern frown, and he doubted he would be able to maintain his charade for long.

<u>19</u>

Brixton held his breath, anxiously waiting for his father to tell him how upset he was with him.

He was not disappointed. Guilt welled up inside of him as Bartholomew began to speak a moment later.

"I am horrified to learn of last night's incident," Bartholomew said softly, his voice full of resentment. Brixton felt the aching, shameful tightness in his chest as much as he had when he was younger. "I was especially disturbed to hear of your role in stealing the Dragon Eye."

"Father, I can explain," Brixton interrupted. "Dr. Winston—"

"You're lucky he was there to protect you as much as he was."

"He was the one who was behind it."

"He was the one who told you to go to Scotland Yard tonight with a pair of wanted burglars and break into the vault?"

"I was going to check the vault for security purposes." Brixton felt his cheeks burn with crimson humiliation.

"That's a lie, lad, and I know it."

Behind him, Ryu cackled, and Brixton lowered his eyes.

Behind Bartholomew, Luella cleared her throat. "Father, you promised I would be able to speak to Brixton, too, please."

Bartholomew glared down at her, obviously upset to be interrupted. But, after a silent battle of their wills, he allowed Luella to step forward.

"Lu." Brixton tried to give her a reassuring smile.

Luella reached in between the bars, patting his cheek in a sisterly manner. "Oh, Brixton," she said.

He was about to tell her his situation was exactly why he did not want her to come along, when she suddenly slapped him across the face.

"Hey!" Brixton jolted back and rubbed his cheek, the sting of Luella's rejection even worse than her attack.

"Luella, stop." Bartholomew stepped forward. "That's not proper."

"You fool," Luella said, still focused on Brixton as their father tugged her shoulders, trying to keep her back.

"Luella, I said you could come with me to see Brixton, but this is unacceptable behavior."

"My behavior is unacceptable?" Luella scoffed. "How about his?"

"His behavior is why he is in here."

"It's not enough!" She shook her head before pointing her finger at Brixton accusingly. "I can't believe that you would do this to us! Have you learned nothing from all the trouble you caused before?"

"Lu … " Brixton felt himself nearly choke as she continued to fight against their father's grip. She managed to escape and pushed herself back in front of Brixton.

She grabbed him by his shirt, pulling his collar hard as she shook him. "I hope you rot in here!"

"Luella Catherine Flew, that is enough," Bartholomew muttered, prying Luella away from the cell. He gave his fervent apologies to the accompanying guards, before he grabbed her by the shoulder. "I do believe it is time for you to leave. Brixton, I will be back later to discuss your indiscretions. For now it seems I have to get your temperamental sister back to her mother."

Luella continued to fight against her father as they left the room. The two other guards helped, each one taking an arm as Bartholomew led them out of the room. "I can only hope you will enjoy your time in here!" she cried back, as the door to the prison block shut. "It'll be too short, that's for sure!"

There was a long moment of silence before Brixton was surprised to hear Jiahao laugh.

"That is your sister?" Jiahao asked. "Well, what do you know? The British even betray their own families."

"You don't know us very well, do you?" Brixton touched the spot on his cheek where Luella had slapped him with one hand, while he patted the small pocket in his shirt, just under his suspenders. Inside the pocket was one of his lockpicks. She had slipped it to him while everyone else was distracted with the clash of her palm on his cheek.

"Didn't seem like she was that excited to see you," Ryu called from across the way.

Brixton ignored him as he pulled out Luella's gift. "My sister has a gift for the dramatic, but she's just as prone to trouble as I am."

Jiahao took a step closer, watching as Brixton held up Luella's gifts. "What is that?"

"Something that will allow us to get out of this cell," Brixton said. He looked back at Ryu. "When are the guards coming again?"

"I'd wait 'til their next round or so, if you're going to escape. You don't want your sister to be the first one they suspect."

"Good." Brixton nodded. "That gives us time to formulate a plan."

"But we don't know anything about this Dr. Winston," Jiahao said.

FAVAN AND FLEW

"We know plenty," Brixton insisted. "We know he wants the Dragon Eyes, and he already has one."

"My brothers are getting the other one."

"Well, we also know Dr. Winston wants to set the dragon free."

"He'll need Adelaide to do that," Ryu said. "She has the Qin curse running through her blood."

"Curse?" Brixton turned back to face him. "Wait. Do you mean there is an actual curse?"

"All of creation is cursed," Ryu said with a snort. "The most powerful creatures in all this world are not able to escape the curse of Eden's fall. Dragons were offered free will, and they faced the same consequences of the choices—and that's why they're extinct now."

"I'm only asking about Adelaide's magic."

"Have you never even wondered where her magic comes from?" Ryu shook his head. "You got yours from your family and their exposure to the dragon magic through the portal. The Qin family carries magic in our blood, just as we have done for millennia. You have had magic here for nearly three centuries, but we have had it since the Age of the Dragons."

"I know the magic here comes from the dragon spirit in the portal," Brixton said.

"The Qin Dragon wasn't always in the portal." Ryu snorted. "After its prestigious empire was established through magic and blood, the last Emperor of the Qin dynasty cut out the eyes of the dragon, all in hopes of winning the heart of the woman he loved. As the dragon lay bleeding and betrayed, the emperor's sister, Wuja, cast a spell cursing the family for its greed, before she fled from the Qin Empire along with the blinded dragon. Since then, the women in our family carry destructive magic, doomed to carry the dragon blood in their veins and bear the brunt of our family's curse. They are destined to kill, especially what they love."

"Can't the Dragon Eyes help us?"

"The Dragon Eyes are said to contain a part of the Qin Dragon's soul. The closer Adelaide—and the power in her blood—gets to them, the more the dragon will seek her out."

Brixton curled his hands into fists. "There has to be something we can do to help Adelaide."

"If you are so desperate to do something, you should go and seek out the Qin clan. They'll be able to help you much more than I will. Jiahao."

"What is it?" Jiahao asked.

"Take him to the haven. You might be injured, but you're not useless. If anyone can find a way to turn this situation around, it's my grandmother."

"Tàitai will not welcome him."

Ryu chuckled. "Well, that's not our problem, is it? It's his." He looked over at Brixton. "If you want to find a way to save her, and destroy her magic, you'll need to prove yourself."

"I'll do anything for Adelaide," Brixton vowed.

"Well, that's a good start, but we'll see how far you actually get." Ryu nodded slowly. "When you see her, tell Tàitai what you told me. Tell her you will prove yourself in combat. That should win her over."

"Combat?" Brixton felt nervous at the thought. He glanced back at Jiahao, who was suddenly smiling, not even bothering to hide his amusement at Brixton's fate.

Ryu cleared his throat. "Yes. My family will not like meeting you, but they will honor your request for a challenge."

"If for no other reason than to enjoy watching you fail," Jiahao said darkly.

"Don't act so high and mighty, Jiahao," Ryu admonished. "They won't like that you've allowed Adelaide to be captured any more than they'll like how you lost one of the Dragon Eyes."

"They will still hate him." Jiahao crossed his arms, and Brixton was almost tempted to thank Adelaide's father for silencing him. He had not cared much for Adelaide's cousin earlier, and he was beginning to believe his first impression was the right one.

"I don't care if they hate me," Brixton said. "I'll do anything if it means saving Adelaide. And maybe they'll be able to help us trap Henry in the process."

He turned back to Jiahao. "I can't wait any longer. We have to go. Take me to your family."

Jiahao glanced back at Ryu, who glared at him under his large, thick eyebrows.

"You heard him, Jiahao," Ryu said. "Those are my orders, too."

"You're a traitor to the Qin family."

"I know," Ryu shot back. "But this is my daughter, and if Tàitai wants her revenge, she still needs Adelaide to get it."

"Revenge?" Brixton looked up from unlocking the cell long enough to see both of them in a silent battle of wills.

Neither of them paid him any attention, so Brixton decided to let it go for now. He had to save Adelaide, and that meant escaping prison and finding the rest of her family. He could worry about the rest later.

Luella's gift worked, and the door unlocked with ease; the door briefly stuck against the suddenly uneven floor,

FAVAN AND FLEW

but Brixton slid out and waited for Jiahao, before hurrying toward the cell block's exit.

"Brixton."

At the sound of his name, Brixton turned back to face the deposed captain. "What is it, sir?"

Ryu leered at him. "If you do save my daughter and the world and such, and if you happen to come and see me again, bring me some more cigars, would you? The guards don't have any fashionable taste in this matter."

"Maybe. If I have the time." Brixton could not think of anything he wanted to do less. But Ryu was Adelaide's father, and whether she loved him or not, and whether Brixton approved of him or not, he did provide something of use to him. "Be safe, sir."

The instant Brixton left the prison block, he felt his magic burst with full power. The suffocating powers of the wielder's prison was broken.

From the look on Jiahao's face, Brixton knew he felt the same. The two of them said nothing as they headed out of the prison.

Just as he was breathing in the fresh, invigorating air, Brixton heard a guard call out behind them.

"Stop right there!"

Brixton flinched and Jiahao groaned. A few guards were waiting outside Tower Hill.

"Do not let them catch you," Jiahao said, as he went on the offensive. Brixton watched him as he began to fight, amazed at his skill. Before he could join him and hope to keep up, Brixton saw a familiar hand reach out.

"Luella."

His sister grinned at him as she grabbed onto the guard Jiahao attacked. Her power caught him, freezing him as easily as she had Reginald the crocodile the day before.

"You told me I could come along with you on your next adventure, Brix."

Jiahao stared at her, looking from the stymied guard to her youthful face. "You are excited about this."

"Of course," Luella said with a giggle. "Why wouldn't I be?"

"Where's Father?" Brixton asked.

"He's gone. He wanted to report back to Inspector Spade. He told me to get home on my own." Luella bit her lip as the guard she held began to twitch. "He was very embarrassed by my behavior and even wondered why my magic couldn't stop me from disappointing him."

"Oh, Lu," Brixton murmured sympathetically.

"That is enough." Jiahao lashed out a kick and sent the guard flying. Once they were safe, he shook his head at her. "You will get in trouble. There will be danger."

Luella gulped, but she looked back at Jiahao, putting on a brave face. "So? Life is as dull as you make it, according to our mother."

"It's fine. She can come," Brixton said, unable to hide his smile as Jiahao frowned. "I'm not sure Mother will be happy to hear you didn't take her advice the way she wanted, Lu."

"That's parenthood for you." Luella snickered.

They started to head down the block, walking among the shadows to keep out of sight. There were other alarms calling out from the prison, but Brixton was determined to remain free this time.

"I'm glad you were able to get out," Luella said, as Jiahao began to open a sewer grate for them. "Sorry for slapping you. I had to make it convincing."

"You certainly fooled me for a few moments." Brixton patted her hand. "But I'm fine. Now we need to go and rescue Adelaide."

"Where are we going?"

"Ask him." Brixton pointed at Jiahao. "We need his family's help if we're going to rescue Adelaide."

Luella turned her attention to Jiahao. "You are taking us to see your family, right?"

"I am not taking you—"

Luella gasped, interrupting him. "Your arm!"

"What?" Jiahao glanced down. "What is it?"

"You're hurt."

"It is nothing. It is just a small cut. I am surprised you noticed."

"You've been bleeding," Luella said. She narrowed her gaze and tapped her chin thoughtfully. "I'll be happy to heal it for you, if you'd like."

Jiahao glanced back at Brixton, who nodded.

"You are a young one to already have command of your magic," Jiahao said.

"I learned everything from my big brother," Luella assured him, already pressing her palms into his arm. There was a flash of multi-colored light, and Jiahao gaped at her as the small cuts along his wrists faded.

"Your magic." He blinked. "It worked."

"Of course it did. I know I'm young yet, but you don't need to be that surprised." Luella smiled triumphantly at him. "I'm not just a good actress, you know."

"Come on, Lu. None of that," Brixton said. "Mother would die of embarrassment if she knew you said that in front of him."

Luella drew herself up proudly. "That just goes to show you how good I am. She has no idea how impetuous I can be."

"I'll give you that," Brixton agreed. He turned back to Jiahao. "Now, where are we going?"

Jiahao frowned. After a moment of thought, he gave in. "I will take you to see my family. They live down this way," he said, gesturing toward the sewers. "Follow me."

"Brixton."

He looked back at Luella as she reached into her pocket. "What is it?" he asked.

"Before I forget, I managed to convince Father to get Ticker back from the police. Here." Luella handed Brixton the tiny pocket watch.

He rubbed his thumb over the casing. While Ticker usually responded to the slightest bit of magic, he remained silent and still.

"His power is nearly gone," Luella said with a hint of sadness.

"It's because of Adelaide's magic."

"I know. But I know if anyone can bring him back to life, it's you."

Brixton carefully tucked Ticker into his back pocket and latched the chain onto his belt. "I'll take care of him as soon as I can."

"Are you two coming or not?" Jiahao's voice was impatient and demanding.

"We are." Brixton did not want to keep him waiting, but what Luella said was true. He took a moment to wrap his arm around her and give her an affectionate hug. "Thank you."

And then together, Brixton and Luella hurried to catch up to Jiahao.

As she regained consciousness, Adelaide slowly felt the world slide back into place. Her eyes blinked open, and she was momentarily confused as she saw the crooked world before her.

Everything was tilted to the right, she thought. As the fog inside her mind cleared, she realized she was lying on a small couch, with her hands cuffed in front of her.

She struggled to sit up. Immediately the room began to whirl around in a dizzying horror, but she shut her eyes long enough to center herself.

One of the many topics Tàitai had instructed her in once she was in Peking was the martial arts the Orient was famous for. Adelaide admitted it was empowering to be able to defend herself, and learning the more acrobatic tricks with the rest of her family allowed for them to gain some respect for her, despite the objection to the circumstances of her birth and upbringing.

She opened her eyes again. This time, there was no accompanying vertigo, but she started to become aware of the stiffness and pain making its way through her body. She tentatively felt her neck, where, wincing as she glanced down, she could just see a few hints of purplish-blue marks.

Dr. Winston had strangled her into silence, all while she had been too weak to stop him. She involuntarily shivered at the memory.

"Where am I?" she muttered. It was strange to hear her voice, but it was even stranger to hear it as she stared at her surroundings.

The familiarity of the room hit her at once, making her even more alert.

She was in Dr. Winston's office at Rembrandt.

Nearly everything was the same as it was the last time she was in here, Adelaide thought. The desk was still neat, with a pile of graded assignments on one side and another that was left untouched on the other. There was a clock hanging just over the door, one that told her it was just after one.

Several hours had passed since she fought Dr. Winston in the vault room at Scotland Yard. It had been more than half a day since she had last seen her friend and cousin.

Adelaide sighed. She did not know when she would be able to see them again.

A faint draft wafted over her from the window. She looked up to see it was covered with the same dreary-colored brocade curtains as before. She followed the small sliver of light that peeked through, landing on the portrait of John Wright that hung just behind the desk chair.

His ancestor.

Adelaide paused for a long moment to look on the imposing figure portrayed in the painting. He was a determined man, one of conviction, and he had paid the ultimate price for his dalliance with rebellion.

She made a silent promise to herself that Dr. Winston would pay, too.

As soon as I can get out of here.

The door opened, and like the devil out of the mist, Dr. Winston appeared.

"So it appears my magic managed to work this time," he said. "Good."

"What do you mean?" Adelaide snapped.

"You are talking to the highest engineering enchanter in the land," Dr. Winston said, his elderly smile full of bitterness. He pointed to a small, eye-shaped automaton on his desktop. "I had this set up to alert me when you began to move. It has a detector inside, one enhanced with magic that alerts me when there is significant movement nearby. I've found it is a great resource to keep intruders from burglarizing my offices."

"I'll bet anything you stole the idea from Brixton," Adelaide muttered. She remembered when he had talked of something similar, back when they were in school.

"Are you sure you wouldn't want to take some of the credit, too?" Dr. Winston picked up the small object, tossing it playfully in his hands. Adelaide saw the dullness of his magic's light, knowing Brixton's was much brighter. "I know you worked with him on plenty of his designs, especially some of the more advanced ones."

She said nothing, only pursing her lips into an angry frown.

"Believe it or not, I was quite sad when you left Rembrandt. Brixton was devastated, too. I don't think his work ever reached the level of potential he had when you were around to *inspire* him."

The way he said it made her blush, both with shame and with pride.

"Where is Brixton? What did you do with him?" she asked.

"Do you really want to know?" Dr. Winston chuckled. "Some things are better off left unknown, after all."

"Tell me where he is," Adelaide grunted, barely able to constrain her fury. She fought against the cuffs on her wrists as Dr. Winston leaned against the back of his desk.

"He's been arrested and imprisoned, tucked away in the same rotting prison as your father." Dr. Winston crossed his arms. "And as long as you cooperate with me, he has nothing to worry about."

"I'll never help you free the dragon," Adelaide objected. "You don't know what kind of trouble you're asking for."

"You wanted the Dragon Eyes, too, didn't you?"

"Only to tame my magic," Adelaide admitted, hating herself for telling him something even remotely helpful. She figured he already knew that the gemstones were able to nullify her magic from before, but the admission still stung. She hoped that her gamble would pay off, and she would be able to save Brixton and his family—somehow.

"Your family wants to free the dragon spirit."

Adelaide tried not to squirm. She knew her great-grandmother wanted to do just that, but she was not completely certain of what went on inside Tàitai's mind, and she was content to keep it that way.

"I wasn't going to help them free it," she said instead, knowing that was the truth.

"I think you will, with the right incentive."

"You will need quite an incentive to manage that."

"Oh, I think I have something that will suffice." Dr. Winston stood up and strolled around to the other side of his desk. He reached down and pulled something out of the drawer.

From what Adelaide could see, it seemed like a transmitter box. She recalled Gloria had one similar to it.

"Do you know what this is?" Dr. Winston asked. "This is a detonator."

"A detonator." Adelaide felt her body go numb and her face turn white at the word. He had some kind of weapon ready to use, she thought.

"I see you know what it's for," he said with a small laugh. "I have planted one of my own creations on Brixton's father. It's a shame he is so jealous of his son's success. It was quite easy to convince him the Board was ready to honor him with a new award."

Adelaide watched him as he chuckled, content with his own cleverness.

"Any given time of the day, I would be able to release a poisonous toxin into the air around him, killing him and anyone who gets close enough to him. While I can't guarantee it will end up killing everyone in Brixton's family, I know the death of his father would surely devastate him," Dr. Winston said. "It would mean Brixton would be left to live the rest of his life knowing he was never able to gain his father's approval. Nothing seems to stop him from wanting that—except where you're concerned, of course."

"How do I know you're not lying?" Adelaide asked.

"You don't," he replied. "But are you really going to take that risk?"

Adelaide felt her heart sink. Brixton did not get along well with his father, but she knew of the ardent devotion he had to his family. If anything were to happen to his family, Dr. Winston was right; Brixton, trapped in prison, unable to do anything, would blame himself.

There was nothing she could do to stop him. She would have to play along with him.

For now.

FAVAN AND FLEW

"You're playing a dangerous game," Adelaide told him. "Brixton will come after you if you do anything to hurt his family."

"What makes you so sure of that?" Dr. Winston shook his head. "He's been trying so hard to be a good boy for the last several years that he's forgotten how to handle any trouble when it comes. And even if he did try to take some form of revenge against me, you're forgetting two very important things."

"What am I forgetting?" Adelaide muttered.

"First, he is locked up in the wielder's prison in Tower Hill. There is no breaking out of there, short of divine intervention, and I think it's quite apparent that God has been content to leave England alone since the portal opened. And second, I have you. And your powers are useless as long as I have this."

Dr. Winston pulled out the Dragon Eye, letting it wink in the light of his office.

"I know Brixton, and he would never do anything to risk you," Dr. Winston said. "He's loyal to a fault, is he not? I imagine he would very easily die for you, as much as I might hope to keep him alive."

Adelaide felt her breathing go shallow at the thought.

It wasn't fair, she thought. She had never wanted to hurt him. She had tried to distance herself from him, and even after all the pain she had caused, he would still suffer because of her.

"What do you need my help for?" Adelaide asked, already knowing the answer.

"I need your help in getting the second Dragon Eye." Dr. Winston tucked the jewel into his other pocket and stood up. "Once I have both, it should be easy to call the dragon forth and offer my body to him as a host. Once I am in control of the kingdom, I may even find a place for you in my court if you cooperate."

Adelaide shook her head. "It would be a shame to ruin Britannia for the sake of your pride."

"It would be a shame to step back from greatness if an opportunity presents itself." Dr. Winston walked over to her, and she bristled as he touched her arm. "But we can discuss history a bit later. I am, after all, more anxious to make it than I am to talk about it."

He hauled Adelaide to her feet, unshackling her from her manacles.

She felt the pull of her blood sink down her body as she stood, her earlier exhaustion still wearing on her despite the hours of rest. She forced herself to balance on her feet, unwilling to allow Dr. Winston to help.

"We will be going to the High Counsel Office," Dr. Winston said. "That is where the Dragon Eye is located. You will not cause me any trouble, or Brixton's father will be the first to pay."

As Dr. Winston elaborated on his threats, Adelaide followed him out of his office, desperately hoping she would be able to find a way to distract him long enough to dislodge the detonator from his hand and escape.

But there was no one around.

Where is everyone?

Dr. Winston started to chuckle, as if he had read her thoughts. "There's no point in trying to find a way to escape. The campus has been evacuated this morning after the terrible incident that occurred last night. Maybe you heard about it while you were at Scotland Yard?"

Adelaide felt numb.

"Three young men tried to break into the High Counsel Office last night, while you and Brixton were out on your

FAVAN AND FLEW

rendezvous. Needless to say, Rembrandt's magical protections are quite powerful, as are the guards who stand watch."

Her eyes fell to the floor as her vision blurred over with tears. She gripped her hands together fiercely, trying to stop her grief from overflowing. Jiahao's brothers had been sent out to retrieve the other Dragon Eye, and it seemed as though they had failed.

"Are they … " Her words were barely a whisper, but they ricocheted against the empty hallways loudly enough Dr. Winston heard them.

"That's right, you must have known them. I could be cruel and tell you that they died," Dr. Winston said. "But I'm not as much of a villain as I seem. They barely survived, but they will require quite a bit of recovery time. The healers at St. Bart's are tending to them, and considering the damage that was done, they will likely be there for the next several months."

So they are alive. Adelaide placed a hand on her chest, pressing down on her rapidly beating heart. "How do you know that won't happen to us?" she asked.

"Your magic allows you to walk away unaffected by the protective spells, just as my authority will allow us to walk in and out of the High Office without issue."

"I see." Adelaide gazed out the windows as they made their way to the high tower, where the central office of the school was located. She caught sight of Tower Hill in the distance and thought of Brixton.

"Keep moving," Dr. Winston muttered. "I'd hate to have to make the Flew family pay even more for your trouble. You've already cost them so much, haven't you?"

Adelaide felt her breath catch, as panic started to paralyze her. She hated how much she heard Jiahao's voice in her head, reminding her what a terrible planner she was. Adelaide did not know how she could ever get out of this.

Brixton...where are you? I need you!

Her mental cry for help went unanswered as Dr. Winston continued to guide her up to the top floor of Rembrandt Academy.

20

"This is where your family *lives*?" Luella bounced with excitement as they entered into the dark corridor of the haven. At the amazed look in her eyes, Brixton recalled her delight in asking Gloria about the penny dreadfuls. He had to smother a laugh.

"Yes." Jiahao did not seem to understand why Luella was so enthralled, but Brixton preferred it that Jiahao dismissed his sister. From the odd looks on Jiahao's face, Brixton decided he did not want Jiahao to get too close to Luella.

As if he knew what Brixton was thinking, Jiahao snapped his attention to the entrance way. "This is where my great-grandmother, Lady Fang Gu Qin, lives and rules over our family."

"Do you have more family in China?" Luella asked.

"Of course we do. But those here are the members who are loyal to her."

"Why wouldn't others be loyal to her?"

Jiahao's mouth went into an exasperated line. "You ask a lot of questions."

"It's a family trait," Brixton assured him, making Luella smile.

Brixton was glad Luella was having fun. He felt smothered as the walls around them began to get tighter. The aroma of incense did nothing to hide the smoldering smell that came with metalworking. There was a large fireplace at the center of their hovel, one that served as a warning as well as a welcome. He knew they were in serious trouble.

"Tàitai!" Jiahao called.

Instantly, a short woman materialized from behind a viewing screen, and Brixton had a feeling she had been watching them as they entered, looking them over for weaknesses. He saw the white of her hair, the wrinkles around her cold, black eyes, and the dignity she used to carry herself. He almost felt like he should bow down, having found the Queen of the Underworld.

"Jiahao."

The crackled voice that stemmed from her ancient face made Brixton flinch, but it was not enough to ruffle Luella's nerves, he noticed. She stared at the lady with wide eyes, so unabashedly Brixton almost felt the need to apologize for her rudeness.

"Jiahao, I see you have lost your cousin. Where is Yaling?"

"She has been kidnapped."

"Well, I am glad to see you at least tell the truth when you disappoint me. I knew that must be the case or else you never would have brought these outsiders into our haven."

At her sharp, unforgiving tone, Jiahao grimaced. "I must apologize. They can help us find her."

"We do not need their help!" Tàitai's voice snapped like a whip. "They will only betray us."

"This one, Yaling says he is her friend." Jiahao pointed at Brixton, who stepped forward.

Brixton was just about to agree with Jiahao when Tàitai spat on the floor.

"Ha! I do not believe it."

Jiahao looked like he wanted to agree with her, but he held firm. "He helped us find the Dragon Eye."

"Oh?" Tàitai came up beside Brixton.

FAVAN AND FLEW

She was even shorter than Adelaide, Brixton thought, watching the older lady as she circled him.

"He has magic, I see," she said.

"Yes, I do, Lady Fang," Brixton said.

"Hush, foreigner!" Tàitai's voice crackled with anger, and he was surprised to find a dagger suddenly pointed at his chest.

Brixton found it hard to breathe as he looked at the fine tip of the blade before him. He saw the edges of a dragon tail on the hilt and stared, torn between admiring the deadly weapon and unwilling to examine it more closely.

"Your life belongs to me now, as you are in my home. One word out of line and I will have you killed on the spot."

"You wouldn't really do that, would you?" Luella's voice was quiet and innocent to a fault, and Brixton could only shake his head at her, hoping that would be enough to keep her quiet.

But his sister seemed determined to break all the rules now that she was free. Luella walked up to Tàitai, no doubt surprised to see such an imposing figure who was shorter than she was. "My brother and I would like to help find Adelaide. We were told we would need your help, and the rest of the Qin family, too."

"Ryu sent us," Jiahao said.

"Ryu." Tàitai furrowed her brow. "So, you went to see that traitor, did you? Why should I not kill you right here and now, Jiahao? Is there a sickness of treason going around my haven?"

Her voice echoed around the atrium where they stood. A low murmuring answered her, and Brixton realized that Tàitai had not been the only one who was waiting behind the different screens. She was the queen bee in a hive of darkness, with layer after layer of protection looking after her.

As Jiahao tried to explain the situation, and Luella added emphatic agreements to his case, Brixton took a closer look at their surroundings. He saw a few different shadows as they moved, and eventually he saw that there was a small crowd of people surrounding them in the darkness.

Roaring fires burned behind the viewing screens, and Brixton could just make out an even larger shadow behind them.

"What is that?" he asked, unable to stop himself from interrupting Jiahao.

Tàitai scoffed at him. "You see, Jiahao? Your friend here continues to disrespect us."

"He is Yaling's friend, not mine." Jiahao went silent at her angry stare.

"Captain Favan already told me I would have to prove myself. I fully expect your distrust and even your ire, Lady Fang, but I want to prove myself to you." Brixton glanced around uncertainly before settling his gaze on Jiahao. "In combat, if I must."

"You wish to be tested?" Tàitai looked at him, weighing out her different options. "Hmmm … What can you and your magic do for me?"

Brixton swallowed hard. "I'm an engineering wielder," he said, calling up a small bubble of light in his palm to prove his word. "I have creation magic."

Her eyebrows raised. "And you are indeed a friend of my great-granddaughter?"

"Yes."

Tàitai's frown deepened. "You won't be for long."

FAVAN AND FLEW

"I already know the danger of her magic." Brixton brought his hands together. "But I won't leave her. I will do anything if you can help us find her and save her from the man who kidnapped her."

"Anything?" Tàitai looked at him again.

"Yes," he replied. His eyes met hers as she came to a stop in front of him. He felt as though he was staring death in the face, as the defining moment of his life came, and he made his decision to admit the truth aloud. "I'm in love with her."

A gleam appeared in her eyes. "Well now. I see. In that case, how could I refuse such an offer? A master wielder has fallen for my great-granddaughter, just as we have been stalled in the last hours before our triumph. What a twist fate has offered to us."

There were laughs and jeers that quietly circled him, but Brixton remained firm.

"We should see what he can do with the dragon," a man called from the back.

"I don't know if I can do anything about the dragon spirit, but I know we don't have much time before Dr. Winston tries to get Adelaide to give him the other Dragon Eye," Brixton said.

He was immediately ignored.

"Xijong." Tàitai called out toward the far end of the atrium, and a man appeared. His skin was as leathery as the apron he wore, while his clothes were covered in ash and coal.

Brixton watched as Tàitai began to talk with him back and forth in rapid Chinese. There was nothing he could tell that indicated anything, but Jiahao looked grim.

"Foreigner," Tàitai called, snapping her fingers.

FAVAN AND FLEW

Brixton took a steadying breath before he walked over to her.

"Come with me. I have a job for you."

Tàitai walked him behind the viewing screens, past the large fire pit. Brixton briefly glanced back at Luella, who gave him a brave smile.

He tried not to worry about her as he faced the large crowd before him.

Brixton knew at once he was in the presence of Adelaide's family. Several of them had dark hair—black, if not darker. Many of the men had their hair pulled back into a braid, while the women wore theirs in buns. All of them watched him with a wide variety of suspicion, uncertainty, and disinterest.

"Allow me to make the proper introductions. This is the honorable remnant of the mighty Qin clan," Tàitai said. "I am their leader, Lady Fang Qin Gu, but they call me by my family title."

"How do you do?" Brixton quickly bowed his head to the crowd.

"These are your crewmembers now, foreigner." Tàitai turned back to Xijong. "Show him."

At once, the crowd began a coordinated effort to pull a blanket of shadows away from a hidden object. Tàitai nodded toward her family again, and the large shadow Brixton had seen earlier suddenly became clear.

He felt his mouth drop open at the sight.

Underneath the London streets, no one would have ever guessed there was a mechanical dragon the length of a small train quietly and steadfastly being assembled on an old, unused Underground track.

Brixton felt his eyes widen with astonishment as the veil slipped and revealed even more of the mechanical

FAVAN AND FLEW

beast; it was easily the largest, oddest automaton he had ever seen.

"It's a dragon," he said, his voice full of awe and terror. The empty, lifeless eyes gleamed at him, and the firelight was just bright enough to light up the special scales they had designed as armor across the lengthy body.

"Of course it is a dragon," Tàitai snapped. "Now that the dragon spirit has been resurrected, all he will need to leave his portal is a proper body and the Dragon Eyes."

Brixton carefully stepped forward, putting his hand on the design. He could see it was squatting on its legs, its wings tucked down, while the body was huddled down as it was hidden in the Underground tunnels. It was nearly prepared for takeoff, ready to fly out from right under the city and into the skies.

At his touch, Brixton felt his magic both spark and rage. There was old power inside of the mechanical dragon, one that was both magic and life, otherworldly as much as it was utterly natural. It was an old design, reconstructed with a combination of ancient and recent material.

The image of Adelaide's dragon heart, the one he had helped her with when they first met, blazed into his mind.

"She was not lying," he whispered. "This is a dragon."

"Do you know why dragons hoard treasure in all the legends that you hear, foreigner?" Tàitai asked.

"No," Brixton breathed, still in awe at the engineering feat before him.

"When dragons die, their bodies become treasure. Gold, silver, gemstones—you name it, and more than likely it has a corresponding body part from a dead dragon." Tàitai patted the head of the beast, rubbing her hand over the nose and up its forehead, just below two large, gaping holes.

The Dragon Eyes.

FAVAN AND FLEW

Adelaide had been telling the truth, Brixton realized. They were real eyes that belonged to a dragon.

"Much like elephants, dragons all go to die in the same place as their family. The last one dies guarding the remainders of their family." Tàitai folded her hands together, staring up into the blank gaze of the large mechanical beast. "My family has spent more than a thousand years tracking down dragon treasure remains. We have built this body with scraps, but once the dragon's spirit is free of the portal, he will be able to use this body as his own."

"How will he do that?" Brixton asked, suddenly wondering if he wanted to know at all.

"Ancient blood magic." Tàitai held up her wrist, where several scars stood out amid the wrinkled skin. "Eastern and Western power has the same root, and its root is true. Life is in the blood, foreigner. I have used my cursed blood to infuse the metal and magic together in this design."

Brixton felt his stomach turn. "But it's not his real body, is it?"

"Not all of it, of course. The British Empire brought pieces of the dragon treasure here to London and, perhaps sensing the dark power inside, buried them under Parliament. Suyan, my own great-great-grandmother, managed to resurrect him by tricking Fawkes and Wright into blowing the portal open over his body's remnants. It was the British government's greatest secret, and she used the revolutionaries' ambitions against themselves, all so our family could break our curse and use the power of the dragon to rule once more."

Tàitai straightened and smiled widely, stretching her thin lips across her wrinkled face as she walked in front of the mechanical beast with pride. "Since then, magic has poured out into this world, and this world did not recognize it for what it was."

"Does Adelaide know about your plans?" Brixton asked.

"Of course she knows. Or at least, she knows what I told her." Tàitai waved her arm. "She was talented at working with machines, so we let her refine our designs. But since she is still a mixed-breed like her father, I did not tell her the exact nature of why we needed her expertise. It's much easier to control people who think they know everything."

"Why are you telling me this, then?" Brixton asked.

"Because no matter what you do, I have full control over you," Tàitai said with a sadistic smirk. "If you want me to help you save Yaling, you will succeed at the tasks I give to you. Starting with completing the construction of our dragon here."

Brixton looked down toward the empty chest of the dragon, where Adelaide's old, egg-shaped machine would have fit perfectly.

"You need a dragon heart."

"Yes." Tàitai nodded to Xijong, who promptly handed Brixton an apron and a set of tools. "Now, get to work."

Brixton looked at the mecha-dragon before him, thinking of all those moments he had shared with Adelaide, working on the energy loops and power snares and everything else—those reminiscences had not been in vain or hopeless despair. He could relive those memories clearly, and it would be that—not so much his magic, or his determination—which would help him save Adelaide now.

"What about Adelaide?" Brixton asked.

Tàitai shook her head. "Her kidnapper will take her to the portal. There is no calling the dragon without blood."

"Blood?" Brixton felt sick again.

"Yes. This man will need Yaling's blood and the Dragon Eyes to summon the dragon spirit out of the portal." Tàitai nodded to her family members. One stepped forward and offered Brixton an array of tools.

Brixton was briefly distracted by the shining display before him. Across the man's arms lay a blanket that held nearly every tool he could possibly ever need. He had thought about stealing the toolkits at the construction yards back when he was a young teenager, but nothing had ever come his way that was this fine.

"Once the dragon spirit leaves the portal, he will come seek out a body." Tàitai looked back at the dragon, her eyes softening ever so slightly. "We need the heart finished and working before Yaling breaks the portal open, or she will die, overcome by the dragon's power."

"She'll die?" Brixton fumbled with the tools, dropping several of them as he whirled around to face Tàitai.

"Yaling does not fully know the cost that her magic and its curse requires of her." Tàitai smirked. "If the dragon spirit does not have a body, it will need a host. Yaling will be the best choice, with her young blood and energy. If you want a chance to save her from such a fate, you should get to work. And make it fast, foreigner."

FAVAN AND FLEW

<u>21</u>

Adelaide glanced back at Dr. Winston as inconspicuously as possible while she worked to remove the Dragon Eye from the Rembrandt coat of arms.

The amethyst gleamed at her as she touched it, warming underneath her palm, the same as the other one had when she removed it from the clock tower and when she handled it in Scotland Yard. She knew it would easily come free at her efforts, but she did not want to hurry.

Adelaide took her time, trying to think of anything that would help. If she wanted to get away from Dr. Winston, she would have to find a way to steal the detonator first. Whether it was pure magic or only mechanical, she did not want to risk the lives of Brixton's father or his family.

Or anyone else who might be around when the poison was released, she thought grimly.

"What's taking so long?" Dr. Winston asked.

"It's been in here for years," Adelaide said, trying to keep her voice calm. "I will need some more time to get it loose."

Would it be possible to get the detonator while handing him the Dragon Eye?

It was worth a try, she decided. If she could find a way to distract him, she would have a better chance of success.

Adelaide glanced back at the gemstone. Her fingers wrapped tightly around its flat top. Her magic called to it.

It was almost another part of her, Adelaide thought, thinking back to the Age of Dragons. According to her family's history, a dragon made a blood oath with the Qin family, finding them of good character. The dragon granted them power to rule in hopes of peace.

For a while, times were good, even if they were hard. The Emperor Qin used the power of the dragon to build up the Great Wall and secure his kingdom.

But the last Emperor of the Qin dynasty fell in love with a beautiful woman, one who did not return his love. In an effort to gain her heart, the emperor cut the Dragon Eyes out of the Qin Dragon while he was asleep.

The dragon awoke, blind and bleeding, as his eyes hardened into amethysts.

Everything fell apart. The dragon fled, along with his remaining power, and the power of the emperor's sister, Wuja, who, devastated at what had been done to her dragon, cursed the Qin family.

The few family members who remained alive at the end of the empire were scattered and sent into hiding.

The dragon itself did not die, though, Adelaide remembered. Not then, anyway. He hid in the Western lands, before he was killed. To his last breath, the dragon had guarded Wuja's grave and then died beside her.

Adelaide looked at the Dragon Eye as it fell into her hand. Inside the darkened heart of the gem, there was a swirl of magic—her own, but not her own—gleaming with ferocious, untapped power.

As she watched, it winked at her. She gasped, nearly dropping it.

"What?" Dr. Winston asked. "What is it? It's not a fake. I know it is not a fake."

"It is not," Adelaide agreed. "My family recognized it from the newsletter picture. The other one took us much more time to find."

She felt the warmth of the gem grow to scorching as she handed it to Dr. Winston.

"Ouch!" He dropped the Dragon Eye onto the ground.

Adelaide saw her chance and took it. She rammed herself into his side, reaching into his pocket for the detonator. The Dragon Eye rolled across the office as Adelaide struggled to grab hold of the device.

"You witch," Dr. Winston muttered, throwing her off him just as her hand clasped firmly around the detonator.

Adelaide went flying backwards before slamming into a desktop. She winced at the pain in her hand as she caught herself on the corner. The pointed end of the wood scraped across her palm. Blood spurted from the line of broken skin, but she was too focused on saving Brixton's family to worry about it.

"Get going," she ordered herself, as Dr. Winston hurried to gather the other Dragon Eye.

She hurried out of the office, running as fast as she could.

As she ran, she studied the detonator and poured her power into it, rendering the magical elements useless. She yanked off the back panel, briefly flustered as her nails broke at the effort. She hurried to examine and pull out the copper wires that laced around the magic center, a loop-like design she recognized as one of Brixton's attempts to refine the core of dragon heart.

In fact, she realized, it *was* the last one they had put together. She pulled it out and held it, watching as the magic push of the batteries wound down to a full stop.

"This is mine." Her steps slowed to a stop out of shock and shame.

Dr. Winston had been lying to her before. He had told her before there was no choice but to destroy her contraption, the dragon heart she had built using the old treasures of her family mixed in with the updated materials.

"I should have known," Adelaide whispered, gripping the core and crushing it, equally angry and sad she had to destroy it in order to save it, now that Dr. Winston had defiled it. "I should have known he was lying."

She turned toward a window and opened it, pushing back the curtains and shattering the lock on the glass. Adelaide tossed the useless remnants of the detonator away.

For a brief moment, she watched the last of the metal as it winked in the daylight. It was hard to mourn properly when there was no time, she thought.

As she turned around to finish her escape, Dr. Winston reappeared in front of her.

"I've got you now," he grumbled, grabbing her by the shoulders and pulling hard.

Adelaide twisted free, pushing him away as she tried to duck around him. Instead, she slipped and fell, and found herself winded. She held up her hands to block him as he stood over her, only to find her hands pressed against the Dragon Eye.

"You cursed witch," Dr. Winston howled, as he gripped her arms. "You might have found a way to save your friends, but now that I have the Dragon Eyes, nothing will stop me. Now, I have no choice but to kill you if you don't obey me."

Adelaide barely listened to him. She was too busy watching the Dragon Eye, as it absorbed her blood.

"What is it?" Dr. Winston asked, before it was too late.

The earth began to rumble, and bright, blood-colored lightning burst out of the portal. Even from her position on the top floor of Rembrandt, Adelaide could make out the light's violet-colored glow as it trembled across the darkening city skies.

She managed to free herself from Dr. Winston's grip as the world began to shake. She hurried to get up and grab the window sill, watching as airships fell down from the sky, as the Thames began to boil, and the streets began to crack with power.

"What's happening?" Adelaide screamed.

"The portal is strengthening in preparation," Dr. Winston shouted. His voice was crazy and triumphant. "The dragon spirit is coming!"

Adelaide could only look on him in horror, watching him revel in the resulting chaos. He was euphoric at the city's destruction, she realized.

She tried to escape, but her ankle twisted, and she fell to the floor once more.

"You're not going anywhere," Dr. Winston yelled, his gaze reflecting the demonic red of the Dragon Eyes. "I need more of your blood to call the dragon; Suyan's blood is stronger in you than it is in me."

Adelaide struggled against him. "Never."

"If you don't come to the portal, you're only going to inflict more damage on the city. The dragon spirit needs a body, after all, and as long as you're not there, he'll only come looking for you."

He took her by the arm, pulling her along, as she remained paralyzed by fear.

What else I can do? Adelaide wondered. She fell into line beside Dr. Winston. She needed to see the dragon anyway, she reminded herself, if she was going to break her family's curse.

Outside, the world continued to rumble as a dragon screech raked through the city.

FAVAN AND FLEW

Brixton wiped the sweat off his brow, breathing in the scent of the warm ashes from the fire. While he was concerned for Adelaide and he did not want to know what his father was thinking at the moment, he felt a rush of pleasure to be back doing what he knew best.

The mecha-dragon behind him began to spark with power as he called out orders. Xijong, Tàitai's leading engineer, was happy to translate the orders in their own Chinese dialect while Brixton assembled parts, sutured wires together, and worked on creating an energy loop that would work for a machine of this size.

Even without using his power, he remembered every detail of Adelaide's first project for him. Brixton could see where her design would fit, right behind the protective metallic skeleton of the dragon's torso. This time, he had weaker material to work with, but he knew he could still make it well enough that it would work.

"This is not going to last long," he warned Tàitai. "It will need a lot of power to keep it going."

"You said you would fix it so it would work," Tàitai said, spitting on the ground between them. "We abhor lies around here."

"I'm trying my best."

"Your best has to be better." Tàitai pulled out her dagger again, waving the dragon-scaled hilt to shine against the firelight. "I would hate to think your incompetence would get Yaling killed, after all I've done to help her."

"Help her with what?" Brixton asked, unable to stop himself. "You didn't help her control her magic, and you only sent her out to break the law."

"I helped her plenty!" Tàitai insisted. She held up a hand, allowing a small, dull spark of black magic to settle inside her wrinkled palm. "Did you know that only another wielder with destruction magic can touch her and not worry death will come?"

Brixton turned away from her, trying to focus on the energy loop in his hand once more. He did not want to hear about the pain Adelaide had gone through.

"Even in my supposed cruelty, I have cared for Yaling in ways you will never be able to," Tàitai hissed as she stormed away from him. "Don't you tell me I haven't done enough for her."

Brixton kept staring at the energy loop in his hands, as the last of her footsteps whispered away. The loop had its wires crossed and curled around, just as it had when he first worked with Adelaide.

It reminded him of another loop, he thought.

He pulled Ticker out of his pocket and carefully removed the melted panel on the back of the pocket watch.

Inside, Ticker's energy snare had gone black from Adelaide's earlier power burst. He tweaked the wires inside, looping two of them together, catching her magic's shadow and sending a spark of light from his.

Just as he finished, Brixton saw the white light of his magic fight with the gray aura of Adelaide's magic. He smiled, watching his magic chase hers, while hers tried to tackle his. The incompatible energy of his white magic and Adelaide's black magic swam into an ongoing, circular dance, much like their own relationship.

Destruction and creation magic.

A breath of excitement escaped him. As long as his power was equal to hers, there was power and light. His own power confirmed his conclusion, and less than a second later, their magic brought the electric battery in Ticker's heart back to life.

Ticker's face blazed on in a flash of bright light, blinking up at him eagerly. "Good evening, sir. I do believe I have dozed off for an inappropriate amount of time, and I must apologize."

"It's all right. But now I need your help, Ticker," Brixton said. He studied the mecha-dragon stretched out behind him, before glancing around him.

Tàitai was nowhere to be seen, and the rest of the crew was putting the finishing touches on the rest of the dragon's body. He was duty-bound to fulfill Tàitai's challenge, and he wanted to be able to save Adelaide from being inhabited by a dragon.

But ...

But Brixton also knew that a such a large mecha-dragon, unleashed upon London, would have to be controlled, and he did not want his power-obsessed professor or Adelaide's revenge-driven great-grandmother to find a way to manage that. With Ticker's programming, he would be able to use his magic to establish some control over the mechanical body, and if something went awry, he would be able to fix everything easily.

Well, not easily, Brixton thought. But more easily than if he did not include a failsafe.

This is the PRISM project all over again, he thought with a slight grimace.

"I hope this works," he murmured, pressing his own power into Ticker's body once more, sending the magnets of the dragon heart whirring. The electricity, goaded by the magical jolt, leaked out little lightning strikes.

FAVAN AND FLEW

Brixton ignored the discharge as he made some quick adjustments.

"Oh my," Ticker exclaimed. His little pocket watch blinked as the rest of the dragon began to power up, trying not to gag at the sight of his magic sparking the electricity to power, sending it rushing through Tàitai's blood in the various joints, all while Brixton's magic, tangled with Adelaide's in a continual chase, supplied more energy and magic to the dragon.

Ticker whistled from inside the heart. "Where am I? And why I do feel … so much heavier, sir?"

Brixton smiled. "I apologize for your discomfort, Ticker. Right now, I need you to watch over this body for me."

"I feel … strange ... not like myself at all, sir."

The small hands of the clock face whirred around. Brixton kept an eye on Ticker's batteries, watching in amazement as the small residue of Adelaide's magic and his own bubble of creation magic began to attack each other. Brixton grinned, unable to hide his satisfaction. The void of her magic chased the fullness of his, and the light of his magic instinctively sought to flood the darkness.

Even if they could not be together, Brixton knew he was meant to find Adelaide. Her magic might have threatened his life, but there was power between the two of them that could make life better for others.

He watched as the power burst through even more, charging through Ticker's body and flowing into the loop of the dragon heart. The energy darted down the length of the mechanical body. The small interlockings and strapped workings snapped, cracking as it stretched and sparked with power and magic.

"Sir? Are you certain I am working correctly?" Ticker's voice deepened as the power surrounding him stretched. "I daresay I have never felt quite this … awake. I do believe I have gained a new set of eyes, too!"

Brixton chuckled. "I'll admit you might have to get creative, Ticker, but everything seems to be working fine."

Hopefully, Brixton thought, Ticker would be able to maintain that control once the dragon's spirit was freed and Tàitai wanted to take over.

"I need you to listen to me carefully," Brixton said as he began to check over the rest of the heart's mechanisms. "I have a few instructions for you."

Several "sirs" and many questions later, Brixton began checking his handiwork one last time, before stepping down with a sense of completion.

He was just about to see if Jiahao would get his great-grandmother to examine his work when the tunnels began to shake.

Dirt fell from the ceiling, and the filters shuttered. Smoke spilled into the haven, and Brixton had a hard time breathing as he called out.

"What's going on?"

"It's the dragon spirit," Tàitai called. "He's coming!"

"What? Already?" Brixton scrambled back, as the mecha-dragon began to move.

"Well, is it ready, boy?" Tàitai shouted as she came up next to him. "Is my dragon ready?"

"Yes," Brixton said.

"Brix?" Luella yelled out to him in the distance.

"Over here, Lu," he called back, before coughing. The ashes in the air clogged his nose and mouth as the atrium began to fill with smoke.

Ticker's altered voice roared out an otherworldly screech. Brixton watched as the eye sockets of the mecha-dragon glowed a dark silver and the beast started to move its legs forward. Its long tail began to swish back and forth as it moved, breaking into the walls of the Underground tunnels.

Tàitai cheered and began issuing marching orders. She turned to Brixton. "Well done, foreigner. I am pleased."

"Did I pass? Will we go and save Adelaide now?" Brixton asked.

Tàitai opened her arms. "Come and give me a hug first, foreigner."

Brixton gave her a strange look, but he did as she requested. He put his arms around her in the most awkward hug of his entire life, wondering if this was her way of thanking him for his hard work.

Then her dagger sliced into his back.

He gasped in unprecedented pain as the metal of her blade, hot and slick as it cut through his shoulder, severed the threads of his shirt and darkened it with his blood.

"I am so happy you were able to finish the dragon for me," she whispered, her voice low and deadly. "But our nations have lied to each other for hundreds of years. What makes you think we will suddenly start working together?"

She pulled her dagger free from his body, watching as he fell to the ground, clutching his chest as he gasped in pain.

"I have to go and take care of my family now," she said. "But I will tell my great-granddaughter you died working to free her from her curse. I am sure she will be truly touched."

Behind her, the mecha-dragon began to creak with movement. Brixton heard Ticker call out in fear as it began to move.

"Where are we going?" Ticker's deep voice suddenly cried out in fear as he slithered out of the Underground tunnels. "What is this? You need to stop!"

Ticker! Brixton went limp against the ground, straining his ears to listen until the last trace of the mechanical beast was gone.

"And now, it is time I go and retrieve the Dragon Eyes." Tàitai laughed before she disappeared behind a screen of smoke and magical discharge.

"Brixton!" Luella's voice called to him out of the darkness as the rest of the tunnels continued to shake.

"Lu," he murmured, unable to speak without feeling a tight clenching in his back. He reached behind him and felt the sticky warmth of running blood.

"Oh my," Luella gasped. "This is awful!"

She called up her magic and Brixton felt the full force of her power as it came rushing out of her palm. After a long, uncertain moment, he found he could breathe more easily.

"What happened?" she asked. "Did something fall on you from the ceiling?"

"No. It was Adelaide's great-grandmother. I suppose her name is not Lady Fang for nothing." Brixton reached back and tentatively touched his lower back, relieved to feel the wound was sealed up. It was still covered in blood, but he was no longer in danger of dying.

"I reversed time on it," Luella explained with a grin.

"Thank you, little sister." Brixton gave her a sheepish smile. "I suppose I do need to start taking you on more adventures."

"Especially where the Favan family is involved, by the looks of it." Luella looked worried as the tunnel began to rumble around them again.

FAVAN AND FLEW

"I'm not going to argue with you there." Brixton shook his head. He would be dead if Luella had not come with them.

Jiahao came up as Brixton stood. "The haven has been weakened by the quakes. We need to leave before this place falls apart."

"What about Adelaide?" Brixton yelled.

"We should go to the portal. Yaling should be there, especially if the dragon is coming. Follow me. I know a shortcut."

Brixton exhaled slowly. He glanced at Jiahao, and then he looked to Luella. Together, they would save Adelaide. They just had to.

As they started down into the darkness of the Underground, another idea formed inside of him, and he quickly pulled Luella off to the side.

"I have another job for you."

"Please, I know this trick. It's not going to work. I want to come with you. I can help!" Luella rolled her eyes as Brixton dug into his pockets.

"Right now, we need to think about the mecha-dragon," Brixton said. He gripped her hand, pressing his Rembrandt identification badge into her palm. "Now, listen. I promise it is important."

Luella gave him a suspicious look, before she sighed. "All right. Tell me what I need to do."

<u>22</u>

Adelaide stumbled across the Parliament courtyard as Dr. Winston marched toward the portal. It was spinning fast, like a tornado unwinding into the sky, its narrow funnel curled into a frenzy; the silver railing surrounded it, binding it in metallic moonlight. Aching dragon cries called out from within its darkened heart.

"This is madness," Adelaide whispered, swearing she could feel the dragon spirit as it rumbled inside the rainbow light.

Adelaide had no substantial reason to doubt her family's myth, but she was floored to see its fulfillment.

She curled her fingers into fists, even more terrified at the thought of reversing its progress. But now that her blood had called to the dragon, it was up to her to find a way to stop it from destroying her city.

And freeing my family from Wuja's curse.

"Keep going, Miss Favan," Dr. Winston yelled, gritting his teeth as the pressure from the magical portal began to clog the atmosphere. His eyes were bloodied with sadistic excitement, and Adelaide felt no inclination to disobey him.

Between a raging dragon spirit and magical madman, Adelaide knew where her better chances of survival lay.

Dr. Winston pressed her against the railing. He took the Dragon Eyes from his pocket and held them out to Adelaide.

"Take them," he said. His voice was full and deep, much more terrifying than ever before.

"You won't be able to stop me from using my power on you," Adelaide warned.

Dr. Winston did not seem to hear her. Instead, he hurried to place her bloodied hands on the Dragon Eyes. The second she touched them, he thrust her over the railing toward the portal.

"Hey!" Adelaide screamed, dropping the Dragon Eyes as she grabbed for the edge of the ground, hoping she would be able to find a way to save herself yet.

A lifetime seemed to pass in the half-second it took her to secure her grip on the broken courtyard cobblestones. She watched as the Dragon Eyes fell beyond her, into the depths of the enchanting light.

The violet light of the gemstones, spotted with her blood, winked at her once more, before they disappeared.

The portal light began to glow, brighter than ever before. Adelaide closed her eyes and ducked her head, unable to bear the shining brilliance. She scrambled to scurry over the railing, hurrying to get away.

There was a rush of wind and a collapsing sound, and then a dragon roared. A gust of power shot up from the portal as the light swirled inward, creating a tighter, deadlier corkscrew.

"He's coming!" Dr. Winston shouted enthusiastically.

Adelaide could just hear Dr. Winston crying out with pleasure as the force of the dragon's roar sent her legs flying over her head.

"Oof," she grumbled as she landed hard on her stomach. She sighed with relief, and then scooted forward awkwardly, clinging to the cobblestone with her fingertips as she reached for the railing.

"Please," she whispered. She cringed at each scrape, unable to do anything but hold as still as possible while the wind spun around her.

Adelaide bit her lip, holding back another scream, briefly and profusely thankful she had ditched her skirts in the alleyway behind Scotland Yard.

There was a moment of brief calm, and then there was another wailing screech from above.

Adelaide looked up and gasped.

"It's really free." She watched, amazed at the dragon's spirit hovering in midair. Its body was translucent, like a ghost, shaded with every color in a rainbow. The Dragon Eyes burned a fiery purple from its eye sockets, black magic coloring their depths, while its belly ran scarlet and the horns on its back ran blue. Dark sea-greens and bright yellows dotted its skin in different colors, while its tail flickered with a changing palette.

Dr. Winston raised his hands to the beast. "Great Qin Dragon, I will now claim you as mine!"

The dragon spirit did not seem to hear him. Instead, it flew down to the ground, whipping past them. Her hair obscured her vision, but Adelaide could feel the power radiating from its body as it flew by her.

She turned and watched Dr. Winston go still as the dragon flew at him.

Her mouth dropped open as the dragon ripped through his body, both flying through him and past him at the same time; the dragon's spirit raced into Dr. Winston, and he cried out in joy, and then terror.

And then he went silent.

For a long moment, Adelaide watched in horror as Dr. Winston fell over, unconscious or worse, hitting the pavement with an ominous *crunch*.

"Dr. Winston!" Adelaide cried out, as she struggled to move. She stumbled and scrapped her knees. With her arms shaking, she looked over to Dr. Winston's still form.

FAVAN AND FLEW

Was it possible he was dead?

She reached for his wrist to check for a pulse. Before she could get to him, his body shook violently, and Adelaide screamed and backed away from him, watching as the dragon spirit reemerged, squawking with rage.

Adelaide watched as the dragon spirit hovered over the old man's body. She stared at it, surprised to see the amethyst eyes looking back at her.

The Qin Dragon. He's here.

The lightning from the portal raged. Adelaide could only stare at the dragon, horrified, as little streaks of fire began to fall from the sky behind them.

"Please," Adelaide murmured, trying to stand up before the dragon. She reached forward, trying to touch him.

The dragon suddenly turned away from her, looking up to the sky, as if something had called its attention.

Before Adelaide could try to catch his attention again, he took off, flicking his tail over Dr. Winston's body.

Adelaide hurriedly checked his pulse, just in time to feel the last of his life energy disappear completely.

Adelaide jolted back, dropping his arm quickly. "I can't touch him," she said, stricken as she remembered her own destructive power. Looking down at her hands, she was horrified to see her palms were glowing black.

Did I just kill him? Adelaide wondered, frightened to think she might have been the one responsible for finishing him off.

The dragon looped around in the sky, crying out, and Adelaide saw a flicker of light bounce off a strangely-shaped cloud.

"Huh?" Adelaide frowned, squinting at the sight. Another dragon was headed her way, and this one was anything but a spirit.

It was a large mechanical dragon, one with steel-lined limbs and hollow eyes that whirled with spiraling gray strikes.

"Yaling."

A voice called from behind her, and Adelaide turned to see her great-grandmother with a large smile on her ancient face.

"Tàitai?" Adelaide whispered, unsure of what to do.

Adelaide looked back to see the dragon's spirit rise to meet the mecha-dragon in midair.

Boom!

The sound was thunderous, as the machine collided with the spirit and melded into one.

At the force of the union, Adelaide flew back, rolling backwards on the ground; her ears clouded, deafened by the collision. Her body was already limp and torn from earlier wounds and bruises. She had to force herself to sit up, even though her arms went heavy and numb.

Lightning and fire rumbled from above as she lay on the ground, unable to do anything but stare at the smoking cloud above Parliament.

Behind her, Tàitai only laughed. "At last, the honor of the Qin clan is restored! Now, we will conquer the world again."

"Adelaide!"

Brixton's voice was a less than a faraway whisper, one that she easily could have imagined if she did not want to believe it so fervently.

"Brixton." Her voice was barely audible as she lay on the ground, struggling to turn over onto her side. She brushed her hair out of her eyes, and then she could see him.

He was running toward her, covered in soot, his suspenders snapping loosely at his side. His white shirt had a large tear reaching around to the back and he had blood on his right shoulder.

He was his usual, messy self, but he was still her hero.

Another figure caught her attention; Jiahao was looking up at the battle between beasts as he tried to run beside Brixton. Behind both of them, she could see an airship starting to darken the sky as it heralded from St. James.

"Ada." Brixton slid down onto his knees as he gathered her up into his arms. "We have to move. Hold onto me!"

"Brixton." Adelaide flinched at the sound of her own voice, as her hearing restored itself. She grabbed his arms, horrified to see her hands remained covered in blackened magic, her power still alive and looking for more magic to consume.

She looked at the dragon and then back at her own hands, before beginning to push Brixton away.

"Ada, please trust me!" Brixton fought with her, eventually flinging her over his shoulders as she fought to get free of him.

"No, I'm going to kill you," she cried, suddenly more terrified than she had ever been in her life. "Let me go."

How can I exist in this world if you are not here with me? I need you. Her desperate thoughts cried out inside of her as she felt a lump in her throat threaten her. She finally managed to wriggle free from Brixton's grasp, falling hard onto the ground.

"Ada!"

Adelaide pushed back onto the courtyard sidewalk, trying to hurry away on her own as Brixton grabbed her hand with his and pulled her behind him.

She saw his own magic conjured in his palms. As the world burned black and red, only the white light of his magic kept her steady.

Brixton was risking his life in order to save her, she realized, staring at him as he helped her run. He was not afraid of her magic, even though he knew its power, and he loved her enough to die for her.

She did not know if it was possible for her to love him enough to let him suffer for her, but she knew as they ran, she loved him enough she would gladly suffer with him.

The light of their magic between their hands glimmered sharply. Adelaide stared at their power, watching as it curled together, forming an ongoing, perpetual bond of creation and destruction. She dropped to her knees at the shock.

Adelaide nearly fainted, breathless as her power flickered out.

"Adelaide." Brixton was short of breath as he scooped her up against his chest. He carried her, his hands gentle even as his grasp remained firm.

Somewhere beyond her sight, Tàitai's howl of triumph echoed from long distances away.

Adelaide was still processing everything around her as a cannon shot rippled across the courtyard.

She jolted, wrapping her arms around Brixton's neck more tightly as he ran.

"It's all right," he said. He paused in his running, putting her down briefly as he tried to catch his breath. "Captain Airey is here with the *Horizon*, thankfully. I wasn't sure Luella would be able to convince him to come."

"What's my family's mecha-dragon doing here?" Adelaide asked. "How did they manage to get it working?"

FAVAN AND FLEW

"How else do you think?" Brixton gave her a teasing smile. "They had me fix it for them."

"Oh, Brixton. You shouldn't have done—"

"They promised if I did it, it would help save you from the dragon using you as a host. I couldn't say no to that."

Adelaide looked down at her palms again, surprised to see all trace of her magic was gone; she tried to call it up again, and it whisked through her, a ghost of its former self. She smothered it a moment later, and it winked away into nothing.

Brixton had not only saved her from the dragon, Adelaide realized. He had saved her from her own fear.

"Brixton." Her eyes watered as she looked up at him. "Brixton, wait."

"What is it?"

"My magic. I can control it." Adelaide pushed herself up against him. "Look! I can touch you and be with you and I won't kill you."

As if to prove her point, she tightened her arms around him and pressed her lips against his. He responded to her at once, pulling her tightly across his chest.

"Brixton." She felt a dizzying passion rise up inside of her, and suddenly their closeness was still too far for her to bear.

Anchored against him, Adelaide placed her hands on either side of his face, running her fingers over the shy stubble of his cheeks before glorying in the ruffled softness of his hair.

"Ada." Even with a mechanical dragon flying around Parliament, there was nothing more irresistible than her name on his lips.

Warmth coursed through her body, and without her magic in the way, Adelaide felt herself drawn in. She wondered for a brief second if this was his magic, if the white light of creation was calling to her now, seeking to fill her voided soul with power.

Brixton pressed against her, his arms wrapping her closer to his body. The warmth inside of her suddenly became a blistering heat, threatening to overtake her in a way her magic never could.

It was not until another cannonball rushed through the air and crashed into the king's Tower behind them that Brixton abruptly pulled himself away from Adelaide, leaving her weak with wanting.

"I always seem to end up kissing you at the worst times," he said, glancing over at the raining debris from the attack.

"The best and the worst," Adelaide agreed with a nervous laugh.

"You have to admit, this is definitely one of the worst," Brixton said. "It's not every day that we need to stop a dragon."

"I was just about to remind you," Jiahao spoke up from behind them. He had a disgruntled look on his face, unhappy he had walked in on their passionate display. "It is not something I thought I would have to do."

"Jiahao." Adelaide pulled away from Brixton long enough to embrace her cousin. Jiahao flinched at her touch before remaining rigid, letting her hang on him. "I'm so glad to see you're safe."

"Not now, Yaling. We have to stop the dragon."

Adelaide let him go and turned back to Brixton. "Do you have any ideas, Brixton?"

"You were the one who first told me that the dragon needs a body to survive in this world," Brixton said. "I can disable the body if I can just get close enough."

FAVAN AND FLEW

"If that is your plan, the airship might be able to help with that," Jiahao said, pointing to the airship just as another cannonball launched.

This time, the ball struck the dragon, nicking it on its leg.

The dragon roared, howling loudly and angrily. Adelaide closed her hands over her ears as it passed overhead, heading for the ship.

Brixton looked over at Jiahao, and then back up to the skies, where the dragon began violently fighting with the *Horizon.* "Ada, stay here and look out for Luella. I don't want you anywhere near the dragon or the portal. It's too dangerous."

"Why?" Adelaide asked. "You'd think I would be able to destroy it."

"Tàitai said she used blood magic in making the dragon's body," Brixton said. "If there's no body for the dragon, she said it's possible the spirit will use you as a host."

Adelaide swallowed hard, before nodding. "All right. But please be careful." Adelaide glanced back over at Dr. Winston's body and shivered.

"I will."

Adelaide watched as he looked over meaningfully at Jiahao, who huffed.

"Just hurry up," Jiahao muttered, speeding off toward the dragon, leaving Brixton with a moment to say his goodbyes.

Brixton grinned and pulled Adelaide close to him once more, pressing into her whole body as he kissed her. She wrapped her arms around his, snuggling into the warmth his body offered hers. There was no magic that surged between them, only desperate yearning and quiet constancy.

And then he put her down, and she let go, and they stepped away from each other.

"You need to be careful, too." He looked back at her with an odd expression in his eyes. "When this is all over, there are things we need to discuss."

She felt her cheeks color over in a modest blush.

"Are you coming yet?" Jiahao called back, clearly upset at their slowness.

Brixton gave her one last kiss on the cheek and then hurried away.

She watched him leave, before turning toward Westminster's palace entrance.

Before Adelaide headed out to look for Luella, she heard Tàitai's cackle behind her. A second later, Adelaide felt her great-grandmother grasp her wrist tightly. "Tàitai, what are you doing?"

"I see your foreigner survived his earlier encounter with me. Let us see if you will have the same fortune as he did, Yaling."

Adelaide felt the sick and sudden heat of a blade against her palms, and the warm splurge of blood.

"Tàitai," she hissed, shocked to see her great-grandmother's old dragon blade covered with her blood.

"If you want to tame a dragon," Tàitai said, "the first thing you must do is feed it. If you want it to come to you, you must offer it a sacrifice. Come, Yaling. We must give blood to the beast."

And then, the dragon's cry resonated around her, mixed with the deafening sound of the *Horizon* as it crashed into the ground and an explosion cut through the skies.

FAVAN AND FLEW

<u>23</u>

Brixton had just caught up with Jiahao when the airship crashed into the courtyard. The two of them jostled, slamming into the cobblestones as the wooden hull of the ship shattered against the ground.

"Look!" Jiahao coughed, pointing toward the ship. "Up there, on the front of the ship."

Brixton looked up in time to see the mecha-dragon come flying down a moment later, its tail caught up in the ballooned sails of the ship. But it was the dragon who held his attention; Brixton felt his eyes widen as he caught sight of the lone figure standing up on the shattered bow, holding a hand up, as if to tell the dragon to stop.

Luella.

"What is she doing?" Brixton grumbled, as he stood up and brushed himself off. "Luella!"

As he shouted her name, his sister stilled for a second before she resumed her self-determined quest. The dragon wiggled around before her, his legs still tangled in the tarped sails, while her feet were balanced precariously on the tip of the bow.

"It's all right, Brixton," Luella called over to him. "I can stop him with my power."

Jiahao clapped him on the shoulder as he stood up next to him. "I will take care of your sister. You get the dragon."

Before Brixton could object, Jiahao hurried off, easily climbing up and over the broken pieces of the fallen airship.

As much as he was still wary of him, Brixton had to admit Jiahao was certainly light on his feet. He watched as

Adelaide's cousin gripped onto the splintered wood, climbing upward despite the ship's dilapidated form.

Luella continued to try to tame the dragon from above while Brixton made his way toward the dragon's heart. His muscles were sore, and his body was worn as he forced himself to move below the mechanical claws of the beast.

"Once you get him, Lu, I'm going to take out his heart," he called up to her.

"Do you think that's a good idea?"

"I can't imagine it's a worse idea than trying to resurrect it in the first place."

"Good point," Luella said with a small laugh.

"Jiahao, be ready," Brixton said, watching Jiahao nod as he stood behind Luella protectively.

He darted around its rearing limbs before grabbing onto the front forearm. Before he could find a good foothold, the dragon went still. A small glimmer of light wrapped around its body, and Brixton felt the warm playfulness of his sister's magic.

"I've got him, Brix," Luella cheered from above.

"Thank you." Brixton grinned as he climbed up the dragon's underbelly.

"You'll need to hurry up," Luella warned. "I don't know how much longer I can keep this up. He's a pretty big beast."

"Just don't fall," Brixton replied, reaching between the armor plates covering the chest area. "Ticker? Can you hear me?"

"I'm here, sir," Ticker's voice was deep and robust as it echoed through the dragon's mechanical body. "The Qin Dragon is not happy with me, though."

"You're talking with him?"

"As best as I can, sir," Ticker replied. "He especially does not like you. He says this is his body and I need to get out of it."

"I'll help you with that right now," Brixton said, reaching his arm into the heart. He felt around the different components of the heart, searching for where he had welded Ticker to the rest of the dragon body. The dragon body twitched, and he bit down on his cheek to keep from squirming in pain at the sudden, if small, movement.

"Sir, you need to be more careful." Ticker's voice was suddenly elevated with fear.

"Brixton," Luella called. "He's fighting me."

"I only need another second," Brixton called back.

But it was too late. He felt the power of Luella's magic break. The dragon shook it off, flinging the layer of light off like raindrops.

"Whoa!" Brixton hollered along with Luella as the dragon leaped into the air, tugging itself free of the airship balloon sails and heading back toward the portal—where he could see Adelaide was fighting off Tàitai and her dragon dagger.

"Adelaide!" Brixton cried, watching as blood dripped down her hands.

Brixton reached into the heart of the dragon again, trying to grab hold of Ticker. Brixton slowed as he felt the heart inside the dragon beating, almost like a real one.

The dragon landed on the ground before Brixton could find Ticker. At the hard, sudden impact, his arm drew blood as he nearly fell.

"You will not interfere with this, Yaling," Tàitai snapped, her attention divided between Adelaide and the dragon that was suddenly leering over her. "I am using your blood to call the dragon."

"Brixton, stay back," Adelaide warned. "I don't know if she will be able to control it or not."

"Yes, foreigner, we wouldn't want to get caught up in a dragon's mouth, would we?" Tàitai snapped, holding her dagger out toward Brixton threateningly.

Brixton hurriedly scrambled up higher on the dragon's belly, grabbing at its neck while shoving his foot further into the joint at its arm.

"Get away from him, Tàitai," Adelaide shouted. "I need him!"

"Finish the blood magic spell, then," Tàitai ordered her. "Or I'll kill him. It would be a shame for me to kill the man who's pledged to do anything to save you at this point, Yaling."

"Ada, don't!" Brixton dug his heels into the scaly metal plates of the dragon. "I've almost got Ticker free."

"Yaling! Now," Tàitai screeched. "Offer up your blood to our dragon. Show your respect!"

"No," Adelaide yelled back.

"Fine." Tàitai yelled as she stepped toward Brixton, aiming her dagger at his heart. "I should have made sure you were dead the first time I stabbed you, foreigner."

"No, Tàitai! Stop," Adelaide screamed.

Suddenly, the dragon lurched forward, striking hard and fast. No one saw it coming—least of all Tàitai.

She screamed and cried out as the dragon opened its jaws. The spikes of its teeth cracked against her body as the dragon grabbed hold of her and swallowed her.

Brixton nearly fell off the dragon at the jerky movements, grunting as he flopped against the dragon's chest. He grimaced as Tàitai's screams slowed and gradually became more muffled.

FAVAN AND FLEW

"Brix," Adelaide called out to him, her voice shaking, as she stood up. "Are you all right?"

"I'm here." He waved at her with his free arm, only daring to let go of the dragon for a quick second. The dragon was still moving its neck up and down as it devoured Tàitai's body, but it slowed as her cries became more muffled. "Stay there. I'm going to take care of the dragon now."

"Wait," Adelaide called out.

"What is it?" Brixton asked.

"What if I can't control my magic once the mecha-dragon is gone?" Adelaide asked. She gripped her hands together before her as he met her gaze.

He did not have to look at her to know the answer to that question. Brixton knew if he stopped the dragon and put its spirit back in the portal, it was possible Adelaide would be right back where she started—unable to control her magic, and unable to be with him.

"My magic has been a curse in my blood all my life," Adelaide told him. "But … if the dragon remains free, maybe I won't have to carry it any longer."

"Ada." Brixton said her name, letting his full affection for her infuse into his speech. He knew she was upset, but there was nothing he could do for her. Even in taking down the dragon for her, he knew he was more likely going to condemn her to life with her destructive power out of control. "I promise, there is nothing I want more than to be with you. But neither of us can pay that price."

"I know." She sighed, her head collapsing into her hands. "I don't know if I'll be able to help you. I might end up doing more damage, like I did to Dr. Winston."

"Dr. Winston?" Brixton briefly looked back at where Henry's body lay.

"I think … I think I killed him," Adelaide whispered. "It was right after the dragon was released, and I didn't know … "

"It's not your fault," Brixton told her.

"I'm not so sure." Adelaide seemed defeated as her voice trailed off, but she gave him a rueful smile. "Slay the dragon for me, Brix."

He nodded. "I will."

Reaching down into the dragon's heart again, Brixton gritted his teeth as he let out a rush of his power, letting it pour out of his hand. The dragon reared up as though in pain, and Adelaide cried out.

Brixton could only hold on as the dragon roared and began to buck, trying to shake him off.

"This is madness," Brixton muttered, briefly chastising himself for putting in so many panels. Ticker clearly did not need that much protection.

Finally, he reached down into the dragon heart and clasped a bundle of wires, grabbing onto Ticker.

"Sir!"

The little automaton's voice washed over him just as the dragon went still.

"Hurry, Brixton!" Luella called, as her magic overtook the dragon again. Brixton nodded, seeing she had grabbed onto the tail with both hands. He was surprised, and then a bit unsettled, to see Jiahao was at her back.

"It's too strong," Luella called. "Be careful, Brixton!"

"You got it." It took him less than a second to send his magic through the dragon's heart. He felt Adelaide's power—no, the dragon's power—start to attack him, but Luella's energy held it in check. Brixton grabbed onto another energy snare and sent more power flying into it, using it to recharge his attack.

"Ticker, shut down," Brixton yelled. "I need you to shut down the body, and then I can pull you free."

"He won't let me, sir," Ticker argued. "Even with your power, it is not enough to allow me to overpower him. It is only because you are here now that I am able to speak. He is not very polite, sir."

"I'll get you free, just shut it down!"

"You cannot free me without damaging me, sir."

"If there's any damage, I will fix you," he promised. "I'll likely need to charge you after this anyway."

Using his other hand, Brixton used his fingers to claw open another gap in the panels, tearing at some of the wires before reaching into the heart of the mecha-dragon. He clasped Ticker with both hands.

Behind him, he could hear Adelaide cry as the mecha-dragon roared again; Luella gasped as the dragon broke free from her power.

"Sir," Ticker cried out. "I do believe the Qin Dragon is quite upset now. He's … trying … to … take … over my systems!"

"I'll get it," Brixton yelled back.

It was the moment Brixton had been waiting for. The spirit inside of the mecha-dragon lashed out, attaching to him just as he unleashed the bright white of his magic.

The ebony swirls of the dragon's spirit and the white lightning clashed, and the dragon roared; Brixton heard his own cry of anguish echo in his ears, and he swore he could hear Adelaide crying out his name.

And then, suddenly, Ticker's voice spoke, both from all around and from inside of Brixton's body.

"So … you are the one my vessel is in love with." There was a small scoffing sound. "I was rather hoping it would be someone else. Of all magic, I hate white magic the most. Even if it is the most delicious to consume."

Brixton stilled. "Ticker?"

"Your toy is no longer here," Ticker's voice replied. "I am the Dragon of Time, the one you know as the Qin Dragon."

"You're the dragon?" Brixton shook his head, suddenly feeling sick. He glanced around, watching as the world stood nearly frozen. The waves of magic from his hand and the heart of the dragon had stalled to slow motion, and he wondered if he was trapped within Luella's power again. While it carried her color, there was no distinctive mark of his sister's character.

The Time Dragon. The dragon was controlling the flow of time around them.

"I am he," Ticker's voice said, the pride in the voice no longer dully automated, but fully animated.

"Is that why I can hear you now?" Brixton asked. "Inside my head?"

"Yes." The dragon's voice did not bother to hide his snicker of glee at Brixton's expense. "Who are you?"

Brixton felt his mouth go dry. "My name is Brixton," he replied slowly. "I'm in love with Adelaide."

"You may love her, but until she believes it, I do not need to give you my blessing."

"I'm not here for your blessing."

"Aren't you, though? It is the only way to break the curse."

Brixton glanced around them. "It is?"

"Yes. A dragon's blessing is an enormous gift. Once we give it, we die. That is the price Wuja demanded of her kin."

Brixton finally understood the full implications of the dragon's revelation. "You have to choose to give Adelaide your blessing, and then the curse will go away, but you will die."

"Yes." Brixton did not have to see the dragon's face to imagine he was smirking. "Now that I have been fully awakened, I do not feel the slightest compulsion to return to hell."

"Instead you'll make Adelaide suffer."

"It is a shame how she must suffer because of choices others have made." The dragon's voice softened. "She is rather like my Wuja. As much as I might not like you, or your magic, I hope you will take care of her until the next time we meet."

"Next time?"

"You ask a lot of questions, don't you?" There was another flash of a smirk, and then time's power resumed.

"Brixton, what's wrong?" Adelaide's voice called out to him again. "Hurry!"

Brixton shook his head, clearing his thoughts. Calling up the remainder of his magic, he thrust his hand into the mechanical beast like a flying sword, blasting Ticker free and dismantling the delicate wirings of the dragon heart.

Brixton caught Ticker and drew his hand back quickly, ignoring the slits the wrecked panels cut into his skin. With his faithful pocket watch tucked carefully away, Brixton slipped down the awkward slide of the dragon's belly, just as the mechanical beast reared back.

Its metal body roared, right before it went limp, pausing as it held steady onto its hind legs. Around its feet, a pool of blood began to form as it leaked from the machinery.

The dragon heaved out one last tired mechanical sigh of rage and fury, before going completely still.

It was at that moment Brixton jumped down and ran for Adelaide.

"Ada," he called, scooping her up against him as soon as he caught hold of her.

"Brix." Adelaide eagerly embraced him, winding her arms tightly around his neck.

"I'm never leaving you again," he whispered, drawing her close to him and placing a kiss on her forehead.

Brixton barely noticed as the dragon shifted once more. He saw the spirit inside of the body struggle, screeching as it tore itself free from the mechanical body before disappearing from sight.

The remaining metal skeleton of the dragon creaked dangerously as it teetered on the edge of its mechanical toes.

"Adelaide, Brixton, move!" Luella's warning called out to them, as the dragon body fell backward and crashed spectacularly into the ground.

A dark cloud bellowed out around them as Brixton reached for Adelaide. The air flushed his feet out from under them, and Adelaide rolled with him at the sudden force.

Brixton looped his arm around her, protecting her, shielding her with his body as best as he could. As the power of the crash scattered dirt and debris upward, Brixton could not see what happened, even with the light of the portal beside them.

He felt Adelaide squirm beneath him, but he only pressed her down further into the grass as the smaller crashes continued around them. It was only when the dust finally settled down that Brixton saw the dragon had toppled over and smashed into several pieces. There were a few small fires burning in different places, no doubt from where the electricity sparked.

"Did we win?" Adelaide asked. Her voice echoed across the newfound silence of the area. "Is the dragon gone?"

Brixton nodded. "He's gone. For now."

"I was so afraid for you."

"Come on. You'd be amazed at what you can get done if the right people are distracted."

Adelaide gave him a weak smile. "You were always so clever."

He grinned in reply, but he saw her own joy was short-lived. He saw her glance down at her hands, watching as power curled up in her palms, whirling into a ball of black light. He watched as she sighed, unable to exercise full control over the magic in her palms. It flickered and then faded, but he knew she was upset to see it once more.

He thought of his encounter with the dragon, between the seconds of time. He did not know if what the dragon revealed to him would comfort Adelaide or not.

He glanced around the courtyard, taking in all the brokenness. Adelaide was not the only one who was in pain. Just beyond the portal's glow, he saw several other airships waiting in reserve as emergency officers were already seeking to help the crew of the *Horizon*. Just a little further down the courtyard, Jiahao and Luella were steadily recovering from their close encounter with the mecha-dragon, holding onto each other in a way that made Brixton frown.

Adelaide sighed, drawing his focus back to her broken heart. They had fought off an ancient spirit, a mechanical dragon, British law enforcement, and her family's

FAVAN AND FLEW

reservations. Surely, he thought, there was a way to find happiness no matter what else they came up against.

"Adelaide?" Brixton reached down and cupped her chin. His eyes met hers and he leaned down.

"Brixton." His name was a whisper on her lips, an inch away from his. "We can't. My magic—"

"I love you, Ada." He watched as her eyes went wide; her breath inhaled sharply, and then he closed the distance between them, kissing her as she trembled against him.

He felt her clutch at his shoulders before she shyly reached up and ran her hands through his hair. Somewhere behind him he could feel Jiahao's angry glare and he could hear Luella's hushed giggling, but all he could think about was how perfect Adelaide felt in his arms.

"You've always been mine." Brixton gathered her to him, cradling her to his chest as he eased away from her. "See? No black magic."

"This time," Adelaide whispered. "It will come back."

"No life is separate from suffering. If I suffer, I suffer for loving you. Create a life with me or destroy me with your kisses. I can't bear the thought of being apart from you. Unless you're with me, I'm only half alive."

"It's still better than fully dead."

"I'll be the judge of that." He brushed his lips over hers again. "We will find a way to be together."

"But—"

"We have time," he said. "We have time to figure out how to make this work, I promise."

"Are you sure?" Adelaide asked. Her hands clasped around his neck as she buried her head into his chest. "Our magic is not compatible, Brix."

FAVAN AND FLEW

"Our magic might not be compatible, but that doesn't mean we can't be happy." He risked another kiss, drawing back more quickly than he would have liked as he felt the menacing shadow of her dragon slowly move between them.

He could feel it move even more as Adelaide began to voice her doubts.

"But what about everything else?" Adelaide asked. "There's your father, and my father, and your job, and what if you have to be arrested again? What about my family? Will you be able to handle their rejection?"

"The only rejection I can't take is yours."

"But the dragon—"

"Are you trying to convince me to stop loving you?" Despite the day's long battle, Brixton chuckled. "You're not going to succeed."

"I've always needed you, but I can't do anything for you," Adelaide said. "It's not fair."

"I've always needed you, whether you could do anything for me or not. This is not one of our usual partnerships, Ada. I love you." He stood up and reached down, pulling her to her feet and steadying her.

"It's not just that I can't add anything to your life," Adelaide said. "I'll only cause you more trouble."

"Then at least let me have the privilege of facing the trouble alongside you."

"But—"

Brixton groaned. "I should have known you would be difficult about this. Do you want me to leave you?"

"No." Adelaide's fingers dug into him. "No, don't go."

"It's nice to see neither of you have changed over the years." Luella laughed weakly as she came up beside them.

She reached down and hugged Adelaide. "I'm glad you're all right. I have been waiting to see you again. My brother has been so depressed without you around to bother."

"Oh, Luella." Adelaide tentatively hugged her back. "I have missed you, too. Thank goodness you're safe."

"Of course I am." Luella glanced back at Jiahao, who was examining the mecha-dragon body. "Jiahao was able to carry me down from the bow of the *Horizon* without trouble."

"Had enough adventure?" Brixton asked.

"Not yet." Luella gave Brixton a teasing smile as Adelaide released her. "I've been waiting nearly all my life to get a sister, and I'm tired of waiting."

"I can't imagine a sister would cause you to sneak into the kingdom's most secure prison and help break out a few prisoners."

"It's not because you're a horrible brother that I wanted a sister. I wanted one precisely because you are so wonderful, Brix. A sister could only add to my joy." Luella knelt down and took hold of Adelaide's hands. "Let me help you with these wounds. Brixton can check the dragon."

As Brixton nodded, the top part of the dragon suddenly gagged. A second later, the body spat Tàitai's body up, sending her flying across the grass.

"It's Tàitai," Jiahao said, his eyes opening wide in shock.

"I'll see to her," Brixton offered. "You stay here and watch these two, Jiahao."

He did not know how he felt about running to check on the woman who had tried to kill him earlier, but Brixton felt it was the least he could do—the very least.

And, he thought, he still had a few questions for her.

FAVAN AND FLEW

He knelt down by Tàitai's broken body, looking for signs of life. He was gratified a moment later when she heaved a dry cackle.

"Come to see me die, have you, foreigner?"

"We can save you," Brixton insisted.

Tàitai's cackle turned into a cough, her shaky laugh mixing with a small splatter of blood.

"There is no point." She closed her eyes. "My soul has been damned from the beginning. A woman who only seeks revenge is already consigned to a hell of her own. It is a matter of honor, of course—but such acute concern dishonored the intent just the same."

"What about Adelaide?" Brixton asked, watching as her chest convulsed. "And her curse?"

"If you truly love Yaling, you already know how to defeat the curse, foreigner." She gave him a small smirk as she fell back, twitching in pain against the grass. "Of course, it may take some time. The Qin Dragon is not easily appeased."

Tàitai went silent, before she fell back against the ground, completely still.

"Lu, I need your help." Brixton cringed. He did not know what to make of her words, as much as she seemed to think he had the answers.

Luella's curls bounced as she hurried to Tàitai's side. As she worked with her magic, Brixton glanced behind him, watching as Jiahao and Adelaide exchanged uncertain glances.

Brixton felt a tidal wave of relief as a group of police officers and medical workers came rushing into the courtyard. He was more than grateful as they took over the scene, ordering people around and tending to the mess in the courtyard.

FAVAN AND FLEW

"I hope we don't have to wait long to get done answering their questions," Luella said as she came up next to him.

"Are you all right?" Brixton could see the tired shadows under her eyes.

"I'll be fine." Luella shrugged, letting her curls bounce. "The medics are tending to that old lady now. I don't know if she'll be all right or not."

"Everything will be fine." Brixton sighed with a mix of contentment and exhaustion as he stood beside Adelaide.

"Have you gone mad, now?" Adelaide asked, giving him a small, teasing smile. "I should remind you that the Favan name has lost quite a bit of luster recently."

Brixton pointed across the courtyard, where Captain Airey descended from the broken hull of the fallen *Horizon.* Together they watched as the captain saluted them before issuing orders to his crew. "We might have more help than you realize."

"We'll need it," Luella said, pointing over toward the guards. "Father is here."

Brixton glanced over to see she was right. He could see his father, dressed in full uniform, his mustache flared with a mix of blatant relief and disgruntled disappointment.

"Well, then, I suppose *most things* will be fine," Brixton amended, suddenly feeling more weary than ever.

"It could be my father instead of yours," Adelaide murmured.

Brixton might have laughed, but he did not have the energy to argue with her; after their long, harrowing day, he did not have any energy at all. "I hope this isn't going to take long."

"Don't worry." Adelaide gave his shoulder a friendly nudge. "We'll get through it together."

FAVAN AND FLEW

<u>24</u>

It was a few days later when Brixton stood on the street, gazing up at Favan Hall. The autumn sunlight was cool and crisp as he stood just outside the townhouse, taking in the full picture before him.

A soft breeze sent loosened leaves flying past him. The London fog had drifted off, almost as if the morning airships had towed it away. The city's grand landscape, including the ever-present portal aura, seemed brighter this morning as repairs were underway on both Parliament's courtyard and the clock tower.

But there was still magic there, Brixton thought, even if it was nothing compared to the magic he felt standing outside Adelaide's door.

As he studied his surroundings with new appreciation, Brixton gripped the letter in his hand tightly. The formal invitation for him to come and spend the day with Adelaide had arrived earlier that morning. After several days of answering questions from the police, the Crown, and even Rembrandt Board members, Brixton was eager to spend time with Adelaide.

The letter served as a talisman, one that would guide his heart to its new home, one that offered hope amid the madness the rest of the world presented.

Brixton stepped forward, walking between several gardeners who were trimming back the unkempt grounds, while other workmen painted the house with a new coat. As Brixton stepped closer to the entrance, he could hear a new vibrancy from inside the walls, the exact opposite of the silent decay he had felt in arriving just a few days before.

A newly installed curtain flicked open on the second floor to the grand townhouse. He did not have to look twice to know it was Adelaide.

She opened the door a moment later.

"I'm surprised you came," Adelaide said, giving him a sardonic look as she pulled him inside. She was wearing a new housedress and a leather apron, one that paired well with her working gloves. Brixton was not surprised to see a new pair of working goggles on her forehead.

"You needed me, remember?" Brixton gripped her hand in his as she led him down the sunny hallways. He tried to recall what it had looked like the last time he arrived, but all he could remember was darkness and shadows.

"I noticed you're getting some housework done," Brixton said, squeezing to the side of a hallway as a pair of maids rushed through with bundles of laundry. "This isn't all for me, is it?"

"No, though I am sorry for the mess," Adelaide said. "Since the haven is facing severe construction damages thanks to the earthquake, everyone agreed it was 'necessarily prudent' for us to open up the house here. Most of them are upstairs, enjoying their new rooms. Only a couple are sulking, worried about what to do now that Tàitai is stuck in St. Bart's."

"So your family is doing well?"

"All except for Tàitai. The best healers at St. Bart's said there is little they can do. It seems her heart is failing her, or at least, the stone she uses instead. At best, she will have a little longer. Although they did not rule out a miracle," Adelaide said. She looked down at the scars on her palms, clearly still sore at her great-grandmother's actions. "Either way, it is about time my family made our formal return to London."

"I guess there is a lot of social pressure on you, given that Gloria was pretty keen on announcing your family's presence when she woke up."

Adelaide frowned. "Gloria was not very happy with the situation, that's for sure. I knew a long time ago we would never be friends, and this past week has certainly guaranteed that."

"I can talk to her if you want."

"There's no need to get along with her now," Adelaide said. "And I doubt she would be eager to do so, for other reasons, too."

"Any chance I could help with the police?" Brixton asked, changing the subject. "Between Rembrandt, Captain Airey, and even my father, I managed to get most of my charges reduced."

"How is your father?" Adelaide asked carefully.

"He was happy to see me and Luella alive, but he is still unsure of what do with us." Brixton shrugged. "It's hard to explain how my father feels."

"My family's name has taken quite a hit, but we're still mostly reputable here. No one important is going to believe Gloria when she tries to tell them Jiahao and I were the ones trying to find the Dragon Eyes before. Especially since Dr. Winston and Tàitai provide excellent scapegoats."

Brixton ran his hand through his hair nervously. "I know you did not like him, but I was still sorry to hear of his death."

Adelaide looked down. "I don't know if it was my fault or not that he died."

"It wasn't. You wouldn't have even been by the portal in the first place if he hadn't taken you there. Don't be so hard on yourself."

"I'm not," she said, but he knew from her tone she was lying.

Brixton nudged her arm companionably. She rested against him for a moment, before pulling him down another hall.

"Come this way," Adelaide said, as her steps picked up with cheer.

Her voice was full of anticipation, and Brixton welcomed the new distraction.

"This room," Adelaide said. "This is the room I've wanted to show you for years now."

Brixton walked through the doorway. He thought he would be entering another room, but he found he was almost in another world as he looked around.

Tinker's tools lined several of the walls, while designs cluttered the desktops. He could see bookshelves lined with golden titles, some of them he recognized from his old textbooks, and others—including well-worn copies of *Beowulf* and *Frankenstein*—were pulled out of their proper placement for easy reach.

"This is your workshop," he said, his voice reverberating into the corners of the high ceiling and around the surrounding walls.

"Yes. What do you think?" Adelaide seemed to bounce with excitement as he circled the room, his eyes wide.

"This is amazing." He ran his hand through his hair as he gazed upward and all around, eager to examine things more closely.

"See? There is still an upside to the Favan name." Adelaide motioned him toward the far end of the room, where the room's large windows allowed for plenty of light to pour onto a pile of unfinished projects. "This is where I'll be working for the next several weeks."

FAVAN AND FLEW

"You are going to stay in London, then?"

"Of course. If you're here, I want to be here, too." She tightened the belt of her apron. "My family is less excited about that than I am, but with my father in prison and Tàitai in the hospital, I am the only one who has proper access to his bank accounts."

"If you have money, what are you going to be working on?" Brixton asked. "Did someone offer you a job, too?"

"Too?"

Brixton grinned, eager to share his own good news with her. "Lu and I went and talked with Captain Airey yesterday. He is willing to bring me on his crew as a contracted consultant for the next few months."

"Oh, Brixton, that's wonderful!" Adelaide leapt into his arms, giving him a swift hug before slipping away just as quickly.

"I am very grateful," Brixton said. "Especially now that my future at Rembrandt is unclear."

She gave him a disgusted look. "Surely you're not going to keep working there? No one had any idea Dr. Winston was so evil, and he's been working there for years."

"The Crown has ordered an investigation." Brixton shrugged, unsure of what to tell her. "Right now, the school has been temporarily shut down. Until then, I can't do anything. They won't even let me give my resignation. And believe me, I tried."

"Will you be able to support yourself? And will your family be fine, too?"

"Captain Airey's contract will be enough for me to pay my remaining loan installments while I wait to hear from Rembrandt." He frowned. "One thing I did find out was that Dr. Winston was behind a lot of my debt. He

FAVAN AND FLEW

purposefully changed the numbers so I would be stuck working there."

"That's terrible." Adelaide shook her head. "Now I'm not actually sorry he died."

"Just that it might be your fault, right?" Brixton gave her a softened look.

She huffed and turned away, beginning to busy herself in her workshop.

"I still have some debt, but not as much as before, although I will have to pay off my new charges," Brixton said. "My father made sure I didn't get off completely for the courtyard debacle."

"That's silly," Adelaide said. "But it does give me a good reason to ask if you want to pick up some work on the side."

He gave her a thoughtful look, seeing the calculating gleam in her silver eyes. "I'm not sure," he said. "Did you have something in mind?"

"Of course I do. The Crown has reached out to me and my family. They would like to see the dragon repaired. They thought it would be a blast to have it at the official November ceremony commemorating the anniversary of the Gunpowder Plot."

Brixton sighed. "I don't think that's a good idea, unless they want a literal blast."

"Neither do I," Adelaide agreed. "But there are enough perks to the idea that I thought I would run the agreement by you. They offered to give my father a new trial in return for my cooperation while I work on it."

"I'm not sure he would want that," Brixton said. "But I guess he did want to go to prison so he could be safe from Lady Fang. Now that she's indisposed, I guess he will get cleared of his charges."

"You don't need to worry about him, you know," Adelaide said. "I'm hoping he'll stay in there for a while yet, considering he was the one who stopped you from coming to see me before."

"Would it have changed your mind?" Brixton asked. "If I had been able to get to you, would you have stayed with me?"

"There's no use wondering what could have happened, since it happened." Adelaide gave him a small smile, but seeing his displeasure at her teasing, she cleared her throat. "What do you think about my offer? Would you want to work on the dragon with me?"

Brixton decided to allow the topic to change—for now.

"Am I allowed to ask if there's money in it for me, without it seeming like I am prostituting you?" He gave her an amused look, one she quickly returned.

"We will split the commission. Sixty-forty, since I'm negotiating the deal."

"Need I remind you that I'm the one who fixed the dragon heart in the first place?" Brixton crossed his arms. "I think I deserve fifty-fifty."

"I'm saving you from discussing things with the government, which allows me to earn the extra ten percent. Especially considering we both hate dealing with authorities." Adelaide gave him a teasing grin. "I'm the one who hasn't been arrested multiple times, after all."

"Only because you were never officially caught. Besides, if you stay with me long enough, you might get there one day. And then you'll get to face the wrath of your father, too."

"I don't ever worry about my father. He has his own scars, and he's stronger in ways I'll never be able to fully understand or appreciate," Adelaide said quietly. She raised

FAVAN AND FLEW

her brow as she looked back at him. "Your father wasn't too upset with you, was he?"

Brixton said nothing for a moment, thinking of his father's reaction. He had been properly horrified to find his son was the one responsible for the large dragon tearing up Her Majesty's Airship Force and destroying the Parliament courtyard.

"It's fine if you don't wish to discuss it." Adelaide put her gloves on and adjusted a new pair of goggles on her forehead. "He'll forgive you one day, if nothing else."

"I won't hold my breath." Brixton sighed. "I did tell my father I would go back home to live with my family for a while, to prove I'm able to stay out of trouble. He seemed content with that compromise, but only because he knew my mother would like it."

"You'll enjoy that, too."

"Of course. I'll have my family's collection of books to entertain me, when I'm not working or finding an excuse to spend time with you."

"I always did approve of your reading habits," Adelaide told him. "I happen to think Luella will approve, too."

"I didn't think of that," Brixton admitted. "I feel better now."

"You really didn't think of your sister?"

"Actually, I was thinking of Jiahao. He promised to come by and check up on her in the future. I'll need to be there to watch him."

"Oh, Brix." Adelaide tried to hide her amusement. "I wish you could see it from my perspective. My cousin chasing down your sister is hilarious to me."

"I wish I could find some joy in it, too, but I know Jiahao too well after our adventures together. I take comfort

FAVAN AND FLEW

in knowing he'll likely have some competition. Captain Airey was noticeably happy to see her today."

"She'll be sixteen next month. It can't be that surprising she's getting some attention." Adelaide brushed against him. "But she can handle herself. I wouldn't worry about Luella."

"You wouldn't. But I will."

"You are too much some days." She put her head on his shoulder briefly, before reaching for her toolkit.

"What about the rest of your family?" Brixton asked. "I thought falling in love with foreigners was forbidden. Wouldn't they be upset with Jiahao?"

"I'm not sure," she admitted. "My family has often derided the British, but they are mostly happy they can use my father's house as an outpost. So who knows what else time will bring us?"

"Time has always played a role of torment for me," Brixton said.

"I thought that was my job." Adelaide reached out and ruffled his hair, clearly enjoying the thrilling risk that came with just touching him.

He exhaled slowly. "I will have to agree with you there. Time has made me suffer, but it is clearly nothing compared to what you can do to me, Ada."

"Brixton, I'm joking, I swear—"

He tugged her close and kissed her, before she could object or even realize what he intended. Her magic was slower to react, and he took as many moments as he could before he felt the looming danger of her power.

"The nice thing," he whispered against her lips, "is that now I can torment you back. It is quite impossible to do that with time."

FAVAN AND FLEW

"And here I thought anyone loving me would be impossible," Adelaide murmured back.

"There are several impossible things when it comes to you, Ada. It was impossible to forget you before, and it is impossible to stop loving you now. Time was only cruel to me because it kept us apart, and now it will be cruel to me in only giving me the rest of my life to spend with you."

Her eyes misted over before they went wide. "Time! Oh, that reminds me. I fixed up your watch for you."

She pushed herself away from him and hurried over to the workbench on the other side of the room. After searching through several boxes, she finally cheered.

"Here it is," she said. "I hope you don't mind the modifications I made to it."

"I'm sure Ticker will like them," Brixton said, glad to see his watch had survived both the dragon's power and Adelaide's modifications. He had been surprised to find how much he missed having Ticker remind him of his appointments in the past few days; he had even missed the accompanying lectures on manners and morals—mostly.

He took the watch from Adelaide and examined it. At the touch of his magic, Ticker opened his eyes.

"Oh, my. Where am I?" The little watch face blinked awake. His eyes roamed around the room, before he let out a sigh of magical discharge. "I seem to be back to my regular size."

"Yes, you are," Brixton said. "It's good to have you back to normal, Ticker."

"Speak for yourself, sir. I was rather beginning to enjoy having some company."

"Company?"

"The magic from my other body, sir," Ticker explained, before he yawned. "He was a little rude, but I do believe he grew on me back there."

"You've had a tiring adventure," Brixton said with a smile. "I'll allow a lapse in judgment."

"I should say so. It's not every day one wakes up to find oneself in a dragon's body," Ticker agreed.

As Ticker continued to describe his experience, Brixton examined Adelaide's handiwork. The casing was on new hinges, the chain had been replaced, but he was surprised to see she had melted and molded the back panel back into pristine condition—with the exception of the inscription.

I love you.

He looked up at her and she eyed him carefully. "I know I never said the words before, but I do. I love you, Brixton."

Adelaide came up close to him, tugging on his shirt, as she drew him as close to her as possible.

"I love you, too."

Adelaide smiled up at him. "I think I loved you from the beginning."

"No you didn't," Brixton said with a laugh. He carefully put Ticker to the side, ignoring his talkative automaton as he focused only on Adelaide. "You barely paid any attention to me when we first met."

"Fine." Adelaide pouted. "But I maintain that it was the second time. At that point, I knew you were someone who believed in the impossible. And there is no denying I needed—need—someone like that."

She laughed and gestured around the room. "Just like I need someone to help me clean up my messes here."

"I don't know if I can help with that," Brixton said. "But it sounds a little safer than the job with the dragon."

FAVAN AND FLEW

He pulled her close as she laughed, leaning down to kiss her again; as he held her, he felt the first pangs of her magic's pull, but he knew there was no staying away from her. The black magic that resided inside her still called out to his, calling for him to be devoured. He would find a way to manage it, he vowed.

"Brixton." Adelaide began to step away from him.

"No. Not yet," he whispered.

"You're sweating."

"It's fine. I can handle it."

She hesitated, but he pressed into her. All other thoughts were forgotten as he held her against him, desperate to keep her where he could still reach her.

It was only moments later when he felt the room begin to spin that he broke away from her. Instantly, he stumbled, falling to his knees.

"Brixton." Adelaide slumped down next to him.

Maybe, Brixton thought as he carefully tested his balance, there was no escaping Adelaide's power. After all, he had never managed to escape her before—or the trouble she brought to his life.

"It'll be fine," he said, doing his best to give her a smile.

"But I don't want you to suffer."

"That's not an option at this point," Brixton murmured, delicately brushing a stray lock of hair out of her eyes.

Adelaide blushed. "But that's not fair."

"Life is not fair, nor is it just," he replied. "But we can still choose to be true to each other. Let me love you, Ada. Please."

She gave him a tremulous smile. "I'm still worth the trouble I cause, right?"

FAVAN AND FLEW

His eyes held hers, his heart resolute. "You've always been worth the trouble."

Brixton had promised her they would find a way to be together, and that was a promise he would keep until the end of time. And as if to prove it to her, and himself, he reached forward and dared to kiss her once more.

FAVAN AND FLEW

C. S. Johnson is the author of several young adult sci-fi and fantasy novels, including *The Starlight Chronicles* series, the *Once Upon a Princess* saga, and the *Divine Space Pirates* trilogy. With a gift for sarcasm and an apologetic heart, she currently lives in Atlanta with her family.

FAVAN AND FLEW

AUTHOR'S NOTE

Dear Reader,

I always adore getting to fall into a new world. It's like setting out on a new adventure, one where you know of where you would like to go, but you end up doubling back and twisting your way around to find the real ending you were looking for all along.

I started toying with the idea to write this story much as I had with some of my other works. The intriguing part of Favan & Flew was in the title this time, *One Flew Through the Dragon Heart*. All I knew at that point was I wanted my male lead to have the last name of Flew, and I wanted the dragon to be both more literal and more figurative, for different reasons.

Sometimes in my work, I see a lot of things I like to play with, often times in multiple ways—I keep joking I fear being a bad mother, because I have so many sad, missing, or sadistic mother figures in my books, for example—and as I worked through this one, it again came back to this idea that I fear I am unlovable, and that even though there are those who love me, I will only make them suffer more for it in the end. Who *can* really love a person such as that? And isn't that a terrible question to even consider: Who *will* really love me, when I am like that?

As always, the writing is secondary to the inspiration. It was wonderful to read this and not only see the answers to my doubt expressed, but the responses. Much as Brixton loves Adelaide despite their incompatibility, my husband loves me and refuses to leave me alone in both the magic and misery of my self-destruction. And while we have a love that exists on a fallen plane of existence, I have full hope that God, in his love for me, has taken on himself the pain of my sin, finding an everlasting way to eradicate all barriers between us. This sort of love, the one that calls to sacrifice and acceptance and suffering, is something I struggle with—not only with knowing it is real, but with believing it, and further with demonstrating it myself.

Of course, as you will see in the next book, it requires courage to respond to such a love, and such love cannot be complete without the answer.

Thank you for reading on to the end, and I promise, this one remains full of surprises. All stories are God's stories, and all truth is God's truth—and all stories of God are filled with grace. I hope you will stick around for the next book in the series as Brixton and Adelaide face off with even more perils and passion, as well as the perils of their passion.

Until We Meet Again,

C. S. Johnson

Thank you for reading! Please leave a review for this book and check out my work for more adventures!

338

FAVAN AND FLEW